Praise For Call Her Janie

"I couldn't turn the pages fast enough. Fabrico does a fantastic job of pulling you into the small-town story. She had me at the prologue. A perfect beach read, I highly recommend."
~Dana Derricks, 12-Time Award-Winning Author

"Call Her Janie is definitely one of the most intense romantic suspense stories I've read. S.R. Fabrico was able to buckle me in on a crazy rollercoaster ride. The ending got me hooked. I'm so ready to read the trilogy and see what disarray comes next."
~Matthew J. Anderson, Author

"S.R. Fabrico grabs you from the very start and will take you on one very suspenseful roller coaster ride filled with twists and turns. It is fast-paced and unputdownable. You will be on the edge of your seat from start to finish!"
~Lisa Wetzel, Bookstagram @mokwip8991

"I couldn't put this book down. I had to finish it just to know what was going to happen. You'll get a small-town romance mixed in with danger and suspense. Truly the best of both worlds. I recommend picking this book up if you're looking for a quick read that'll make you fall in love with the characters."

~Sam, Bookstagram @court_of_reading

Also by S.R. Fabrico

Fiction:
The Secrets We Conceal
Keeping Janie – Coming 2024

Non-Fiction:
My Firefly Journal
My Dance Journal
My Cheer Journal
My Gymnastics Journal
My Soccer Journal
My Swim Journal

Call Her Janie

S.R. Fabrico

SRF Creations

Copyright © 2023 by S.R. Fabrico

All rights reserved.

No portion of this book may be reproduced in any form without written permission from the publisher or author, except as permitted by U.S. copyright law.

This book is a work of fiction. Any reference to historical events, real people, or real places are used fictionally. Other names, characters, places, and events are products of the author's imagination, and any resemblance to actual events or places or persons, living or dead, is entirely coincidental.

Hardcover ISBN – 979-8-9867938-3-2

Paperback AMAZON - 979-8-9867938-4-9

Paperback INGRAM - 979-8-9867938-5-6

To Al, Danielle, Dave, and Jen, you're the best siblings a little sister could ask for. You have impacted my life in ways I cannot put into words. I love you.

Al, thanks for teaching me how to be brave by dangling me by my ankles over the staircase when I was little.

Danielle, I'm sorry I used to throw my clean clothes into the dirty laundry for you to rewash them.

Call Her Janie

ONE

A muffled beep and pumping sound filled the room like a beating metronome. *Something's in my mouth; I can't breathe.* Anxiety moved through my veins like a freight train. I wanted to move, but my limbs were heavy; they ignored my commands.

My head throbbed as I opened my eyes and then immediately slammed them shut as the light blinded my corneas. Finally, I managed to move my arm, and I felt a cold metal rail and clutched it in my fingers.

"She's waking up," I heard a woman's voice call out. "Oh my God, she's finally waking up."

What's going on? Where am I?

Immediately, my mind thought of my little girl. I slowly moved my hand from the rail and slid it gently onto my stomach. Tears formed behind my closed eyelids, trickled out of the corners, and slid down my cheeks.

Where's my daughter? What's happening?

Panic grew with each passing moment. I needed answers, I needed to move, and I needed whatever was in my mouth to get the hell out.

"Hello, Lizzie. I'm Dr. White. We're going to sedate you so that we can remove the breathing tube from your mouth."

Sedate me? Breathing tube?

Filled with fear, I opened my eyes wide to look directly at the doctor. I tried to shake my head, and I wanted to scream.

"We're so glad to see you awake. We'll explain everything properly as soon as we can get you situated."

I felt like an animal trapped in a cage, and my body was the cage.

Oh, the throbbing. Please, God, make the throbbing stop.

"You have a long road to recovery, but with our help and hard work from you, you'll pull through. You woke up. That's a miracle, and I have no doubt you'll be good as new."

So many questions and not enough answers. I wasn't even sure what I was experiencing was real.

"Lizzie, I'm Kit. I've been taking care of you. Relax," she said in a soothing voice. "You're going to fall asleep any minute now."

Kit? Her voice sounded familiar. *Did I know her? She's been taking care of me. Where am I?*

"Relax, my friend," Kit said as she gently rubbed my arm. "I'm here for you. I'll be here the entire time."

My eyelids grew heavy, and I wanted to sit up and scream, but sleep took me over as I drifted out of consciousness.

TWO

Early October

The sun burned brightly in the sky as birds sang like choirs of angels. The warm temperature brought instant, much-needed comfort. The smell of fresh salt air washed over my body like a baptism of renewed energy. Getting out of the Uber was the first step toward a new, simpler life.

I thanked the driver as I shut the car door. I pulled my sweatshirt over my head and tied it around my waist as the driver took off, leaving me to begin this new chapter of my life. I picked up my black Vera Bradley backpack and put it over my shoulder. North Carolina was warmer than New York in October. The quaint little town was spectacular. Golf carts eased down the street of this charming seaside community. The vacation vibe immediately drew me in and put me at ease.

My usually neatly styled hair was tied into a messy brown bun, like a bird's nest on top of my head, and I was slightly disheveled from traveling. Needing to move my legs from the thirteen-hour train ride, I wheeled my suitcase down the path to a brown wooden bench a few feet from the water's edge. I reveled in the magnificence of the sapphire blue sky. *I've never seen a sky this beautiful. Then again, maybe I never bothered to look up.*

Taking in my new world, I stood and stretched. On my right was a long, thin pier that extended into the water. Moms and dads sat along the edge and watched their curious children play as bicycles and pedestrians passed, oblivious to the stranger who had entered their small town. I leaned my head back and let the sun's rays shower my face with warmth. I closed my eyes, took a deep breath, and questioned every life choice that brought me to this moment.

I thought I had everything figured out. For the last ten years, I had been on a mission, and I was sure I was on the right path. Clocking at least seventy hours a week and hustling to climb to the top of the mountain as the only female executive in my firm would indeed make me happy. Somehow, in the process, I lost myself.

"Hello sweetie, mind if I sit here?" a woman said in a Southern accent.

Yes, I do mind, but I replied with a smile, "Of course, please sit."

"How long ya in town for?" she said as she sat down. I noticed her green leggings and matching quarter-zip pullover.

She looks sporty.

"Is it that obvious that I'm not from around here?"

She chuckled. "Well, I haven't seen you before, but the suitcase kind of gave you away."

Trapped between not wanting to talk to her and feeling rude, I said, "You from here?"

"Born and raised," she said proudly. "What brings you to Southport?"

"I'm visiting my brother and sister-in-law."

Beaming, she said, "That's nice. You've come at a great time. We're having so many fun fall events. We've got the annual fish fry, the harvest festival at the Baptist church, you know, the one around the corner, Oktoberfest, the ghost walk tour, Lord child, that's a scary one, and of course, you can't miss the Halloween parade."

I definitely need to keep moving.

"Sounds nice. I'll be sure to check them out. I should probably be on my way. It was nice to meet you." I grabbed the handle of my suitcase and turned to walk away.

"Bye now," she said as she waved.

I knew my brother lived on Caswell Avenue, only a few blocks from the waterfront, but I didn't know the exact address. I should have called to tell him I was coming. *Oh well, too late now.* I pushed my suitcase down the sidewalk along Bay Street in search of Caswell Avenue.

Beep! Beep!

The sound of a high-pitched horn squeaked as a man in a bright salmon golf cart adorned with seashells and twinkling lights pulled up beside me.

"Hello, do you need a ride? *Cruisin' Through Town* at your service. I'm Chuck," he said, eager to please.

I wasn't in the mood for another conversation with a stranger, but I didn't know where I was going. Reluctantly, I said, "Sure, Chuck. I'd love a ride. Thanks."

"All righty then, hop on board. You can throw your bags in the back seat if you'd like. Do you need a hand?"

"I think I can manage."

Chuck appeared to be in his late teens. His huge mop of blond, curly hair covered most of his forehead, with a few unruly curls dangling in his eyes. His faded blue shirt said Southport Provision Company 1993 in white block letters on the back.

"What's your name?" Chuck asked.

"Lizzie."

"Nice to meet you, Lizzie. Make sure to put your buckle on. The police around here aren't too keen on golf cart riders not wearing buckles. It's the law," he said and laughed. "Where to, ma'am?"

Ma'am? Do I look that old?

Embarrassed, I said, "Caswell Avenue, but I'm not sure which house."

"Um, okay. Do you know the name of the person that owns the house? I know almost everyone in town, so maybe I know your people too."

"I'm here to visit my brother, Randolph. Randolph Levine."

"Randy, the handyman? He lives past Leonard Street."

I had to stifle a laugh because I hadn't called him that since we were kids. He decided as an adult that when he started working, he wanted to be called Randolph. He said it was more sophisticated. So, I guess down here, he was Randy again.

"Yes, take me to Randy's house on Caswell Avenue, please."

Buzz, buzz. My phone vibrated in my hand. I had a text message from Kit. My thumb pressed against the screen and clicked open the message.

Kit: How ya feeling?

Me: I'm good.

Kit: Checking on my favorite patient.

Me: Thanks. I'm good. Looking forward to visiting my brother.

Kit: Enjoy. Text me if you need anything at all. Hug emoji.

She's so nice.

The house was brick with green, hardy plank. A powder blue golf cart and an emerald-green 1980s Ford pickup truck sat in the driveway. The front yard was a dedicated bird sanctuary. I imagined myself sitting on the bench swing in the morning, surrounded by bird feeders and birdhouses, and drinking coffee. The front porch was bright white and looked to have been recently painted. Fall bows decorated with pumpkins and pickup trucks dressed the railings. The home looked warm and inviting. I stood there and took it all in as I hoped and prayed that my brother and sister-in-law would be as warm and inviting toward my unannounced arrival.

I talked to Randolph at least once a month, but we hadn't seen each other in over ten years. He moved away, and my work always consumed me. *Why didn't I make time for anything else?* My hands started to sweat, and my throat went dry. *Lizzie, you're so stupid. Why'd you come here? This was a bad idea.* I was about to grab the handle on my suitcase and bolt when I heard my name.

"Lizzie? Elizabeth Anne Levine, is that you?" Randy said with a dazed look on his face.

He looked good, a little older than the last time I saw him. *Of course, he looks older. You haven't seen him in ten years.* His auburn hair was longer, bringing out his hair's natural wave, the wave we both got from our mother. He was thinner, too, but towered over me as always.

"Surprise," I said with a frog in my throat. I thought the bile in my stomach might project out of my mouth and across the lawn directly in front of his feet. "I thought I'd come visit you, bro." My neck was on fire, and I could feel my skin turning red. Randolph stood there blinking. I think he was trying to decide whether I was actually standing in front of him or if I was a figment of his imagination.

"Oh my God, sis!" He beamed. "Come over here right now." He opened his arms for a hug, and we held each other for what seemed like fifteen minutes. He wouldn't let go, and I let him hold me tighter as warm wet tears trickled down my cheeks.

THREE

"So, who died, and how long do you plan to stay?" Randolph snickered as we walked through the front door. Renee, Randolph's wife, was washing dishes at the kitchen sink. Her long black hair was tied in a ponytail at the base of her neck and flowed down her back.

Never looking up from the dishes, Renee asked, "Who died? Who's staying where? Randy, are you talking to me?"

"Look who's here, Ren," my brother said. Randolph set my bags down by the stairs and walked into the kitchen. "Are you thirsty? Can I get you something to drink?" he asked me.

"Some water would be great, thanks," I said as I dried my tears.

Renee looked up at me and gasped. Concerned, she said, "Lizzie? Oh, my word, it's been so long. Randy forgot to mention you were coming to visit. Is everything okay?" Renee was beautiful in every sense of the word, and her smooth olive skin complemented her dark hair and eyes.

"I'm okay, just emotional," I said as I moved toward her. "Randolph didn't know I was coming. Hell, I'm not sure I knew. I just kind of ended up here and decided to visit."

The house was immaculate. *I could eat off the floor.* The entrance was an open floor plan with a large kitchen, living room, and dining room. Letting in tremendous sunlight, the windows in the house lit up the entire space. Paintings of beaches and seashells decorated the walls, and pillows with hearts and peace signs were nestled in the corners of the couch. I could feel this was a happy home filled with love.

"Come sit. Tell us about life. Did I hear Randy say someone died?" Renee asked.

Laughing loudly, Randy said, "No, Ren, no one died. I was kidding. My sister showed up out of the blue for the first time after years of us living here. You know, like who died and brought you here? It was a joke, right, Lizzie?" my brother said, looking at me to make sure he didn't put his foot in his mouth.

"I desperately needed a change," I said. "Life's short. Sometimes, less is more. I've been chasing my career for so long, I forgot what's important. I'm tired of city life. I'm tired of the stress and pressure that comes with my job." I paused to sip my water and considered how much I would share with them.

"I quit my job. Yep, there you have it. I just up and quit, packed a bag with a few clothes, and decided to leave it all behind. I don't have any specific plans. I've been traveling around for a while and ended up here." Fidgeting with the hem of my T-shirt, I looked at them momentarily and said, "You've talked about how much you love it here and how you adore the community and small-town feel. So, I thought maybe it was time I came to check it out."

"We're glad you're here. Truly, sis. It's great to see you," Randy said. He sat at the kitchen table beside me and rested his hand on my shoulder. "You don't have to tell us what's going on, but promise me you're okay." He placed his hand on mine and said, "We love you no matter what."

"Thanks, Randolph. I appreciate that, but I'm okay. I don't want to impose. I've got a little bit of money saved. I hope to find a place to rent for a while until I figure out where I'm going and what I'm doing with my life."

"Nonsense, there's no reason for you to rent a place. We've plenty of room here. You can stay for as long as you want. No questions asked," he insisted.

"Of course, you can stay here," Renee said.

"Thank you," I responded sincerely. "I'd love to take a shower and get cleaned up. I've been traveling for a few days."

All I wanted to do was lie down. I was emotionally and physically exhausted. The spare bedroom was as immaculate as the main part of the house. The queen-size bed, covered with a soft mint green blanket and the fluffiest pillows I'd felt, was calling my name. Matching cream nightstands sat on each side of the bed, and there was a long dresser with a flat-screen TV in the center of it. Also sitting on top of the dresser was a pink bath towel with a matching washcloth and a bar of soap. I chuckled and shook my head. Of course, Renee would be prepared for guests. She was ready for everything.

With no idea what life would bring, I opened my suitcase and unpacked my clothes.

How could I know what life was going to bring? I didn't even know what tomorrow would bring.

My entire life, I thought about the future, worked for the future, and prepared for the future. For the first time, I had no future. I had only today. The feeling was unsettling, but it was what I needed for now. Time to find myself.

I walked to the bathroom attached to my bedroom and put away the few toiletries I had packed. While I brushed my teeth, I turned on the shower to let the water get warm. Catching a glimpse of myself in the mirror, I saw shame and regret looking back at me. I bent over to spit out my toothpaste, and tears trickled down my face again. *This, too, shall pass.*

I stood tall, looked at myself in the mirror, and said, "You'll find happiness. Dammit, Lizzie, you'll find your way, and you will be whole once again."

FOUR

"Good morning, Lizzie. Did you sleep well?" Renee asked.

"I slept like a rock. The bed is so comfortable, and the pillows—wow—I love the pillows. They're like sleeping on a cloud," I said as I filled my cup with coffee.

Renee was dressed in a long cotton skirt, a T-shirt that said, *Learning is Fun*, and a light pink cardigan. Her dark hair was neatly rolled into a bun that rested on the back of her head. "Randy has to put in a tile backsplash around the corner, so he took off early this morning. I'm off to school to teach the kiddos, but make yourself at home. We should be back around four o'clock. Will you be eating dinner with us tonight? We'll eat around 5:30," she said as she packed her things to leave.

"Sure, I'll be here for dinner. I plan to look for a job today. I'm also going to hit the grocery store at some point. Do you guys need anything?"

Today was a new day, and I was determined to move forward and begin my new life.

"Actually, yes, that would be great. I have a list of a few things we need on the fridge," Renee said as she grabbed the list and handed it to me. "*The Pilot's* on the counter. You might find some jobs there. The garage door opener is hanging by the side door. You can come and go through there until we can get a key made for you. I've gotta run. I don't want to be late."

She grabbed her tote bag and hurried out the door. I picked up *The Pilot* and thumbed through the pages. The stranger on the wooden bench wasn't kidding. The paper had at least four pages dedicated to fall festivities over the next several weeks.

First, there was a story about a man named Wilbur who caught a large fish. Apparently, the largest ever reeled in from land. Next to Wilbur and his large fish was an image of a beautiful new bookstore. The article boasted that Bayview Books celebrated its grand opening with owner Helen Loughlin last week. Helen was a Southport native who always dreamed of providing a bookstore for locals and visitors to enjoy. "A meeting place to sit and enjoy your favorite books," the paper quoted.

I continued flipping through the pages, but saw no job listings. I scanned through one more time for good measure, but no luck. The paper provided gobs of things to do, information on how to donate to the food pantry, missing dogs, the local Axe League stats, and future weather predictions, but no jobs. I set the paper down and poured myself a second cup of coffee.

I needed to get dressed, but I wanted to sit and listen to the birds for a while. So, I grabbed my book, *The Dictionary of Obscure Sorrows,* and sat on the bench swing in the bird sanctuary.

I forgot how much I enjoyed reading. For several years, I was so focused on work that I didn't make time for fun books. Sure, I had read plenty of leadership, marketing, and "how to" books for work, but I hadn't read a book for myself in years.

Swinging gently, I cracked open the book and devoured the words on the page. There are an estimated 171,146 words in the English language, yet only about 131 of those words describe human feelings or emotions. In *The Dictionary of Obscure Sorrows,* the author crafts made-up words to help provide new ways to express human emotion. It was the most satisfying book I had read in a long time, and reading a few pages was the best way to start each morning.

After thirty minutes, I returned to the house and rinsed out my coffee cup. Then I glanced at the back door to ensure it was locked and headed up the stairs to my room.

I didn't have much, but I was thoughtful enough to pack a flowery sundress and a matching blue lightweight sweater, the perfect attire for job hunting. I washed my face and applied a little concealer. I added some blush and bronzer and then applied mascara. My hair looked a little tousled. My thick, wavy locks were challenging to manage, so I grabbed my brush and attempted to tame my lion's mane. Feeling excited for the first time I could remember, I heated up my straightening iron, hoping it would control my stray hairs.

Applying some gloss to my lips, I looked at myself in the mirror and felt ready to attack the day.

Determined to find a job today, I threw my cell phone in my backpack and headed to lock the front door. Just because the paper had no listings didn't mean there wasn't a job out there with my name on it. So, I grabbed Renee's list on the counter and headed out the garage door.

Moore Street was downtown and full of local shops, each as quaint and unique as the previous. On the corner was a beautiful two-story white house with a sign out front, THE CHRISTMAS SHOPPE. The house's front porch was decorated with outdoor fall decor and several rocking chairs for people to sit and gather. I walked up the steps and into the shop to the checkout counter. The wall behind the counter was covered with bows of all shapes and sizes. *This must be where Renee gets her bows.*

"Hello, my name is Lizzie. I'm new in town and looking for a job. I thought I'd pop in to see if you had any jobs available or an application I could fill out."

Wearing an orange shirt that said *Happy Fall Y'all* in black cursive letters, the lady behind the counter looked to be in her mid-fifties. She said, "Hello, darlin'. I don't own the place. I make the bows. Not sure Velma has an opening right now. But, I'll grab an application if you want to fill it out. We get busy around the holidays, so she might be hiring then."

She shuffled around under the counter and popped back up with an application in her hand. "Aren't you sweet," she said as she handed it to me. "You can fill it out now or bring it back later. Up to you."

"Thanks again. I'll bring it back. Have a nice day." I waved goodbye and walked toward the exit.

I put the application into my backpack, pulled out the shopping list, and continued to the Southport Market general store across the street. Inside the store was an assortment of homemade jams and jellies, novelty kitchen items, T-shirts, sweatshirts, and hats. My attention was drawn to a shelf of barbeque sauces, each locally made in the Carolina Beaches.

The store was full of a myriad of wonderful goods, but it was clear that I wouldn't find any of the items on my list. I slipped my backpack off my shoulder to put the list back inside when someone shoved me.

I was knocked on my ass, which caused me to tip over a rack of keychains that clattered loudly as they hit the floor, and alerted the entire store to my fall. Stunned with a massive slice of embarrassment, I sat there trying to process what had just happened.

"I'm so sorry. I thought I'd squeeze past, but you turned, and I …"

"You knocked me over," I said in a huff. I was mortified. I wanted to be invisible, and now everyone in the entire store was looking at me. I grabbed the black rack, put it back in place, and picked up the keychains that now littered the floor.

"Please let me help you pick those up. It's the least I can do." His tone was smooth, and I felt the pitch of his voice deep down inside my stomach. Looking up, our eyes connected, and I noticed his tan skin and burly muscles in all the right places.

"I don't need your help. Thanks, anyway. Don't you have someplace to be in such a hurry?" I knew men like this with their delicious looks and smooth attitude. He was easy on the eyes, but no doubt an asshole like the rest of them.

I'm so done with men.

"That's fine. I won't help you. I'll help Tessa, the owner. She has a huge mess here because some crazy person knocked over her display," he said with a flirtatious smile.

"Suit yourself." I rolled my eyes, intentionally not looking at him, as I placed a handful of keychains that said *Beach Please* onto their hook.

"My name's Josh. Are you from around here? I've never seen you before."

I ignored him. I just wanted to get out of the store.

He seemed nice, but I had my fill of men and small talk, but mostly men. *You've been down this road before, Lizzie. Don't be fooled by his Southern charm. You're here to figure life out, not to find a man.*

"You don't have to answer. No pressure," Josh said as he looked at me with his piercing, ice-blue eyes. His dark black hair was slightly longer on top than on the sides. His blue jeans hugged his hips just right, and his biceps wore out the sleeves of his shirt. He had a five o'clock shadow that perfectly highlighted his square jawline.

"I'm not from around here," I finally answered.

"Too bad. I was going to see if I could buy you dinner to apologize."

"I'm in town visiting. I won't have time, sorry." *I can't get hurt again.*

"Well, that's the last one. I better get going. Thanks for the help," I said, practically running out of the store. As I stepped onto the sidewalk, my heart was racing, my face felt flushed, and the butterflies in my stomach could have carried me away. *What's wrong with me? I've got to get it together.*

Up the road a little, I could see a white sign with blue letters that read SOUTHPORT COFFEE CO. *Perfect. Coffee's exactly what I need.* Entering the cute side entrance, I walked to the counter and placed my order.

"Do you have pumpkin spice?"

"We just ran out yesterday."

"Well, shoot. I'll take a medium iced vanilla latte with a pump of caramel, please."

The young girl behind the counter said, "Absolutely. Can I get a name for your order?"

"Lizzie," I replied. "Can you tell me how to get to Bayview Books?"

"It's across the street, above the thrift shop. The entrance is on the right side of the building," she replied.

"Thank you," I said as I nodded at her and smiled.

I grabbed my coffee and walked out the front door onto the porch. Southport Coffee Co. was also a two-story white house with a large front porch filled with adorable bistro tables and chairs. I wandered over to the corner, where I spotted an empty chair. Putting my backpack in my lap, I unzipped the front pocket, reached inside, and pulled out the latest novel I was reading, *The Secrets We Conceal*. I sipped my coffee and read a chapter before packing up to leave.

Crossing the street to the thrift shop, I watched people stroll along the road. *This is a cool town, slow and quiet. Exactly what I need. I could be happy here.* I walked up and looked closer at the craftily painted little chalkboard sign outside the door.

BAYVIEW BOOKS
COME ON UP

I climbed the old cement stairs to the landing. A thick wooden door with iron hinges and a rectangular metal slot at eye level opened to the most incredible book heaven.

The woman behind the counter greeted me. "Welcome to Bayview Books. Buy a book, bring a book, read a book. We don't care—come on in and hang out. I'm Helen. My book haven is your book haven. Are you looking for something specific?" Her light brown hair hung just above her shoulders. Shining through the window, the sunlight behind her caused a few strands of gray to sparkle like tinsel on her head.

Antique wooden shelves lined the walls. Tan leather couches and chairs were scattered throughout the center of the store. In the far corner stood a beautifully crafted spiral staircase leading to a small loft with more shelves full of books.

"Now, you wait a hot minute," her voice grew more excited. "We met yesterday by the waterfront. I almost didn't recognize you looking all spiffy in your pretty sundress, but I'll be darned."

I was so busy taking in the surrounding beauty that I had not noticed the owner. "Helen? You're the owner? Wow, I had no idea. You must be so proud."

Standing at five foot six, Helen was a few inches taller than me, with subtle wrinkles on her face. The kind of wrinkles that implied she had worked hard throughout her life but took care of herself. She was a thick woman, but her curves went with her personality. I found her intriguing.

A children's section in the opposite corner was brightly painted with various colors, and beanbag chairs were scattered around the small shelves of books.

Helen grinned from ear to ear. "I'm thrilled you decided to stop by. She's small, and she's quaint, but she's all mine. The town's never had a bookstore, and it's always been a dream of mine. I've saved most of my life to open Bayview Books. When I turned fifty-five, I decided to take the plunge. I retired from my job as a paralegal and opened the store."

Crystal chandeliers hanging from the ceiling gave the store just the right amount of light. Next to the couches and chairs were small lamps for additional light. My eyes were filled with adoration for this authentic, little reading space.

Along the back wall was an antique wooden armoire with a mirrored glass door from top to bottom. Immediately drawn to its uniqueness, I had to take a closer look.

Following me, Helen said, "That's where I store my antique books."

"It's exquisite."

"The books I keep in there are only for display. I won't sell them. My great-grandfather collected old pirate manuscripts, and they've been passed down to me. I keep them under lock and key, but people can view them while they're in the store."

"Incredible. Pirates, huh?"

Helen chuckled. "Pirates, indeed. Southport has a history of pirates. We even celebrate Pirate Day. The town folks dress up like their favorite pirate, and we drink a variety of rums."

Of course, there's a Pirate Day.

"What an accomplishment. Your store's rich with unique treasures, history, and tremendous character. You've done an amazing job. I love it," I said, marveling at the chess pieces on the two-seater table beside me. "I've been out job hunting and getting acquainted with the town."

"I didn't realize you were staying. I thought you were visiting."

"I decided to stay for now. It's time to slow down. So, here I am, slowing down," I said with a shrug.

"What did you use to do?" Helen asked.

"I was an executive at a marketing firm in New York City. I worked all the time. I needed a change of pace." Answering honestly felt easy with Helen.

"I don't have full-time hours I can give you, but the store is much busier than I expected. If you'd like to help around here, I can hire you at least a few days a week. Maybe you can market the store too," Helen said.

"Are you serious? I'd love to work here." My legs felt jittery, and I couldn't keep my smile from filling my face.

"Girl, yes, I'm serious," she replied. "Come back Monday morning at nine o'clock to get started. You can wear anything that makes you comfortable, but look presentable. I'm not too picky."

"I'll be here, ready to go. Thank you so much, Helen," I said as I perused the books on the shelf in front of me.

Walking toward the exit, I turned and said, "Hey Helen, what's the story behind this incredible door? There must be a story."

Helen walked toward me, ran her hand along the wood, and said, "The door came with the place. As the story goes, in the late 1800s and 1900s, during prohibition, my bookstore was an illegal bar. Entry required a special knock and password. Supposedly, it's the original door." Helen used her fingers to push the flap on the metal slot in the door. "Apparently, they wanted to ensure the sheriff couldn't break down the door." She laughed.

"What a cool piece of history. You should put a little plaque on the wall telling the door's story."

Helen laughed and said, "Great idea. See, totally glad I hired you."

"Me too," I said. "See you Monday."

FIVE

The lasagna in the oven smelled so delicious that I thought spittle might drool right out of my mouth.

"Can I help set the table?" I asked Renee.

"Sure, the plates are over there." She nodded to a cabinet above the dishwasher. "Silverware's in the drawer over here." She pointed to a large drawer on the island. "Did you have a good day?"

Grinning from ear to ear, I said, "I had an awesome day. Downtown is beautiful. It has an incredible personality."

The town enthralled me. I did not realize that places like Southport existed. It reminded me of Stars Hollow from *Gilmore Girls* and was precisely what I needed. I was unsure I would recover emotionally, but living here was my best chance to heal and move forward, at least for now.

"Hey babe, sorry I'm late," Randy shouted as he walked through the garage door into the kitchen. "The tile cutter broke, so I had to cut the last few pieces by hand. What a pain in the ass."

"It's all good. The lasagna still has a few minutes, so you're just in time," Renee said as Randy scooted toward her and kissed her cheek.

"Ooh-wee, lasagna. My favorite. What's the occasion?"

"Celebrating Lizzie's visit," she said.

I enjoyed watching them live their peaceful life. They left the chaos behind years ago and had made a beautiful home here. They worked hard, and I am sure things weren't perfect all the time, but they chose happiness. Life is too short, and they lived it to the fullest. I admired that quality in Randy and Renee. I admired how they cared for each other, and I was in awe of their deep friendship and genuine desire to spend time together. But most of all, I admired the work they put into their marriage and how they did life together. Together.

Together was an interesting word. The adverb together means, in one place, in contact, connection, or union. Webster defined it as harmony or an integrated whole. One could say I was "together" with someone back in New York City. We were in one place. In connection? That's a hard no. In harmony, that's an even harder no.

"So, Lizzie, how was your day?" Randy asked, his question snapping me away from my thoughts.

"I was telling Renee before you came in how much I loved downtown. The bows, oh my God, the bows at the Christmas Shoppe."

Chuckling, Randy said, "Oh yeah, the Christmas Shoppe is the best. Renee buys bows for every occasion. And I don't just mean the traditional holidays. Any reason to buy new bows."

Renee narrowed her eyes as she set the lasagna on the table and said, "Whatever, Randolph Michael, you know you love my bows."

"I do, you know I do. I'm just having some fun with ya," he said, his lips curling into a colossal smile.

"Well, I love your bows. Don't let Randy steal your bow joy, Renee." I grinned at Randy. "I grabbed an application from the Christmas Shoppe, hoping to learn how to make them, but they aren't hiring. However, I did get a different job today."

"You did? That was fast." Randy sat down at the table.

"Yes, I did. I'm super excited about it. It's only part-time, but I'll be helping Helen at Bayview Books, the new bookstore that just opened." I took a seat at the table. "I'll be helping customers pick out books, stock shelves, and whatever else she needs me to do. She also said that I could promote the store for her. The job is kind of perfect for me. I can use my marketing skills, but it's low-key and simple."

"That's fantastic. I'm happy for you," Renee said as she pushed a serving spoon into the lasagna. "Dig in."

"So cool, sis. I'm pumped for you." Randy scooped a massive helping of lasagna onto his plate. He stared at the food like he hadn't eaten in weeks.

"Thanks. I start Monday, but enough about me. How about you guys?"

"I had a pretty eventful day," Renee said. "My class worked on a family tree project. They collected family photos and brought them into class to paste onto their trees." She sat down once she had her plate filled. "So, there I am, walking around the room helping the students, and I stop at Jameson's desk. He had an eight-by-ten family photo filled with people that caught my eye. There were probably thirty people in the photo. I guess he planned to cut each person out and place them on his family tree. Who knows? It was the only photo he'd brought. I reached down, picked up the photo, and said, 'Wow, Jameson, you have a large family. Why aren't you in the picture?' He blurts out, 'I was still swimming in my daddy's balls.'"

Water shot right out of my mouth and across the table. I thought my brother might choke on his garlic bread because he was laughing so hard. Renee jumped up and grabbed a dish towel to clean the mess. We all laughed hysterically.

"Yep, that happened. Never a dull moment in the first grade class at Brunswick Elementary," Renee said as she wiped tears from her eyes.

"I can't even imagine. What'd you do?" I asked.

Renee replied in between bursts of laughter. "I set the picture on his desk and said, 'All righty then. Just keep swimming.' It was the first thing that popped into my head. I was so caught off guard."

We all burst out laughing again.

"My stomach hurts," Randy said through his laughter.

Once we finished eating, I got up from my chair and cleared the table. I washed the dishes at the sink to put them in the dishwasher while Renee wiped down the table. Randy was taking a sip of wine and swallowed just in time before laughing again.

"Ahh, I don't know why I can't stop laughing. I keep imagining you standing there looking at this boy. I'm sure you would've never guessed that would be his reply." Randy kept taking deep breaths as he tried to collect himself.

Shrugging her shoulders, she said, "Yeah, it was one of those moments. You know, out of the mouths of babes. I mean, he wasn't wrong, I suppose."

Randy pushed his chair away from the table. "Dinner was delicious, babe. Thanks for cooking. I guess I'll head out back and get to work."

"What's out back?" I asked.

"We've decided to convert my work shed into an Airbnb. I need to get it cleaned out and ready to go. Which reminds me, the contractor will start in a few weeks. So, don't be alarmed if you see a crew back there working."

"Very cool, an Airbnb. Do you want some help?"

"Sure. You can at least keep me company. I want to hear all about New York."

"Wouldn't you love to know?" I said with a twinge of sarcasm. "Let me run upstairs and change, and I'll be right out."

I put the last dish into the dishwasher and went upstairs. Closing the bedroom door behind me, I caught a glimpse of the small pink blanket poking out of my suitcase. I pulled the blanket up to my face. Rubbing the soft blanket against my cheek, I closed my eyes and blew out all the air in my lungs. My chest ached. Sitting on the corner of the bed, I ran the blanket's edges through my fingers and traced the white silk elephant stitched in the corner.

"It's a lot bigger inside than it appears from the outside," I said to Randy as I stood in the center of his workshed.

"Yeah, it's a great space. I imagine a small kitchen over here," he said and pointed to the corner of the room. "A nice little island facing out into the center of the room. Against the other wall will be a living room. The bathroom will go in the other corner." He moved farther in and pointed up. "I'm thinking about a loft above the kitchen for the bedroom. That will make the living areas larger and more spacious."

"I love it all. Where will you work?"

"I'm considering renting a little space downtown to display my craftier items, with a workspace in the back."

"What a great idea. I'm so proud of you. You and Renee seem happy here. I'm sorry I haven't visited more," I said, feeling my gut tense.

I felt terrible. My brother and I are close, but I haven't bothered to visit him in years. *I chose my career over everything.*

The regret from my past choices oozed from the pit of my stomach and must have shown on my face because Randy looked at me with sad, curious eyes and said, "Lizzie, what happened? Don't get me wrong. I'm thrilled you're here, and you can stay as long as you need. But I can feel your sadness. I don't know how to help because I don't know what you're going through."

I sucked in as much air as my lungs allowed and exhaled slowly. "So much has happened."

"Oh, Lizzie, whatever it is, you can tell me. You're my sister. Let me help you."

"I appreciate that, but I need to work this out myself." *I needed to forgive myself.* "Welcoming me here is help enough."

"Okay, little sis. I won't push, but please know I'm here for you when you're ready to talk."

SIX

Late October

The streets were packed shoulder to shoulder with locals and vacationers lining the sidewalks. Many shades of blue embraced the clouds that looked like cotton balls sweeping across the sky. Waiting for the parade to kick off, Renee and I stood on the corner outside the Southport Market.

Children with bright eyes and smiles, dressed in an array of costumes, danced along the street. There were princesses, mummies, *Fortnite* characters, grim reapers, *Stranger Things* characters, and several costumes I didn't recognize. The air was cool, but it was the perfect day for the Spooktacular Parade.

The Southport fire trucks slowly rolled down the street with their sirens blaring. Not the typical emergency siren, but a beep-beep to kick off the parade. The gleaming bright red trucks stopped in the street, giving the nearby children a chance to get a better look, while firefighters wearing pumpkin hats waved happily at the crowd. It had been only three weeks since my arrival, but this place was starting to feel like home.

"Oh look, Lizzie, here they come," Renee said and pointed at the zombies riding in figure eights down the street.

The local axe-throwing team was in the parade, and Randy was the ringleader. They decorated their golf carts with cobwebs and leaves to make them look old and dirty. A sign hung from the lead cart: LUMBER JAX. Their clothes were ripped, tattered, and covered in dirt and blood. Randy's face was painted pale white with dark circles under his eyes and fake stitches painted on his cheek. His auburn hair was teased up and sticking out in different directions with sticks and leaves scattered throughout like he had just woken up from a weeklong slumber in the woods.

"This is too funny. These guys look like they're having a ball," I said to Renee.

A remix hip-hop version of The Cranberries, *Zombie*, bellowed from the golf cart speakers as they drove past.

Behind the Zombie axe-throwing team was the local Zumba club. They were dancing to Michael Jackson's *Thriller*. They looked like they came straight out of an '80s MTV Video. I began moonwalking in the street and finished it off with a spin and Michael's famous knee kick.

Renee cheered me on. "Yes, girl. Do your thing."

I was having the most fun I had in a while. Feeling light and hopeful, I enjoyed the moment. I knew it wouldn't last, but for today … I let my past go.

The parade continued down the street with the local high school band playing *The Monster Mash,* followed by a float of dancing skeletons. Next, a *Ghostbusters* wagon crept along the street with giant green ghost balloons floating in the sky. Three men and three women waving and dancing were dressed in gray ghost-busting suits as they walked on either side of the wagon.

"This is so much fun. I'm glad you insisted I come," I said to Renee.

"Now we can tease Randy and our axe-throwing friends together," she said and laughed.

"Oh yeah, lots of teasing for sure. For real, though, I think it's great they participated. It's marvelous you guys are so involved in the town."

"The fire trucks kick off the parade, and the police pull up the rear," Renee said as the police car passed us on the street.

"Perfect timing. I need to head to the bookstore and get ready for the Haunted Read tonight," I said, then hugged her goodbye.

Going over the list of things I needed to do when I arrived, I walked down the street toward the bookstore. Helen and I had become fast friends. She trusted me to host the Haunted Read, one of my marketing ideas for the store, and I didn't want to let her down. I was about to cross the street when something rubbed against my leg.

"Well, hello there, little guy. Where'd you come from?" I bent down to pet the adorable Goldendoodle nudging my leg.

He was so soft and gentle. His fur was a golden brown and adorned with a bright green collar. I could see a tag dangling from his collar, so I crouched lower to get a better look.

"Come here, little cutie. Let's see who you belong to." He sat on his hind legs and set his paw on my wrist. Tilting his head to the side, he let out a little groan as I located a phone number on the back of the tag. I needed to get to the store, but I didn't want to leave the dog on the side of the road. I dug through my backpack to find my phone when I heard a voice call, "Lizzie."

Who could possibly be calling my name? I know three people in town. As I rubbed the top of the dog's head with my hand, I heard the voice say, "I see you found my dog, Cooper."

I looked up and saw Josh trying to catch his breath.

"You," I said flatly. "This is your dog? You don't strike me as the doodle dog type."

"My dad bought the dog. He's such a good pup." Josh rubbed the dog's ears and said, "Except for today. You little stinker, running away from me like that."

"He's a cutie. Your dad chose well," I said. "I need to get going. I'm glad you found him."

"Wait. Lizzie, hold on a sec," Josh called after me, but I was already crossing the street. I turned and waved to him, shouting, "I'm sorry. I've gotta run."

"Thirty more minutes until the doors open," Helen exclaimed. Bayview Books looked incredible. "Oh, Lizzie, this is going to be so much fun. I can't believe you came up with this idea. Thank you for putting in the extra hours to get everything ready. I feel giddy. I could burst with excitement."

I had worked my ass off going door to door to get the local businesses to participate in tonight's event. The Christmas Shoppe loaned us one hundred jack-o'-lanterns placed throughout the store with battery-operated flicker candles inside each one. Southport Coffee Co. provided a hot chocolate stand and cookie decorating station, and the Southport Market provided black cauldrons filled with candy.

Helen gave me a budget for supplies and decorations, and I went all out. Randy helped me build a life-size coffin that I propped in the corner by the front entrance. He also agreed to play the vampire sleeping inside. Renee offered to help work at the event too. I bought Dollar General out of every bag of spiderwebs that now draped from each chandelier in the store. A fog machine sprayed haze every ten minutes, giving Bayview Books an ominous feel.

Helen was dressed like a Victorian queen. She wore a typical court dress, complete with a hoop skirt. Her short hair was slicked back and fastened into a bun accessory. I was a fortune teller, the perfect costume to play my part for the evening. Helen borrowed a projector from Renee's school that displayed a fire that flickered life-like on a large screen against the far wall. Eerie Halloween music played throughout the store speaker system to set the mood.

"Helen, do I look okay? It's almost time," I said, straightening the bandanna on my head.

"You look great." She was beaming from ear to ear.

"Randy, you ready to get into the coffin? Don't scare the kids too much." Laughing, I said, "Know your audience before you get crazy."

"I got this. Don't worry. I won't scare anyone to tears."

Dressed as Raggedy Ann, Renee was by the cookie station to help the kids decorate pumpkin-shaped sugar cookies. Helen had rounded up some friends from town who were also dressed in costumes scattered around the store to help make sure the evening was a success.

"Places, everyone," Helen shouted. She turned off the overhead chandeliers, so the only light in the building came from the jack-o'-lanterns and a few lamps she strategically chose to leave on. "I'm going to open the door. Here we go."

Everyone hurried to their places as Helen opened the door.

"Welcome to the Haunted Read," Helen curtsied and greeted the first guests who entered the bookstore. "We have loads of adult and child activities planned this evening. Take an activity card. This will help you follow along during the evening. Please enter at your own risk."

I designed small notecards to pass out. One side was purple with pumpkins and said kids in large capital letters.

KIDS

7:00 p.m. Welcome to the Haunted Read. Enjoy some hot chocolate and decorate sugar cookies. Have your fortune read by Madame Vondula, if you dare.

7:45 p.m. Queen Helen reads Book Of Ghost Stories

8:15 p.m. Games

9:00 p.m. Hocus Pocus

The other side of the card was orange, with spiderwebs and spiders decorating the edges.

ADULTS

7:00 p.m. Welcome to the Haunted Read. Enjoy special adult Halloween punch and snacks. Mingle with adults, if you dare.

7:45 p.m. The Queen reads Book Of Ghost Stories

8:15 p.m. Adult Games

9:00 p.m. Hocus Pocus

"Mwahaha," Randy said in a deep Transylvanian accent as he came to life and popped out of the coffin.

"Oh my God, I totally thought you were a prop," a man chuckled as he entered the store with his wife and twin daughters.

"Happy Halloween," I said, bending down on my knee to be at eye level with the twins. "I love your pretty Cinderella dresses."

By 7:30 p.m., the bookstore was filled to capacity. The event far exceeded my expectations. Wall to wall, children and adults were dressed in a variety of costumes, and the vibe was incredible.

Sitting at a small table for two outside the children's reading area with a fake crystal ball, I was ready to tell fortunes.

"Come closer, child," I said in my best fortune teller accent. I took special care to roll my r's as hard as possible. "Let me look into your eyes. Ahh, you are a brave one, I see."

The boy was dressed like a pirate, with one eye covered by a patch, but I could still see the surprise and wonder in his uncovered eye. He looked to be about seven years old. I saw him enter the store with his family, so I knew he had a little sister.

I continued. "You are strong like bull, and although you might pester your little sister at home, you love her. Your secret's safe with me. I see cookie decorating in your future. Off with you now." Pointing my finger toward the cookie station, I peered into his eyes.

The younger kids were mesmerized by learning their fortune, but the older kids knew I was a fraud. Playing Madame Vondula was a much-needed distraction, and I had fun pretending.

"Is this seat taken?" a stranger asked and pointed to the empty chair across from me at the table.

The stranger was dressed like V for Vendetta, complete with a Guy Fawkes mask, black hat, black suit, and a long black cape.

Playing along, I asked, "Would you like Madame Vondula to read your fortune?" They nodded.

Shuffling the deck of Go Fish cards used instead of actual tarot cards, I said, "Let's see what the cards tell us."

I flipped the first card onto the table. It was a red oyster shell with a pink pearl. "Ooh, this is a lucky card—the luckiest card of all. You'll come into a massive fortune. More fortune than you could ever imagine," I prophesied and did my best to maintain my silly accent.

"Well, wouldn't that be something," the stranger said and laughed playfully.

I flipped a second card onto the table. This time, the card was a conch shell with red tentacles dancing through the opening. Raising an eyebrow, I teased, "Ahh, this card tells me you have a secret. Perhaps you're keeping something from a friend or a significant other?"

The stranger's back stiffened as they sat up a little taller. Menacing eyes peered through the slits in their white mask. *If looks could kill. Are they being serious?* I wasn't sure, but the hairs on the back of my neck sending chills down my spine sure thought so.

"My apologies. I was having fun, playing a role. I didn't intend to offend or upset you. Please accept my apology," I said genuinely in my normal voice.

"Sure, you never intended to hurt anyone, did you? Karma, Lizzie Levine. Karma will come for you," the stranger spat.

My heartbeat quickened, and I could feel the cortisol pumping furiously through my veins. *How did this person know my name? What were they talking about?* Confused, I opened my mouth to speak, but my throat felt like I had devoured handfuls of sand. Closing my mouth, I worked hard to swallow my spit and clear my throat to respond when I saw Renee from the corner of my eye. I turned toward her.

"Lizzie, Helen is getting ready to start the reading. She asked us to help get the kids seated in the children's room," Renee said as she walked toward me.

"Okay, I'll be right there," I waved to her. I turned back to the table, and the stranger was gone. I scanned the room, but it was dimly lit and crowded, with people shuffling around to find a seat for the main attraction.

SEVEN

The sun danced on the horizon, painting a canvas of pink, orange, and faint purples in the sky. Quiet had fallen over the town after the hustle and bustle of yesterday. The serenity was a welcome change. I had to be at work soon, but I wanted a few minutes alone by the water. I inhaled deeply, filling my lungs with cool air until I thought they might burst. Closing my eyes, I exhaled slowly. I continued taking slow deep breaths as I reminded myself to appreciate the slowness of my new reality.

Buzzing through my bag against the wooden bench, my phone snapped me out of my peaceful calm. I unzipped the front pouch and dug for my phone. Then, like a sledgehammer, reality came crashing down on me. The text was from an unknown number. The words, "I'll find you," displayed on the screen. The phone buzzed again. "I see you. Eye emoji. I'm watching."

The hair on the back of my neck stood like tiny soldiers marching along my skin. My senses kicked into overdrive. I stood from the bench and spun around to glance behind me. No one was there. My heart was racing, and I felt like I might hyperventilate.

Stop it. Pull yourself together. It's probably a wrong number. Trying to calm my nerves, I deleted the text, gathered my things, and headed to the bookstore. I couldn't shake the feeling of being watched, so I picked up my pace. I was practically jogging as I approached the bookstore and bumped into Helen as she opened the door.

"Jeez, Lizzie. Why the hurry?" she asked curiously. "I mean, the store's great, and you're my favorite employee, but damn, girl. Such excitement to open the store." She laughed.

"I'm your only employee," I said as I rolled my eyes and smiled back at her. "I didn't want to be late." I shrugged my shoulders.

She gave me a side-eye as she put the key in the door's lock. "Maybe you should try again. You aren't due to be here for another hour."

I sighed. The noise that escaped from my mouth was much louder than I anticipated. I attempted to cover my anxiety by turning the corners of my mouth into an enormous fake smile.

"Come on, let's head upstairs. I'm glad you're here early." I was thankful that she didn't push the topic.

Helen set her bags down at the top of the stairs and flicked on the lights. I scooped up her things and followed behind her.

"Whew, last night was a fantastic success," Helen said with a huge smile. "Several children's books sold out, and we sold quite a few other books too."

"Wow, that's great. I'll count the drawer after we clean up since we didn't do that last night." I set our bags by the checkout counter.

Bayview Books was looking back at me, begging to be cleaned. Crowds of people came and went through the store last night, and the space looked tired and worn today. The spiderwebs that were neatly hung from the chandeliers were now ripped and drooping, some hanging almost to the floor. The children's reading area was a total disaster. Beanbag chairs were strewn around, books littered the floor, and several bookshelves were empty.

"This place got a lot of love last night. You're brilliant, Lizzie," Helen praised as she pulled webbing from the chandeliers.

My nerves were starting to settle, but I was afraid that Helen would hear the lingering anxiety in my voice if I spoke. *Deep breaths, Lizzie. It was a wrong number.*

"The party was great. I think the customers had a blast. The store needs some love today, but this is what Bayview Books was meant to do. Bring people together to celebrate and have fun. You know, make reading exciting. If kids enjoy coming to the bookstore, they'll read. I want people to have fond memories here," Helen said.

Finally collecting myself, I said, "It was fun. Your reading was epic. The kids seemed to have a blast. I think the adults even had a good time. They could be with their kids, but also have adult fun. The poker game in the corner might have gotten a little out of hand, though." I laughed. "The special adult punch was a hit."

"I couldn't believe the costumes. Not just the kids, either. I was shocked at how many adults dressed up," Helen said.

This is my chance. "Did you see the person dressed as V for Vendetta?" I was doing my best to seem nonchalant.

"Hmm, V for Vendetta? I don't think so. I don't remember that costume. Why?"

"Just curious. Whoever it was, acted like they knew me, but I didn't recognize them through the mask. It was a little odd. I thought you might know who they were."

"Sorry, I'm not much help."

"It's okay. Probably nothing." I was disappointed, for I had hoped that Helen would know who the mysterious V was. *"Karma, Lizzie Levine. Karma will come for you,"* the stranger's words, like a broken record, continued in my head. *Who was this person?*

"Oh, and I forgot to tell you the book club idea you suggested was fabulous. Three clubs are full: Colleen Hoover book club, Historical Fiction book club, and Sci-Fi book club. We have two others with people on the list," Helen chirped as she organized the bookshelves.

Absentmindedly picking up the cups and napkins that littered the floor, I said, "I'll start planning meeting times for each book club and create e-blasts to send to the groups. We can start in November. I can't wait to choose the books for each club. We have five clubs, right?" I didn't wait for an answer, I continued, "Maybe we do Tuesday and Thursday nights each week to host book clubs, so it's consistent." I pulled down a string of cobwebs and wadded it into a ball. "We'll let the club bring wine and cheese, pretzels and beer, or whatever they want. We can provide space for them to meet. I can create a link in the e-blast where they can easily order the book online, swing by, and pick it up." I did a little tap dance of excitement for my idea. "We can also make a book club table to display the current month's books. This way, when people are in the store and want to participate, they can go straight to the table and see what the group's reading."

Helen clapped her hands. "I love it. I love it all. This is going to be so much fun."

Exhausted, Helen and I plopped onto the couch in the center of the room. We had cleaned for hours, and the store looked great. Bayview Books was alive again, and work was exactly what I needed to clear my mind.

"I'm starving," I said.

"Me too. Ooh, let's order soup from No Soup For You. You call. I'll walk over and pick it up." She was already walking out the door as she spoke.

"Wait, Helen. What do you want?" I called after her.

"Silly me, I'll take a bowl of tomato soup and a grilled cheese sandwich. What do you want to drink? I'll grab those when I get there."

I opened my mouth to answer, but Helen cut me off. "Never mind. You want coffee, a pumpkin spice latte, hot with skim milk, right?"

Blinking at her, I stood there, my mouth still open. "Yes, that's exactly what I want. Are you secretly a mind reader?"

She giggled. "Nah, I just pay attention."

I walked over to the checkout counter and rummaged through my bag for my cell phone. Glancing at the screen, I realized I had a text message from Kit. *I'll read it later.* I Googled No Soup For You, Southport, NC, and tapped the call button. The phone rang several times before Dave answered. "Hello, No Soup For You, we have sandwiches, and if you're nice, we have soup. I'm Dave. What can I get you?"

"That was a mouthful, Dave," I said playfully. I could hear him laughing light-heartedly through the phone. "Well, I'll take a bowl of tomato and a bowl of potato soup, please. I'd also like to get two grilled cheese sandwiches. My friend Helen's on her way to pick it up."

He repeated the order back to me; I confirmed, then thanked him, and we disconnected.

I clicked open the text message from Kit.

Kit: Hope you're enjoying time with your brother. I forgot to tell you. I'm an aunt.

Kit: My sister had a baby girl. Celebration horn emoji.

Kit: She's beautiful. I spend every minute with her that I can. Smiley face emoji.

My heart sank, and my shoulders slumped, but my sadness was instantly replaced by guilt. I exhaled and texted back.

Me: That's fantastic news.

Don't be an ass, Lizzie. This is good news, so put your shit aside.

Me: I'm so happy for you, Auntie.

I settled in behind the register and began counting the drawer from last night. Helen wasn't kidding; the Haunted Read was a huge success. The event itself was free, but the customers bought loads of books. I carefully organized the bills, taking special care to ensure they were facing the same direction, when I heard the front door beep. I quickly placed the money in the safe under the counter and looked up to greet the customer.

"Hello, welcome to Bayview Books. I'm Lizzie. If you need help, let me know," I said, happiness spilling out of my mouth. Then, noticing it was Josh who entered the store, I gasped, "You!"

"It's lovely to see you too, Lizzie," he said. His voice was creamy like butter. "I read occasionally. My niece was here last night for the party. She went on and on about it this morning at breakfast. So, I wanted to come by and see what all the fuss was about."

"I'm glad your niece had fun. Are you looking for a particular book?"

He looked at me squarely and said, "I'm not sure. Do you have any books on how to land the girl of your dreams?"

His piercing blue eyes sent tingles pulsating through every inch of my body. He was extraordinarily handsome, but I refused to give in. "You mean you haven't written that book? I bet you know all the tricks," I said sarcastically, but deep down, I wanted to flirt with him.

He raised his hands to surrender and said, "It was a joke, but I'll wear you down eventually." He winked. "Don't say I didn't warn you."

"Good luck with that. You can try, but you'll fail. I'm not interested, I've given up on men." Doing my best to play coy, I allowed a flirtatious tone to escape with my words just as Helen interrupted with lunch in her hands.

"Get it while it's hot," she yelled as she bebopped through the door. "Whoops, I'm sorry I didn't realize we had a customer."

"Josh, this is Helen, the bookstore owner," I said and looked toward Helen.

"Hello, Josh. Are you a friend of Lizzie's?"

Josh walked toward Helen to help her with the food. He took the bags from her hand and set them on the counter. "I'd like to be."

"Do you need help choosing a book, or did you only come here to flirt with me?" I raised an eyebrow as I spoke.

"I'm good for now, but I'll be back. Maybe you can recommend a good Sci-Fi book for me when I return." He turned and walked toward the door to leave, but paused and turned back around. "You look beautiful, Lizzie. I'm glad I ran into you today."

I smiled and waved my hand as if I was shooshing him out the door. Rolling my eyes, I pretended I wished he had not come to the store today.

"Woowee, girl. He's H-O-T hot. Like smoking hot. Seems nice too. Why haven't you told me about this fine specimen of a man?" Helen took the containers of soup and sandwiches out of the bag and placed them on the counter.

"It's complicated. I'm not looking for a relationship right now," I said. Unfortunately, my voice sounded like I was trying to convince myself rather than speaking like I meant it.

"Well, he sure seems interested in you."

"I'm sure he is. Interested in the chase. You know the type. The kind that wants to add me to the list of girls he's conquered. I don't want any part of that," I said with conviction. Irrational fear sent ice through my veins, which helped convince me I was doing the right thing.

"Whatever you say, Lizzie." She sounded slightly annoyed. "Maybe he's actually a good guy, and he's into you. You might consider giving him a chance."

I didn't want to talk about Josh. I didn't want anything to do with him right now. My soup was scalding hot, but I didn't care. I shoveled a gigantic spoonful into my mouth so I wouldn't have to speak.

"Look, honey. I don't know what you've been through, but you can't push everyone away forever. You could miss out on the great moments life has intended for you. Life is worth experiencing, the good and the bad. You can't protect yourself from everything." Helen's eyes were filled with tenderness, and her tone was candid.

"Thanks," I said. "I'm working on healing my heart. I'm trying, but I need time." My head fell back on my shoulders, and I stared at the ceiling. "I've made too many bad decisions and suffered the consequences. I need to forgive, but it isn't easy."

"No, forgiveness isn't easy. But I have faith that in time you'll find it in your heart to forgive him," Helen said.

"Ironically, it's not a him. It's me. I need to forgive myself." Tears were forming in my eyes as I looked at her. That was the first time I had admitted that out loud. *I need to forgive myself.* "I don't feel that I deserve forgiveness."

Helen jumped from her seat and wrapped her arms around me. Her hug felt warm and necessary. Like a mother's embrace, her arms melted the pain away. I was grateful for Helen. Leaving my hands on her shoulders, I backed away and said, "Thank you. I really do appreciate you."

"Maybe you can start by telling me about your old job. How'd you get into marketing? I've visited Washington, DC once but never been to New York." She rubbed my arms once more and then gave me some space. "I'd love to hear all about it. You don't need to share anything that makes you uncomfortable. But I'd love to hear about the big city and enjoy it vicariously through you." She laughed.

"Okay, Helen. That sounds like a plan, but can we start tomorrow? I'm talked out for today." I was ready to get back to work.

EIGHT

Lying in bed, I forced myself to get a few more minutes of sleep. The past two days were long, and I was exhausted. I clung to the pink blanket beneath the covers. Drifting in and out of sleep, I dreamed my little girl was with me. I could feel her soft skin, and my heart swelled with love. I woke an hour later to the sound of my alarm screaming. Realizing she wasn't with me, I peeled my eyes open and released my tight grip on the baby blanket. I felt empty. Hollow. I dragged myself out of bed and staggered to the shower. My body felt heavy, like each limb was without function, and unwilling to move.

The water rained down on my skin, and I welcomed the warmth. Every day began as a struggle. I leaned against the wall and let the steam engulf me in the tiny space. Like an exorcism, I hoped the shower might cause the sadness to ooze out of my enlarged pores.

Two steps forward, one step back, I reminded myself. Two steps forward, one step back. *This is life, Lizzie. Right foot, left foot, right foot, left foot, keep moving forward.* I've been cheering myself on every morning in the shower for several months, and I couldn't remember the last time I was excited to tackle the day.

Anger swept over me in a flash, and my inner voice raged. *Other people go through far worse. Suck it up. You're not the only person on the planet having a hard time. Remember the people and happy moments you do have. Stop feeling sorry for yourself.*

From sadness to anger, this ritual had become the cable that jump-started my engine every day. I reached for the shower knob and turned off the water.

I slid the towel from the rack hanging on the wall and dried myself off. Catching a glimpse of my body in the bathroom mirror, I smeared my hand along the glass to clear the fog. My rib cage protruded through my skin, and I could count each rib. I hadn't realized I had lost so much weight.

Standing in front of the mirror, my eyes were drawn to my scars. A reddish, slightly curved scar was a few inches below my belly button. Another along my right hip bone still itched and bothered me occasionally. I applied Vaseline to help calm the itching and keep my skin from getting dry. I scooped another glob and applied it to the long scar down my left thigh.

Most of my bruises had faded away, but a few light brownish-green spots still lingered. My invisible bruises were the ones that hurt the most. Bruises to my heart, my self-confidence, and my soul.

Mentally, I still felt broken. Shattered like a fragile piece of glass, wandering through life and collecting the shards to put them back together someday.

I poured toner on a fresh cotton pad and wiped my face. Then, I applied Rodan and Fields Multi-Function Eye Cream and topped it off with the Eye Brightening Complex. The combination was magical, erasing any trace of bags or puffiness under my eyes. Grabbing the moisturizing lotion next to the sink, I swiped the inside of the round container with my finger and massaged the cream into my face.

I threw on jeans and a long sleeve T-shirt and ran a brush through my hair. Helen had given me the day off, and I was looking forward to the break. My twenty hours a week had turned into fifty. I didn't complain. I needed the money and enjoyed working at the store, but a day to myself was long overdue.

Feeling somewhat better, I straightened up my room, grabbed my bag, and walked downstairs to the kitchen. Renee was standing by the island and talking to Randy, who was eating a stack of pancakes at the kitchen table.

"Good morning," Renee said. "I made pancakes if you're hungry. Oh, and there are fresh-picked strawberries on the table."

I walked to the coffeepot and poured myself a cup. I didn't want to eat, but the image of my starved body flashed through my mind. "Thank you. I'd love some pancakes. Sounds delicious."

"You have plans today?" Randy asked.

"I'm not sure what I'm going to do yet. I'll probably run some errands at some point. I need to grab a few things. Or I might read. I don't know," I said. "What're you guys doing today?"

"I'm going fishing this morning, then probably work on the shed out back. The contractor and his crew start next week, so I want to make sure everything's ready for them." Randy pushed the bowl of strawberries toward me.

As Renee wiped the countertop, she looked up and said, "We should have a game night. Ask Helen if she wants to come."

"Okay, sure, that sounds fun. I'll text her in a little bit. What time?" I said as I drizzled syrup on my pancakes. I had not eaten them in years. Breakfast in New York consisted of coffee and a bagel, sometimes a croissant, or a doughnut on rare occasions. "I can make taco dip if you want."

"Sure, that'd be great. I'll take care of everything else. See if Helen wants to come around seven," Renee said.

"Will do." Finishing my breakfast, I grabbed my plate and washed it in the sink before placing it in the dishwasher. I poured myself another cup of coffee, grabbed my book, and headed out front to read.

Sitting on the bench, I watched the birds and heard a loud drumming, drill-like sound. I glanced around and searched for the noise. The sound was coming from a woodpecker beating his beak furiously into an oak tree across the street. Smiling, I chuckled internally, for I could relate. There were many times I felt the need to bang my head against a wall. Wanting to know more, I reached for my phone and typed in black and white woodpecker, Southport, NC.

This particular bird species was called a Downy woodpecker, known for its black and white feathers with a touch of red on the top of its head. They mostly pecked trees, but were sometimes known to wreak havoc on the wooden siding of houses.

Oh, the wonder of Google. Information at your fingertips.

I wondered what life must be like living on a diet of wood. I also wanted to know if the wood tasted different, perhaps a sweet and savory oak or some pine with a spicy kick. I admired the bird's beauty and work ethic as he pecked away at the tree. Perhaps mama woodpeckers stored wood chips in their beaks to feed their babies, or maybe the babies pecked for themselves. Curious, I went to *Google* again and was pleased to learn that woodpeckers do not enjoy a delicatessen of tree bark. They eat the insects that take up residence inside the wood.

Today had been restful. Relaxing. Now, it was time to have fun with my brother, his wife, and Helen. Several games were stacked neatly on the corner of the table. Three kinds of cheese placed on the kitchen island were cut into thin square slices and put in alternating rows with pepperoni on a beautiful glass tray. Small pumpkin-shaped dishes lined the edge of the glass tray and held a variety of mustards. Matching fall ceramic bowls filled with pretzels, chips, and Tostitos were organized in the shape of a triangle. A folded square card with Lizzie's Taco Dip written with blue ink in perfect penmanship was placed next to the Tostitos bowl.

"I have meatballs cooking in the Crock-Pot," Renee said happily.

"Yum, Ren. You know how to speak to my heart," Randy said as he pecked a gentle kiss on her cheek.

I adored the two of them, such sweetness. I looked forward to game night and spending time with Helen outside the store. She was the only person I considered a friend, and having some good old-fashioned fun would be nice.

I had positioned my taco dip in the designated spot on the counter when a knock bellowed through the house.

"I'll get it," I said as I walked toward the door. Helen stood on the porch smiling. She wore one of her typical outfits, leggings with a sporty matching quarter-zip top. "Hey, Helen. Come on in. I'm so glad you could make it."

"Thanks for having me."

"Welcome. Let me take that from you." Renee took the bottle of wine from Helen's hands.

"Okay, let's eat. The meatballs are calling my name," Randy said as he hovered over the Crock-Pot. The smell of homemade tomato sauce made everyone's mouth water.

Looking at Renee as she entered the kitchen, Helen said, "Your home is lovely." Then, she looked at the evening feast. "Wow. Look at all the food. I'm glad I came hungry."

"All right, everyone. Don't be shy. Grab a plate." Renee pointed to the stack of tan plates covered in fall leaves.

"You don't have to tell me twice." Randy scooped three meatballs, extra sauce, and dipping bread onto his plate. He chuckled. "I'll have snacks after."

Helen and I made our plates and sat at the table.

"What can I get you to drink?" Renee asked politely.

"I'll get it, Renee. Sit and eat," I said. "Wine for everyone?"

When everyone nodded, I poured four glasses of wine and listened to the chatter at the table. Helen thanked my brother and Renee for their help at the Haunted Read. Randy told Helen he enjoyed helping and was thrilled to have a bookstore in town. He commended her courage in opening the store. "It takes guts to go into business for yourself."

I set a glass on the table next to each person and took my seat. "The bookstore's remarkable. I'm grateful for the opportunity to work alongside Helen." I loved the job and appreciated that she trusted me to explore my ideas. Although, she did not agree with every idea I presented, she did agree with most of them.

"I'm grateful Lizzie walked into my store that day. She's been a godsend," Helen said to Renee and Randy. "I didn't realize how much work the store would be, and Lizzie's been there every step of the way."

"Aww, thanks, Helen," I said and blushed. I was not good at accepting compliments. I never quite knew how to react or what to say.

"Has Lizzie told you about the chess tournament or the book clubs?" Helen asked Randy and Renee.

"I told them about the book clubs but not the chess tournament," I said.

"Well, she has loads of plans. Plans for years to come." Helen laughed. "The chess tournament should be fun. We've planned it for January. Anyone can enter, and we'll have different ability levels and age groups depending on the number of people who enter. The winners will get a medal, Bayview Books credit, and, of course, bragging rights. We've even discussed taking pictures of the winners to display in the store."

"That sounds great. We aren't chess people, but I know Mr. Paul across the street loves to play. I'll make sure he knows about the tournament," Randy said.

"If it's half as successful as the Haunted Read, it'll be worth it," Helen said.

Randy nodded. "Yeah, the place was packed. I didn't realize that many people could fit inside the building."

"So many people." I gulped down the rest of my wine. "Speaking of, did you guys see the person dressed like V for Vendetta?"

Confused, Randy asked, "At the bookstore?"

"Yes, someone dressed as V for Vendetta at the Haunted Read. You know, with a white mask and a big black hat. Whoever it was sat at my table and asked me to tell their fortune. It seemed like they knew me. I thought maybe you'd have noticed a person dressed in that costume."

Randy looked thoughtful. "I don't remember a V."

Pouring more wine into her glass, Renee said, "I vaguely remember seeing someone in a white mask, but I was so busy I can't be sure." Then, she tipped the bottle in the air, signaling she could refill my glass too.

"No thanks. I'm going to have some water for now. I need to clear my palate for the stiff drinks I plan to consume later," I said, chuckling.

Pictionary can be a violent game when playing with the Levines. Born with a competitive streak and an unbreakable determination to win, Randy and I can become quite rowdy, but Renee might be the most aggressive of all.

Initially, I was concerned for Helen. She didn't know what she was getting into coming here for game night. Then, as I was about to apologize to her and suggest we calm down, she jumped into the battle, flailing her arms and defending her sketch of a sheepdog. The image looked like two blobs with eyes. I had no idea what she was drawing.

"It's so clear. How can you not see? Sheep, right here, this is a sheep." She snorted. "And this right here is a dog. Sheepdog. Ugh, so easy." She rolled her eyes playfully.

"Maybe I'm not thinking clearly and need a drink," I said as I stood up to walk to the counter and poured myself a glass.

"What're you making?" Randy asked.

"Fatorade," I replied.

"Fatorade?" everyone chorused.

"Yep, Fatorade. Keeps you hydrated and drunk. It's a two-for-one. Vodka and Gatorade." I lifted the bottle of vodka in the air. "It's time to get serious."

"Hell, I'll take one," Randy said. "Why not? Sounds interesting."

"Oh shit, here we go. The party's getting started now," Renee said.

Wrinkling his nose at her flirtatiously, he said, "Renny Ren Ren, you hush it."

We went from Pictionary to Catch Phrase and rounded out the night with a traditional game of Spades. Laughter was the best medicine, and I had several doses tonight. Glimmers of happiness and a future free from regret shimmered throughout the evening like glitter sparkling in the sky.

Randy shared the story of when he met Renee and their wedding. He told Helen how the bridesmaids, including me, stood in the center of the dance floor, turned around, lifted their dresses, and mooned everyone. Helen gasped, but leaned forward to hear more. He explained through his laughter that the bridesmaids wore white boxers with black letters painted on them that spelled BEST WISHES.

"My poor old Aunt Phoebe almost had a heart attack," Renee said. "We were so young. That was a long time ago."

Helen grinned. "Marriage is a splendid rollercoaster of ups and downs, twists and turns."

"Are you married?" Randy said to Helen.

My body clenched as he asked her the question. For myself, I had no plans to marry, ever. I'd been through enough. Hell, I'd practically sworn off men altogether. I admired my brother's marriage and the life he had created, but married life was not for everyone, especially someone like me.

"I was married for thirty years," Helen answered. She shifted in her seat before she spoke again. "My husband, Kenny, was a kind and decent man. God took him when he had a stroke a few years ago."

Laughter was replaced with genuine sincerity. I did not know Helen had been married. *I'm a shitty friend. How did I not know this*? My heart was sad for her, and I was sure that Randy did not enjoy the taste of his foot in his mouth.

"I'm so sorry. I couldn't imagine losing Ren," Randy said softly.

"I didn't realize. I'm so sorry, Helen," I said. The words weren't enough, but it was all I had to offer at the moment. I figured if she wanted to talk about it with me, she would have.

"I have good days and bad days. Kenny's why I opened the store. Life's too short, you know. I'd made excuses to justify not taking the leap sooner. After he died, I said screw it. Now's the time. It keeps me busy, and that's good." Helen fidgeted with her napkin.

"Good for you, Helen. You're a strong woman," Randy said to lighten the mood and bring back the good vibes.

"I take it one day at a time."

"We can't always control the things that happen to us," I said as I exhaled a little louder than I intended. "But we move forward and do the best we can."

"Isn't that the truth," Helen said.

"Spoken like a woman who's been through some shit. Huh, little sis." Randy began packing up the games. "Are you ever going to tell us what brought you here? What happened?"

"Randolph," Renee scoffed at the directness of his question. "We have a guest. Besides, Lizzie will tell us when she's ready."

"I've been patient, and I've been supportive. For Christ's sake, she's living with us. I think we deserve to know," he said, indignation in his voice.

Perhaps his boldness was the vodka talking. Did it matter? He was right. He deserved to know, but I wasn't ready to discuss what had happened. I needed time and space. Space was difficult to come by since I didn't have a place of my own, and time, well, time, was just that. Time moved forward at the pace of sixty seconds per minute. No matter how much I wanted to, I couldn't speed it up or slow it down.

Politely, Helen said, "I had a lovely evening. Thank you for having me over, but I think it's time for me to head home." She got up from her chair and collected her things. "I didn't realize how late it was. I'm surprised I haven't already turned into a pumpkin."

"Thank you for coming. I'll see you tomorrow at work." I hugged her and waved goodbye. Closing the door, I spun around and glared at Randy.

Outraged, I said, "How could you?"

"We deserve to know. Maybe my timing was bad, but I want some answers," he shouted.

I began pulling and tugging at my pant leg. "What do you want to hear? Do you want me to tell you I fell in love with a man, and it almost broke me? Or that I cared about my career over everything else?"

I finally worked my pant leg up to my hip. Pointing to the scar on my thigh, now in full view, I said, "Do you want to know that this is one of several reminders of the stupid mistakes I've made?" Tears rolled down my cheeks, and I continued, "Thanks for everything you've done. I'll start looking for my own place tomorrow. You've both been extremely gracious, but I've overstayed my welcome."

"Oh, sweetie, please don't be hasty. Let's all get some rest and regroup in the morning." Fixated on my scar, Renee's eyes filled to the brim with tears. "Your brother loves you. He's concerned. We both are. We want to make sure you're okay."

"Look, you don't have to tell us until you're ready. But please tell me if you've done something illegal or are in legal trouble." Randy dropped his head into his hands.

"Of course, you'd think that. No. I'm not mixed up in anything illegal, and I don't have any legal troubles. I'm done having this conversation. I'm going to bed," I shouted. "Good night." I turned and stomped up the stairs.

How could he? How could he bring this up in front of my friend? My boss. And then insinuate that I had done something illegal. No matter how many years pass, I'm still his stupid, bad-decision-making little sister.

I flopped onto the bed in a huff and buried my face in the blue decorative pillow with the word JOY stitched on the center in a soft script. Pressing my face into the letters on the pillow, I practically suffocated myself as I convulsed through my tears. I wouldn't dare let Randy hear me crying.

I woke to a burst of sunlight, smacking me straight across the face through a slit in the curtain. My eyes burned, and my head ached. I squinted and blinked frantically to give my pupils time to adjust to the light.

For a moment, I thought the Downy woodpecker was pecking my skull, the pounding increasingly more painful with each inhale. Then, I pulled the covers over my head, rolled over, and slammed my eyes shut.

Unfortunately, the bed began to spin like a top. I barely reached the bathroom before the vomit projected from my mouth. Foul-smelling puke mixed with vodka, red Gatorade, and meatballs splashed into the toilet bowl.

On the bright side, my head was feeling slightly better now. I pushed myself off the floor and dragged my body into the shower. I didn't have time to feel like shit. Helen was expecting me to come to work today. The bookstore was closed, but she had planned to restock shelves and take inventory. At some point today, I also needed to look for a place to live.

I grabbed the bottle of Tylenol from the medicine cabinet and popped two into my mouth. I gulped a glass of water to wash them down. As I entered the bedroom, I noticed a note on my dresser.

Lizzie,

> I'm sorry. My words came out wrong. I love you. You're welcome to stay as long as you need. Truly.

Randolph

NINE

I pushed open the heavy wooden door to the bookstore and found Helen organizing the mystery section. My sunglasses still rested on top of my nose to protect my eyes from all forms of light.

"One too many Fatorades last night?" Helen said, her comment more like a statement rather than a question.

I put my things behind the counter and slowly wandered over to help her.

"I'll be fine. I just need a few more minutes for the Tylenol to kick in. I've brought vats of water and coffee to help flush my system." I began taking books from the boxes she had set on the table and placed them alphabetically on the shelves.

"I'm thinking about rearranging some of the shelves. You know, to switch things up a bit. Keep the customers on their toes. What do you think?" Helen asked as she bent over to clean the bottom shelf.

"Sure. Changing things around can make old displays look new and potentially increase sales. Let's create some new highlight tables too." I sipped my coffee.

"Great. Love it. Let's get to work." Helen snapped into action. She was moving a little too fast for me this morning. I needed the room to stop spinning, and I really needed the damn Tylenol to kick in.

We worked around the outer edge of the store. Helen decided which sections would stay in their place and which would move to a different home on a new shelf. We emptied each shelf and wiped and cleaned them from top to bottom. Then, she logged each book into inventory on the iPad.

"I'm sorry things got a little crazy last night," I said softly to hide the lump in my throat. "We both had too much to drink and—"

"No need to explain. I have siblings, and I had a good time. I'm curious, though, about your life in New York City. You did say that you'd tell me." She pursed her lips and tilted her head playfully.

Raising my hands in surrender, I said, "Okay, okay. Where do you want me to start?" I figured I couldn't feel much worse today, so I might as well share small pieces of my past with her. Helen was my friend. Perhaps sharing some of my experiences would help bring me peace.

"Start at the beginning."

I took a deep breath and slowly exhaled as I placed each book back on the shelf. Finally, I opened my mouth to speak, but my throat felt dry like I had sucked on a paper towel. I reached for my water and took a gigantic gulp. I wished I had more coffee, but I had already polished that off.

"My parents died in a car accident when I was a senior in high school—drunk driver. Randy handled everything that came after, and he told me I'd have access to a trust fund when I turned eighteen." My headache was fading, and I continued to organize the books.

"He said the money was mine to spend how I pleased, and he wouldn't control my choices. He pleaded with me to make smart decisions and use the trust fund wisely. I don't remember much of the first year after high school. I shared an apartment with a friend and spent most days completely wasted. Losing your parents leaves a deep hole in your heart, and I had a pile of money to fill that emptiness. The two make a deadly combination."

Helen nodded in agreement.

"One day, I was lying in bed, and I swear I could hear my mom screaming in my ear. She said, 'I didn't raise you to waste your life. Get up. Get your ass out of bed and do something.' I know it sounds crazy, but I felt like she was in the room. Chills ran down my spine, and I promised at that moment that I would do everything I could to be someone she and my dad could be proud of. Grief has a funny way of changing your life. Grief provides perspective, whether you want that perspective or not."

"Amen to that," Helen said.

Helen and I were sitting on the floor, and I had to shift my weight before my legs went numb as I continued. "I applied to fifteen colleges over the next few weeks, but I wasn't accepted to any. Not one. So, I enrolled in the local community college and received my Associate's degree in business administration, but I didn't stop there."

"You weren't accepted to a single University?" Helen said in disbelief. "And you didn't quit? I'm amazed. After fifteen rejections, I'm not sure I'd have bothered to keep trying."

I laughed. "Nope. I didn't quit. After community college, I attended Villanova University, where I received my degree in marketing. I worked for a local firm in Pennsylvania for a year but knew I wanted more. I wanted to be an executive at a marketing firm in New York City. So, I worked my ass off, and Harvard eventually accepted me, where I received my master's degree."

Nodding her head in approval, Helen said, "Harvard."

I smiled and continued.

"After Harvard, I applied to several marketing firms in New York City. My Harvard degree should've gotten me a job immediately, but it didn't. Six months and a dozen interviews later, I was hired as an executive assistant at Gray Stone Marketing, the largest and most prestigious firm in the country. So, off I went to New York City around the time Randy and Renee moved here. I guess they figured I had my life on track, and it was finally time for them to move from the Northeast to the South."

"I'm still soaking in that you have a master's degree from Harvard University. My marketing muse is a Harvard graduate," she said proudly. "So you got the job, and then what happened?"

I laughed. "A Harvard degree has a costly price tag attached to it. I suppose it did the trick because I eventually worked my way up to the Chief Operating Officer at Gray Stone, and now I'm here working for you."

She punched me in the arm. "What? Bayview Books isn't worthy of a Harvard degree?"

"No. No. That's not what I meant. I don't want that life anymore. I'm happy here, and I love working for you. But let's be honest—I don't need a Harvard degree to work here. In hindsight, I could have saved a lot of money," I said.

"Fair point. Tell me more about Gray Stone Marketing."

I took a deep breath and plowed on. "I was an executive assistant, but barely made enough money to survive. I had a little money left from my parents, but by then, I was older and wiser." I snickered. "And I didn't want to blow it all. I'd invested quite a bit in my education. In the beginning, I worked for a woman named Serena. She was the only female executive at the firm. I also worked for a man named Daryl. He was short, round, and bald."

Helen chuckled at my description. "Short, round, and bald, eh?"

"Each morning, I'd swing by the Starbucks on the corner and order their coffee. Venti Pike Place with oat milk, two pumps of vanilla, and one pump of caramel for Serena. Grande Café Americano for Daryl." As I remembered, I shook my head. "I didn't dare be late. I scheduled their appointments and maintained their calendars. Occasionally, I had to pick up and drop off dry cleaning. I didn't mind running that errand because I could visit Giovanni," I said.

"Do tell. Giovanni sounds divine." Helen rested her chin on her hands with a dreamy look on her face.

"He was Italian, complete with the accent and all. Tall, dark, and handsome. He spoke decent English but often mixed up his words, which was completely adorable. We never dated or anything, but I enjoyed the view and his accent every time I went."

Helen giggled like a schoolgirl and climbed the steps to the loft. She wanted to move the history books up there, so I lifted the boxes over my head for her to grab.

"My favorite part of the job was preparing their marketing pitches. They would meet with their teams and create proposals for large and small companies. Once the smarter, higher-paid people developed the ideas, I would package them in a presentation to use during their pitch meetings. I had to work for months to earn their trust to be awarded that opportunity." I sighed. "I never imagined how hard adulting would be."

Helen scoffed. "Who you telling? Adulting's the pits."

"I wasn't a small fish in a large pond. I was a small fish in a sea of sharks. Everyone scratching and clawing their way to the top. Girls were sleeping their way up the corporate ladder."

Helen raised an eyebrow and glared at me, the way a mother's eyes glare at their child.

Twirling my finger in front of her face, I said, "You can put that eyebrow back in its place. I didn't sleep my way to the top. I'd never go that route. I earned my stripes. I do feel for those girls, though. Corporate life is difficult. Powerful men, practically throwing themselves at the young, fresh fish in the sea. Some girls think a quickie in the office or a BJ in secret under the desk will advance their careers faster. In some cases, they were right. In other cases, they got nowhere. They were talked about as the office tramp and eventually moved on to another job elsewhere."

Shocked, Helen asked, "Why didn't they say no? I thought those types of things were only in the movies."

I grunted. "Oh, it's real. You should hear the men talk about the young women they interview. The first comment is always about their looks, never what they bring to the table. Those girls lacked the confidence and self-esteem to say no, and that's why they did it. I think for some girls, the attention feels good. Men in powerful positions know this and take advantage of their naivety."

Helen's face twisted in understanding, and she opened her mouth to speak and then paused. She sighed, then said, "Did this happen to you? Were you hit on by men you worked with?"

"All the time," I said without hesitation. "Every day, honestly."

"Every day," Helen said, emphasizing the word *every*.

"Yeah, every day. The advances varied depending on who was dishing them out. Lower-level executives were more playful and mostly harmless. Almost like they were practicing for the main event someday or hoping for the off chance that one girl would say yes." I rolled my eyes.

"I typically replied to them with, 'You wish,' or 'Maybe never.' The more money they made, the more straightforward and less playful the advances became." I handed Helen another box. "I made it clear immediately that I was not that kind of person, and eventually, they stopped. The word spread, I guess. For a woman to get ahead in the corporate world, she needs to outwork and outsmart the other women, but she also needs to do the same with all the men. Sometimes, even then, it isn't enough."

"Isn't that the truth."

TEN

Helen put on her coat and picked up her bag as I stood at the door waiting for her. She closed the store a few hours earlier than usual on the second Friday of each month because she played bunco with her neighbors.

"I know you can stay and run the store," she said. "But honestly, it's dark out by five now, and the store doesn't need to be open. I don't want you here until nine by yourself."

"I appreciate that, but I'd do it if you needed me to."

"I know you would," she said, wrapping her scarf around her neck.

We left the store together, and Helen locked the door behind us.

"I'll email you the schedule for the next few weeks tomorrow. If you have a chance, can you send me the Stories with Santa event plan? We have some time, but I'd like to have a plan sooner rather than later." I followed Helen down the steps and out the door to the sidewalk. "I know you're off tomorrow, so it can wait until Sunday. No biggie."

"Not a problem. I'll get that together for you." I walked with Helen to her golf cart parked along the side of the road.

She climbed into the sleek, black, brand new golf cart and asked, "Do you want a ride?"

"No, thanks. It's out of your way, plus I enjoy the exercise. Have fun at Bunco, and I'll see you Sunday."

"Have a great night. I can't wait to hear more about New York," she said.

I hugged Helen goodbye and waved as I walked a few blocks toward the beach. Sitting by the water sounded nice. Seagulls danced through the sky, and the sun had almost laid itself to rest. Sitting on the wooden bench that had become my personal sanctuary, I watched the gentle waves slap onto the shore. The sound was incredibly soothing. I let the calmness sink into every cell in my body, and lure me to sleep. For the first time in a long time, I let my mind wander to the future. *Would I be happy alone? Would I be happy here? Would I someday get over myself and marry and have children? What am I doing with my life?*

I could feel the anxiety creeping back into my gut like a snake slithering along the grass, watching its prey. I inhaled the cool salt air to fill my lungs. Then, exhaling slowly, I gently pushed my breath out of my mouth and closed my eyes. I let the ocean breeze wash over me like an absolution of forgiveness. I repeated the breathing ritual, and for a short while, I allowed myself to believe that I deserved forgiveness.

I knew Renee would start cooking dinner soon, so I reluctantly stood up. I didn't want to leave the moment, so I commanded my legs to carry me home.

As I suspected, my mind snapped back to reality as visions of the apartments I had found online rushed into my mind. None were viable. Two were out of my price range, one was forty-five minutes away, and the last apartment had black mold. The landlord quickly responded to my email and said he would fix it before I moved in, but it would take a few months. I wasn't too sure about the moldy place, even if it was fixed. Finding a place I could afford was much more complicated than I expected. However, I found a tiny house I planned to look at tomorrow.

I stopped, realizing I had passed my street. I turned, then looked at my phone to check the time. It was 6:35 p.m.

Out of the corner of my eye, I saw a shadow move. *Am I being followed?* I picked up my pace, but I could hear footsteps behind me. Maybe they were going in the same direction. That wouldn't be so strange.

I urged myself to calm down, but the hairs on my neck disagreed. *Let's assume I am being followed. Should I start running?* I decided to take a more passive approach and turned left on Third Street. I stretched my eyes as far as my peripheral vision could see. As I sensed the footsteps that followed, alarm bells sounded throughout every inch of my body, but I refused to listen. Instead,

I steadied my breathing, continued to the next block, and turned right. Forcing myself to keep my pace even, I racked my brain for a place to hide. The last thing I wanted to do was lead this person to Randy's house.

I could hear their footsteps on the pavement behind me as tiny pebbles crunched under the stranger's shoes. I had to do something. I hooked another right at the next block and headed back toward Caswell. Praying that I was making the correct decision, I crossed the street and walked up a little sidewalk that led to a tan house. A Honda Accord and an older Ford Mustang were parked in the driveway. I continued to the front door and pushed the button to ring the bell.

Breathing a sigh of relief, I saw my shadow continue past the house and turn right at the next block. Luckily, no one was home at the tan house; that would have been awkward. *Hi, I think I'm being followed. Can I come inside and hide?* I rolled my eyes and turned to leave when I noticed a man sitting on his porch across the street. I smiled and waved as I walked back across the street. "Did you see someone else walk past?"

"I didn't see anyone, sorry," he said.

"Okay. Thanks. Your Christmas lights are beautiful. How do you get all those lights on your giant oak tree?"

He stood from his porch swing, moved toward the rail, and grinned. "Oh no, honey. We pay someone to do that for us. That's way too high for me."

"Well, good. I love looking at them, but I'd be terrified knowing you climbed a ladder and put those lights up," I said. "Have a good night."

Standing at least sixty feet tall, the oak tree was beautiful. White twinkling lights covered the trunk and hung perfectly through the branches. It was gorgeous. A bit early for Christmas lights, but I suppose when you're paying someone to do them, you want to enjoy them for as long as possible.

A familiar aroma tickled my nostrils as I entered the front door.

"Do I smell chili?" I asked.

"You don't smell chili. You smell the Chili Cook Off People's Choice Award Winning Chili," Randy said, patting Renee on the shoulder. "Ren's the champ. Best chili for miles."

"It smells delicious," I said as I closed the door. "I'll set the table. Do you need help with anything else?" I asked Renee.

"Everything's almost ready," she said, and pointed toward the pantry. "You can grab the Fritos."

Randy was at the sink washing his hands and asked, "How was your day?"

"Fine," I said flatly.

"Fine, huh? I've been married long enough to know that fine means not fine. What happened?"

"Apartment hunting was a bust, and I'm bummed. Work was great, though, except for my walk home. I swear I was being followed." I scooped a heaping bowl of chili.

"Followed?" Randy asked, more surprised than inquisitive. "That doesn't make sense, not here. Are you sure?"

"Honestly, no, I'm not sure." I described the entire experience block by block for them to draw their own conclusion.

"I don't know, sis. Sounds crazy. We have zero crime here. Who would want to hurt you? They probably were going in the same direction."

He may be right. That was the thing; I wasn't even sure myself.

"I don't think you should walk home alone after dark, anyway. We can pick you up, or you can use the golf cart," Renee said as she wiped her mouth with her napkin after eating a spoonful of chili. "Pass me the Fritos. I need more." She laughed.

"We'll see. You guys are doing so much for me already. I don't want to ask you to do more. Helen offered to bring me home, too. Maybe I can catch a ride with her."

"We'll figure it out. But you don't need to walk home alone at night, period," she said with conviction.

"I agree." Randy squeezed some sour cream into his bowl. "Oh, before I forget, the construction workers will be here tomorrow. They shouldn't be in your way, but I wanted you to be aware."

"Got it," I said quickly. I wanted to shovel more chili into my mouth. The taste was like a fiesta of deliciousness dancing on my taste buds. The diced tomatoes had a hint of garlic flavor, and the ground beef was cooked just right.

Renee must have been reading my mind. She looked at me and said, "I use eighty percent fat ground beef. It adds flavor. I also like to use kidney and pinto beans. But the real secret is my homemade chili seasoning and a little bit of sugar."

"Sugar? In chili?"

"Yup. Sugar. That's the secret." She smiled and winked.

ELEVEN

Bang, Bang, Bang!

I shot out of bed like a cannonball, sprang to my feet, and rushed to the door. Still groggy and unsure of my surroundings, I thought a burglar had broken into the house, and then it hit me. Construction started today on the Airbnb. Yearning for more sleep, I dragged my weary legs back to the bed and flopped like a beached whale onto the mattress.

I lay in bed, but my mind was unable to rest. Ideas for Stories with Santa circled in my head, like a disco ball turning on the dance floor. I hoisted myself out of bed and skipped the morning shower ritual. Instead, I tied my hair in a messy bun, brushed my teeth, freshened up yesterday's makeup, and threw on some sweats.

Grabbing my laptop off the dresser, I headed downstairs to the kitchen, where Randy and Renee sat at the table. I said good morning to them, set my laptop on the counter, and walked straight to the coffeepot.

"We have fresh croissants from Burney's this morning," Renee said. "And as you can hear, the construction workers are here."

"Sounds great. I thought the pounding was in my head." I laughed and poured a cup of coffee. "I have event planning work to do for Helen today, so I might sit out front and work for a while."

"It's such a nice day to sit outside. I wish I could join you, but I have a shiplap wall to build down the street. Ren's going to be my assistant. So, we won't be around most of the day," Randy said as he stood up from the table. He was wearing an old gray Philadelphia Eagles shirt and red mesh shorts. His socks, covered with brightly colored turkeys, were pulled up to his calves.

Laughing, I looked him up and down. "You're very colorful today."

Shrugging, Randy looked down at himself. "What, you don't like my work attire?"

I opened the box of croissants, peered inside, and gazed at the various choices. My options were plain, chocolate drizzle, pumpkin flavor, and chocolate cream stuffed. I should probably have two. Surely, these will help pack on some pounds. I picked up the chocolate drizzle, placed it on my napkin, and sat at the table.

"After I finish my work, I'm going to check out a room for rent on Clarendon." I bit into my croissant. "Oh my God, this is the most delicious pastry I've ever eaten. It's literally melting in my mouth."

"They're so good," Renee said. She looked at Randy and shook her head. "All right, Mr. Rainbow Bright, we should probably get going."

"I'll see you guys later tonight," I said as I took another sip of my coffee.

"We're going to take the truck. I've left the key to the golf cart on the counter if you need it." Randy waved goodbye and walked out.

Sounds of drilling and banging drowned out the silence and made it difficult for me to focus. I thought about leaving to find a quiet workplace but didn't feel like going out in public. Some days, I didn't want to be around people.

I poured myself a second cup of coffee and stirred in my Stevia and creamer. I picked up my mug and laptop and went out front. Setting my things on the tiny table, I sat on the bench and watched the little blue bird flapping and splashing his wings in the bath. Carefree and full of spirit, he flitted around and seemed not to notice the human who entered his territory.

I took a few minutes to sip my coffee and watch the birds. Suddenly, a beautiful red cardinal flew from the oak tree branch to the birdhouse, where he paused and sang a soft tune. I wondered if he was telling friends about the fantastic sanctuary he had found or if he was singing a love song to attract a mate. Then, he sprang from the birdhouse and perched himself on the feeder. The feeder held a variety of food, but Mr. Cardinal was interested only in the sunflower seeds. I watched him pick through the feeder to find them, eat them, and spit out the shells. I guess that's where the saying, "You eat like a bird," comes from.

You can't sit and watch the birds all day.

After an hour of the nature channel live in Randy's front yard, I decided I needed to get to work. I powered on my laptop, created an event plan, and then a list for Stories with Santa.

NEEDED STAFF AND SUPPLIES

Santa – Ask Randy

Mrs. Claus – Helen

Santa's Elf – Me

Hot Chocolate Bar – Southport Coffee Co.

Reindeer Food – Buy Supplies

Candy Canes – Buy Supplies

Christmas Carolers – From the church

'Twas The Night Before Christmas – Santa

Movie – Polar Express

Photographer – Me

I finished creating the list and was packing up when I heard a branch crackle behind me. I turned to see what it was.

"You again," I said, annoyed.

"Hey, Lizzie. What are you doing here?" Josh asked.

"I could ask you the same question."

Feeling embarrassed about my appearance, I rubbed my hands on the top of my head in an attempt to flatten my stray hairs as if that would magically make me look put together.

He pointed to the backyard and said, "Um, well, my company is doing the renovation."

"Your company?"

"Yes, I own a construction company. We do most of the renovations and build homes in the area." He stood tall with his legs spread wide. There was a gleam in his eyes.

"Of course you do," I said as I rolled my eyes to tease him.

He was dressed as usual, in jeans, work boots, and a long sleeve T-shirt that accentuated his muscles.

I was certain he was smug, self-centered, and only focused on one thing: sex. But damn, he was fine. I couldn't take my eyes off him as he walked to his truck.

The sun glistened over his dark brown hair and highlighted the five o'clock shadow on his chiseled jawline. His ass filled the backside of his jeans so perfectly. I stared in awe at his fine body and momentarily disconnected from reality as he hopped onto the back of his truck and leaned over into the bed. There was no denying he was nice to look at, but that's where the relationship needed to end. He had to be an asshole, after all, no different from every other man.

He hopped down from the truck and turned toward me. Catching me looking at him, he raised an eyebrow and smiled. Electricity shot through every nerve in my body. I could feel each impulse transmitted from cell to cell and back again. *Jesus Christ, if his smile could supercharge my senses like this, I could never trust myself with him.*

"I-I need to go," I said, my voice cracking. "I have someplace to be." I stood up, grabbed my things, and hurried toward the house.

"Wait," he called, jogging after me. "Wait, slow down. Why are you always running away from me?"

"I can't …" I said, less shaky this time as I collected myself. He jogged past me up the stairs onto the porch and blocked my way to the front door.

"Lizzie, I liked you from the moment I knocked you down in the store." He chuckled nervously. "I haven't been able to get you off my mind. I want to get to know you. Will you at least give me a chance? I think fate keeps putting us together."

His words felt genuine. Every fiber in my body wanted to jump into his arms and lock my lips onto his. But my mind screamed no. *Hell no.*

"You don't want to hop on my crazy train. That's all I can say. Trust me." I eased past him toward the door.

He grabbed my waist, spun me around, and pressed my back against the door. His arms extended on either side of my head. Our bodies were so close I could feel his heartbeat. He leaned closer, his face only inches from mine, and said, "I'm not giving up, Lizzie Levine. I know you feel the energy between us. You can't deny your feelings forever."

He leaned even closer, and my body tingled from head to toe. I mustered every ounce of strength I had and said, "I don't deny there's chemistry between us, but not all elements are meant to mix. Some can explode when combined." I leaned in even closer, with only a sliver of air separating our lips, giving him a glimmer of hope, and said, "I'm going back inside now."

His body went slack, and I could tell I had taken the wind out of his sails. I turned, opened the door, and disappeared inside.

TWELVE

Christmas carols blared from the overhead speaker as I walked through the door. Several regulars were playing chess and reading books on the couch in the store. Helen allowed them to hang out in the morning for a bit, but she had closed the store today to decorate.

"Great. You're here. It's time to decorate the storefront. The holiday window competition is coming soon," Helen said. She was singing and dancing as she handed me a box of lights.

I raised my eyebrow. "Window competition?"

"Oh yes. Every store on Moore Street decorates its windows, and the residents vote on their favorite. I'm thinking a 'Twas The Night Before Christmas's theme." She clapped her hands together as her mouth spread into a huge smile.

"Well, all righty then, let's do this." I reached into the box, pulled out a strand of lights, and started to untangle the knotted mess. "Speaking of Christmas, I sent you the plans for Stories with Santa."

"Yep. Looks great. A few details to figure out, but I saw the plan and think it'll be awesome. Did you have a good day off yesterday?"

"Nothing special, but it was nice to have time for myself," I said and grabbed a second strand of lights. "My brother's turning his workshop into an Airbnb, and you'll never guess who's doing the work."

"Who?" she said curiously.

"Josh." I could feel my cheeks heating up as his name came out of my mouth.

"Josh the hottie?"

"Yes. That Josh. He owns the construction company that Randy hired. He cornered me and practically begged me to give him a chance."

"And did you?" Helen asked with a gleam in her eye as she stood up to hang the strand of lights in her hand.

"No. I can't. Josh is handsome and seems genuine, but every time I'm around him, alarm bells sound, and stamp out the butterflies his good looks and charm bring fluttering in my stomach."

Helen's face wrinkled with disappointment. She looked at me and said, "What's holding you back? You should go for it. Accept a dinner date with the man. You're not getting married. Give him a chance."

"It's not that simple," I said somberly. I tilted my head down and took a deep breath. "My heart is hurt, and I need to heal it first."

"New York?"

I nod.

"Did a New York City man hurt you, Lizzie? I don't mean to overstep, but clearly, you're guarding your heart from something. I'm your friend, and I want to help," Helen said as she placed her hand gently on my shoulder. "Plus, I like Josh." She smiled.

"A man broke my heart, and my world was shattered, but he didn't physically hurt me." I kept my gaze on the floor.

We allowed the Christmas music to fill the silence as we continued decorating. Helen knew me so well and understood that I needed a moment. We strung garland and twinkling lights around the edge of the store windows. Helen had planned to hand paint a scene of Santa reading a book to three small children by the fire. She projected the image onto the window and traced it with a window marker.

"That part's done. Now we're ready to paint," Helen said. "Tell me more about your job in New York while I work."

I stiffened. "Seriously, why?"

"One, because I've been a paralegal my entire life, I've never been farther north than Maryland, and two, because you need to talk about whatever happened there. It's healthy for you to get it out of your system," she counseled.

I inhaled slowly through my nose and exhaled. "All right." I lifted my chin and looked firmly at her. She was correct; I needed to share my story.

"I worked twelve-hour days. I didn't take vacations, and I never visited my brother. My career was everything. I was determined to be an executive and willing to do the work. No shortcuts for me, if you get my drift."

Helen laughed and said, "I have no doubt."

"I went from executive assistant to product designer, team lead, project manager, senior project manager, VP of marketing, and when I resigned, I was the Chief Operating Officer. I worked out every day to stay in shape. Looking good was part of the job, and I enjoyed the occasional boxing class."

Helen grunted. "Sounds awful. I love the attire, but I hate working out."

I chuckled, but continued. "Gray Stone started the company. He was extremely wealthy and powerful. But the company was publicly traded and run by a board of men. Every executive except me was a man. My old boss, Serena, had left before I took the position."

I began fidgeting with the paint tubes Helen had laid out.

"I can't tell you how many board meetings I attended as the only woman. At first, I rarely spoke. I would take notes and listen, taking in every word of the meeting. I knew I was smart, which is why they gave me the position, but they had a natural way of making me feel small in those meetings. I'm not even sure they were consciously doing it. So, I made sure that when I spoke, it was purposeful, concise, and straight to the point."

"Damn straight." Helen reached down and scooped green paint onto her brush.

"Everyone thought I was a bitch because I was so direct. It was important to me to be fair, and as a woman, I didn't have room for error, or I'd be seen as not fit for the job."

Helen's eyes sparkled with mischief. "I would have loved to see you handling a group of men at that boardroom table."

I grinned, even as my insides began to churn from the memories. "During our quarterly meetings, each executive would present on their department. I would wear a blouse tucked into a short black skirt and my power shoes."

"What are power shoes?"

"Six-inch heels. You know—shoes that can whoop ass if needed." I laughed. "When I presented on operations, they grilled me relentlessly. Each board member took his turn, firing questions like damn drill sergeants." I grimaced as their questions flashed through my mind. *Why is this project over budget? What are your plans for growth? Why do we need this new hire? Should we have taken on that client? What processes and systems will you put in place to ensure success?*

"If I were a baseball player, I would've been Barry Bonds, knocking balls out of the park left and right because I always answered brilliantly. Most of them wouldn't even look me in the eye when I spoke." I shifted in my seat and watched paint drip onto Helen's pants.

"Helen. Your pants."

She looked down and frowned. "Damn it." She tried wiping the paint with her pinky, but it smeared. "Ugh. Keep talking. I'm listening."

I pressed on as Helen ignored the smear on her pants and kept painting. "In one meeting, I presented a growth plan. I mapped out a strategy to allow the company to grow by fifteen percent by implementing online marketing coaching—low-level stuff to help people grow their small businesses. Normally, we targeted the big fish. My idea was to capture the little guys with an affordable product. The product was a subscription designed to run itself. We would need a team of two for every one hundred clients to handle the workload."

"Sounds like a good plan, Lizzie."

"The board didn't think so. They argued with me for an hour that it would fail and cost the company over a million dollars. It got a little tense." I smirked, and Helen giggled. "Frank, the oldest board member, started screaming across the table. 'This will never work. You're wasting our time.'"

"Some men are assholes." Helen continued to swipe her brush over the glass storefront, but now with white paint.

"I calmly explained that it would increase our footprint, diversify our portfolio, and create job opportunities for new and current employees. Enraged, he screamed at me, 'I don't see how any of this works. This is getting out of hand. You're yelling.'"

Helen stopped painting. "The nerve of that guy."

I gripped the edges of the chair I was sitting in as I felt the old anger return. "I had crossed my legs with my six-inch power heels and matter-of-factly said, 'I'm not yelling, but you are.' My eyes were unblinking, and my face was utterly void of expression. It was epic. Frank's face turned beet red as he looked around and realized he was the only one yelling. The tension in the room released like a deflating balloon, and they started murmuring like a bunch of little boys."

Helen mocked. "No, you didn't. I would have loved to be a fly on the wall in that room." Her eyes sparkled with pride.

"You're damn right I did. I earned my seat at the table and was tired of their shit. That day earned me respect. It felt good to stand my ground."

"What happened next?" Helen said, her expression growing more curious.

"Frank said we'd circle back at the next meeting. After we left the conference room, Gray Stone called me to his office."

His office was in the corner of the building, and the view from his window was gorgeous. The floor was covered in hardwood with a plush white carpet in the center of the room. Glass shelves covered one entire wall, housing books, expensive sculptures, and modern art. He even had a private bathroom.

"Gray said that he thought my idea was brilliant and wanted to help me develop the subscription model for small businesses. He asked me if I could stay after work a few nights a week to work on the project."

Helen was working on Santa's boots. "Please tell me you said yes."

"Of course, I said yes. He was my boss. The late-night work sessions were strictly platonic at first. We were focused on developing the project. He was brilliant, and I was elated at the opportunity to work alongside him. I was completely enamored with his brain."

Helen raised an eyebrow. "You were enamored with his brain, huh?"

"In the beginning, yes. He was Gray Stone, one of the wealthiest, most intelligent, and most arrogant people in New York City. To be perfectly honest, the thought never crossed my mind to fall for him. He was way out of my league, and he was married."

"Oh my God, Lizzie." She put her hand on her hip, but as she did, more paint smeared. Trying to keep a straight face, I shook my head.

"He was my boss, and I didn't cross those lines. We spent months together in his office, brainstorming and collaborating. I noticed his comments becoming increasingly flirtatious, but I blew them off, thinking he was just being nice. I constantly reminded myself that he was married and refused to give in to any crazy impulses. One night we were drinking wine and—"

"Wine. Mm-hmm."

I ignored her. "—discussing the final touches to the project. We worked for months to finalize our subscription, which was finally complete. Gray jumped up to high-five me and spilled red wine all over his white dress shirt."

Helen choked.

"I ran to his bathroom to grab paper towels to clean up the mess. He came in behind me, unbuttoning his shirt."

I had Helen's full attention. Her eyes were glued to me, her paintbrush paused in midair.

"He put his shirt in the sink and started the water. It was a small space, and he brushed against me when he walked past."

I remembered trying to keep my eyes from looking at him and went back into the office to pack my things. I was about to tell him I was leaving when he exited the bathroom. His skin was glistening, and his abdominal muscles were pure perfection.

I sighed. "I had spent over one hundred nights ignoring every advance and every hint of flirting, but at that moment, my defenses were shot."

His bright green eyes had penetrated me and filled me with desire. My jaw had gone slack as I eyed him up and down. His black pants rested on his hips and showcased his impeccable love handles. I wanted to run.

"I knew this decision would change everything, but I was frozen. He said nothing, Helen. Not one single word. His eyes and body said everything. I just stood there, unable to move, waiting for him to take me. I wanted him."

My spine stiffened as the memories washed over me. He had tenderly put his hands along my jaw and placed his lips onto mine. My toes had curled in my shoes. With our lips locked together, he sucked in a breath, sending a rush through my body. His hands had slid down my body to my thighs, and under my skirt. He grabbed my ass cheeks and firmly lifted me off the floor. I folded my legs around his waist as he carried me to his desk. He kissed my neck, down to my chest, and back to my lips. His passion was like nothing I'd ever felt before. Taking his time, he savored every moment.

I never knew that sex on an executive's desk could be so incredible. He'd told me he'd wanted to do that for a long time. I told him we would always have this night, but we couldn't do it again. He'd kissed my shoulders gently and said, "I'm separated, Lizzie. Catalina and I are getting a divorce. I wanted to wait and ask you out on a proper date when the divorce was final, but I couldn't wait any longer."

"Helen, I slept with another woman's husband. It didn't matter that he was getting a divorce. I hated myself for it. I still hate myself, but I couldn't leave. We slept on the leather couch in his office most of the night."

Blinking at me, Helen stood, mouth open. "You slept with Gray Stone, your boss. I mean, I'm not judging. I probably would've too." She laughed. "Is that when you came to stay with your brother?"

I looked at her and started to speak, but no words emerged. A knock on the heavy door startled us both. Helen almost fell off the ladder. She giggled. I giggled, too, and went to open the door.

"It's a delivery. I'll accept it and get to work on inputting it into inventory."

"Perfect. Cause I'm covered in paint."

We returned to work, and before we knew it, it was time to close the store for the night. I couldn't help but think how one choice can change everything.

THIRTEEN

Decorations adorned every inch of the store. The window decor was as exquisite as the view of the bay. Helen's vision came to life perfectly. She had strung twinkling lights from every bookcase, and a garland hung from each chandelier. Each table had a Christmas centerpiece, and Christmas pillows sat neatly on each couch and chair. Carols continued to play over the sound system. I was able to convince Helen to add some variety because her choice of Michael Bublé, on repeat, was stuck in my head day and night.

Looking up at me, Helen said, "Lizzie, it's about time you got here."

Confused, I furrowed my brow. "Am I late?"

"Nah. I'm dying to know more about the rich hottie, Gray. After your night with him, is that when you quit your job?"

"I wish. I wish I could go back in time and resign the next day and never look back," I said with a pained look. "The opposite happened. He was magnetic. He said and did all the right things."

I placed my bag behind the counter and started organizing the new shipment of books on the shelves while Helen sat on the couch placing the next order, or so I assumed.

"When I returned to work, my office was filled with red roses. Dozens of them. A card was tied to a single rose on my desk."

I had smiled and sat on my purple velvet desk chair as remnants of our night together flowed through my veins. My heart had swelled with warmth when I'd read the card.

From memory, I recited the card to Helen:

Lizzie,

> Last night was magical. I want many more nights. Be out front of your apartment tonight at 6:30 p.m. My driver already has the address. Wear a semiformal evening gown. If you don't have one, I took the liberty of purchasing one for you, along with accessories. The package has already been delivered. If you aren't outside, I'll take that as a no. I promise I'll understand and respect your decision. Hope to see you tonight.

Lovingly, Gray

Sitting on the tan leather couch in the center of the store, Helen looked up from her laptop and said, "He signed the card 'lovingly'? Wow, this guy knows how to put on the full-court press, huh?" Pretending to overheat, she fanned her face with a magazine from the table. "Did you show up at 6:30 p.m.? Oh wait, tell me about the dress? Never mind, tell me everything!" she said, bouncing her feet up and down, eager to hear more.

I smiled as I remembered the good times I had with Gray. For a moment, my body tingled, recollecting old memories, and I could feel my cheeks get hot. No matter how much I tried to make myself hate him, I couldn't completely shed my love for him.

"Whew, girl. You're getting all flushed just thinking about him, aren't you?"

"Ugh. Yes, I am. He was like ecstasy and poison, enveloped in a beautiful body with unlimited money. I knew he would be my undoing from the first night, but I couldn't stay away. To answer your question, yes, I did stand outside of my apartment promptly at 6:30 p.m. I ended up wearing the dress that he had purchased for me."

"Please describe the dress. Or I'll have to fire you." Helen chuckled.

"Okay, okay. Keep your pants on." I stood to act out my best impression of the dress. "The gown was floor-length and made with Mulberry Silk in a beautiful deep navy. We're talking about a hundred dollars per yard kind-of-silk. With long, formfitting sleeves, the V-neckline plunged to my navel."

"Very sexy."

"You have no idea. Under the V part of the dress, there was a thick band decorated with Swarovski crystals. The dress had a large slit up to my mid-thigh, and I had to wear my extra high heels to keep the dress from hanging on the floor. My short little legs didn't fill the length of the dress." Remembering the struggle, I laughed.

"It sounds beautiful," Helen said dreamily. "Like Cinderella going to the ball."

"But that wasn't the best part. Gray included a necklace, lined with teardrop diamonds that rested perfectly above my breasts." At the look on Helen's face, I added: "And yes, matching diamond earrings. I was terrified to stand on the street and wait for fear that someone might mug me, but I did feel like Cinderella on the way to meet her prince. I asked God what I did to deserve this man."

"Honey, you deserve the best."

"Thanks."

"So, then your carriage arrived …?"

"You bet. Gray's driver was already out front with the door open to a black Bentley, waiting for my arrival. His name was Ray."

I allowed myself to enjoy the memory. "You must be Miss Levine," Ray had said, ushering me into the car. He'd taken my hand, helped me into my seat, and closed the door. He'd walked around the car, got into the driver's seat, looked at me through the rearview mirror, and said, "Mr. Stone is waiting. I'll take you to see him now."

Helen cleared her throat. "Should I leave you and your thoughts alone?" She wiggled her eyebrows.

"You're hilarious. When I arrived at Central Park about ten minutes later, Gray was standing in front of a carriage." I widened my eyes at Helen, who pretended to swoon.

"An actual carriage? Do tell."

"Yep. It was white and red, with twinkling lights decorating the roof. I remember how beautiful the horse had been, with a white feather plume atop his head. Gray was holding a wool blanket and two champagne glasses. Inside the carriage was a bucket of ice and champagne. He'd told me, 'Your beauty captivates me. I'm honored that you chose to join me this evening.' So, I'm pretty sure I fell in love with him right then and there. No matter how much I saw the signs that he was a bad idea."

"Wow. You really didn't stand a chance, did you?"

I shook my head.

"He'd kissed my cheek and helped me into the carriage. I did my best not to fall on my face getting in, but he was a complete gentleman. He climbed in next to me, covered us with the blanket, and then poured us a glass of champagne. At that moment, I thought to myself, is this real? Who knew there were men on Earth that orchestrated dates like that? I thought these kinds of nights were only for the movies."

The carriage had taken off slowly, and escorted us through Central Park. Sounds of hooves clattering filled the air, and I had glanced around, taking in the sights. When he'd turned toward me, his emerald-green eyes meeting mine, I had been utterly mesmerized. He'd leaned in, kissed me gently, and the sparks flew.

"There was no escaping how he made me feel, Helen. He was attentive, masterful even. I had dated before but never had a serious partner. He had me eating out of his palm from that first night."

Helen was nodding in agreement. "You were a goner, for sure."

"I enjoyed the ride, but hardly paid attention to the beauty the park offered. I couldn't take my eyes off him. Honestly, I wanted to skip the date and fast-forward to dessert. He made me feel alive. He made me feel desired and sexy, and I couldn't get enough."

Helen looked wistful. "I know the feeling."

"We ate dinner at this place called Marea near the Museum of Arts and Design. He arranged a private table with candlelight in the back corner."

"He sounds romantic," Helen said.

I nodded. He definitely was. My insides began to tingle at the memory. Even now, thoughts of Gray Stone still warmed me up a touch on the inside. "The food was delicious, and the chef came to the table to thank us for dining."

Gray and I had talked throughout dinner. He'd told me he married his wife too young. He said their marriage had been over for years, but Catalina wouldn't agree to a divorce. He had been renting her an apartment close to her work for three years. He'd told me he couldn't remember when he had fallen out of love with her, but that it had been a long time. She finally agreed to sign the divorce papers, which would be final in a few weeks. "I believed him when he said he was getting a divorce, and that they've been living apart for three years."

"Like I said, Lizzie. You were hook, line, and sinker."

"I told him about my parents' accident and my depression. We'd talked about college and dating, about the firm, and we celebrated our new project. I drank wine, lots of wine. He'd slid his chair closer to mine, reached his hand under the table, and had rubbed the slit in my dress to my thigh. Normally, I would've swatted his hand away, but he drove me insane."

"What did you do?" Helen rested her chin on her hands and gazed at me intently. I felt guilty we weren't working, but it was a slow day, and Helen didn't seem to care, so I continued.

"I stared into his eyes while he teased me under the table. I needed to make him think I could control myself. I never broke eye contact with him and never acknowledged what he was doing to me."

"You were a much stronger woman than I'd have been."

"Believe me, it wasn't easy. I told him I was a prize that deserved better than to be fondled under a table in public. I deserved respect."

To this day, my stomach reeled with fire from his touch. "I grabbed his tie, pulled him close, and whispered in his ear, 'If you want me, take me home to a proper bed.' Helen, you can imagine what happened next."

Fanning herself again, Helen said, "I need some water. I'm not sure if it's your story or a hot flash, but I'm sweating."

Helen and I went to the back room, and she grabbed a bottle of water from the fridge.

"Imagine how I felt living the story. I was mesmerized by him in every way, completely unable to control myself," I said as we walked back into the store.

"This went on for over a year. Gray took me to Broadway at least once a month and fancy dinners several times a week. He showered me with gifts, massaged my body, or arranged for me to go to the spa. I spent most nights at his brownstone, living the life of a millionaire. I wanted for nothing physically, emotionally, or materialistically. He provided for me in every way. I thought I was the luckiest girl in the world."

"It sounds like you were. So, what happened with the project you guys worked on?"

"It was eventually accepted and was a huge success. We managed to keep our hands off each other at work. Professionalism had been important to me. I'd worked hard for my position and didn't want to be seen as just another girl who slept her way to the top. Gray respected that. At work, we were coworkers. I was happy, living my best life, and thought I'd marry him."

Sitting by the counter, I gazed out the window at the water, and my heart ached. So much hurt filled the void that had been left.

Finally, I looked at Helen and said, "Hindsight is twenty-twenty, and most days, I regret ever allowing myself to sleep with him in the first place. But, on other days, I'm grateful for my experiences with Gray. I have many fond memories, and he was unbelievable in the bedroom. In the end, I learned some damn valuable lessons by dating him."

"Silver lining and all that, right?" Sensing that I didn't want to continue telling her the story, Helen stood up and said, "We should rearrange the specialty tables and showcase new books before the store gets busy, so let's get to work. You can tell me more next time."

I pushed my thoughts back into their box as I stood to help Helen. "What do you think about a table of holiday love stories? We don't have one of those yet. And December's right around the corner."

"Perfect," Helen said, smiling.

Helen pulled a list of books we had in stock, and I decorated a sign for the table. Thoughts of Gray fluttered around my head, but they turned to paramount sadness as my mind wandered to thoughts of my baby girl. I clenched my jaw to fight back the tears welling up in my eyes. I prayed that my new path would bring the serenity I desperately needed.

FOURTEEN

December

Randy was standing on the roof, attaching white Christmas lights to the house, while Renee was tying bows to the porch. Red, green, and white ribbons decorated with holly leaves molded and shaped like spring flowers blooming made the porch a merry sight. Neighboring houses shined brightly in the night as each home started decorating for the holidays.

"We'll be hosting the Stories with Santa event at the bookstore in a few weeks," I said as I grabbed a bow and tied it neatly to the railing.

"That's great," Renee said. "You've been working hard at the bookstore. I'm glad you like it, and Helen seems like a good boss."

"Yeah. I enjoy working there. Helen's great, and we've become good friends."

"You're keeping busy, that's for sure," Randy shouted from the roof.

"I'm trying," I said. "Do you think he'd be willing to be our Santa?" I directed my question to Renee. I was afraid Randy might fall off the roof if he didn't pay attention to what he was doing.

Renee laughed loudly and said, "Oh, that'll be fun. I'm sure he will, but ask him when he gets down."

"Yay. I'm going to be an elf. You're welcome to join me if you'd like," I said as I danced around impersonating a silly elf. "How's the Airbnb coming?" I secretly wanted to know how much longer Josh would be around.

"It's coming along," Renee said as she placed Christmas pillows on the bench swing. "I think they have two more months of work. The crew can't come every day, so the remodel is moving slowly, but what they've done so far looks great. They should be back tomorrow."

Butterflies swirled in my stomach at the thought, but I quickly pushed the feelings aside. Standing on the porch with my back to the door, I said, "I can't wait to see it. I'm sure it'll be awesome." I turned to go in and bumped right into Randy, who had sneaked up inches behind me. I screamed and jumped off the porch. Randy doubled over from laughing so hard.

"Oh my God," he said, laughing even louder. "You should've seen the look on your face." Tears streamed down his cheeks as he gulped air and tried to collect himself. "I sneaked in through the upstairs window and came out to see if you two needed help. But, sis, you weren't paying attention, and I couldn't help myself." His laughter bellowing so loud now, that the entire block could hear.

"Randolph, you scared your sister half to death," Renee said, fighting back her laughter.

I punched him in the shoulder and said, "You're a punk." I waffled between my heart racing and laughter, and I might have peed my pants a little.

"C'mon, let's see what it looks like," Randy said.

We walked to the street to admire our handiwork. Christmas spirit was alive and well on Caswell Avenue. The lights glistened like stars in the sky, and Frosty, wearing his red scarf and top hat, sparkled on the front lawn.

"Oh, Randy, it looks beautiful," Renee said, a twinge of nostalgia in her voice.

"Great job, bro," I said. "I'll start cleaning up. Then I'm going to bed."

Standing at the kitchen sink, I washed the coffeepot and looked out the window at the Airbnb. I could see three men, but I didn't recognize them. One of the workers was short and stout, with a receding hairline. He was cutting wood trim in the yard. The other two appeared to be carrying the cut pieces inside. They were both tall and slim, built like twins, but they didn't look alike. One had black hair, and the other was blond.

Disappointment crept into my heart as I searched for Josh, but saw no sign of him. I shouldn't be disappointed. I told him not to bother, and that dating was not an option for me. Maybe he needed to be on another job site today, or maybe he was avoiding me. Given my track record, he was probably avoiding me.

I picked up the dish towel and dried the coffeepot when I heard a knock at the door. Sitting in the living room watching Sports Center on TV, Randy called, "I'll get it."

"Hey Randy," I heard the smooth tone from the front door. The butterflies in my stomach whirled into action, and I could feel my heartbeats speeding up.

"Are those for me?" Randy asked sarcastically.

Laughing nervously, Josh replied, "Well, uh. I was hoping to leave them here for Lizzie."

"Oh," Randy said, confused. "I didn't realize you two knew each other."

"Yeah, we've met a few times, and I thought she might like these. I can leave them with you if that's okay. There's a note," Josh said.

Randy opened the door wider, waved his arm to motion Josh to come in, and said, "She's right in the kitchen. Come on in."

"Thanks. I'll only be a minute. I need to check on the guys out back," Josh said as he walked toward the kitchen counter.

He looked tired, but he was still handsome as hell. He had slight bags under his eyes, making the blue in his irises look grayish. His hair was tucked under a trucker-style hat adorned with his company's logo, Miller Construction.

"Hi, Lizzie. I saw these today and thought you'd like them," he said, handing me the bouquet sheathed in clear plastic paper. At least a dozen white, yellow, red, and pink lilies in full bloom were tucked neatly inside. Attached was a card stuffed inside a pink envelope, with Lizzie scribbled on the front.

"They're beautiful." I reached into the cabinet for a vase. "Thank you. You've brightened my day." I smiled from ear to ear as I filled the vase with water and arranged the flowers inside.

Josh looked into my eyes and said, "You can read the card whenever. It's great to see you. Enjoy the flowers." Then, he turned to Randy and said, "Headed out back. You want to check out the job?"

Slack-jawed, Randy looked from Josh to me and back to Josh. "You go ahead. I'll be right out."

Randy's eyes fixated on me as I watched Josh exit through the back door to the yard. "What's happening here? I could practically see the sparks flying. I thought I might need to grab the fire extinguisher."

"I don't know. We've bumped into each other a few times here and there. He asked me out, and I turned him down. But he doesn't seem interested in taking no for an answer." I fiddled with the flowers to position them in the vase.

"Well, the sparks seemed to fly both ways, sis. I'm just saying. He's a nice guy. You should give him a chance." Randy patted me on the shoulder.

"I might. I haven't decided yet." Shooshing him toward the back door, I said, "Go on now. Go check his handiwork. I'll fill you in on my love life later."

I wasn't sure I could even think about starting a new relationship, and I certainly didn't need or want Randy involved in my love life. However, he gave me his approval of Josh. I was unsure if that made me want to draw a hard line in the sand on dating him or if it made me like him even more.

Staring at the card, I hesitated. I had been down this road before. The butterflies swirling around in my stomach turned into a sour taste in my mouth, causing me to feel nauseous.

Josh isn't Gray, I told myself as I swiped my index finger along the edge of the flap. I ripped open the envelope, took a long calming deep breath, exhaled, and began reading.

Dear Lizzie,

> I can feel our chemistry, and I want a chance to prove to you that I'm a good guy. I promise I'm worth the risk. White Lilies for virtue. I'll respect you, always. Yellow Lilies for desire. I'll fulfill your greatest desires. Pink Lilies for abundance. I'm wishing you eternal happiness. Red Lilies for passion. I feel it, and I think you do too. I'll be here whenever you're ready. You know where to find me.

Yours Truly, Josh - Here's my number, just in case 555.892.7484

I could at least try to be nicer to him. Baby steps, Lizzie, baby steps. Remember what Helen said. There's no harm in giving him a chance. I pulled my phone out of my back pocket, punched in his number, and wrote out a quick text, "Thank you for the flowers and the beautiful note. I could use a friend if you want to grab a coffee sometime."

Staring at my phone, I hesitated. Finally, the voice in my head shouted, *do it, Lizzie! Push the button.* My thumb, seeming to have a mind of its own, pressed send on the message, and my heart skipped a beat.

Three dots appeared, and I thought my heart might completely stop.

...

...

...

I waited for what seemed like an eternity but was more like fifteen seconds, and then the dots disappeared.

No message.

My heart sank to my toes, but I brushed the feeling off. A knock at the back door startled me, and I looked up to see Josh standing by the door. Doing my best to hide my excitement, I hustled to the door and calmly said, "Hey."

"I'd love coffee." He held up his phone with a giant grin on his face. "Anytime. You let me know."

Smiling back at him, I replied, "Sounds good." He stood awkwardly, waiting for me to give him a time. "I'll text you. How's that?"

"Okay, great," he said and walked back toward the Airbnb.

FIFTEEN

As I approached the bookstore, a beautiful bronze ribbon displayed in the window greeted me. Helen was thrilled that the store received third place in the window decorating contest. Christmas was over a week away, and the air was cool. Bustled up in a light winter coat and knit hat, I stopped at Southport Coffee Co. for a coffee before going to work. I ordered my usual and a hot chocolate for Helen.

Smiling, I asked Sam, "Can I have two doughnuts, please?"

"Of course, Lizzie. It's always good to see you. How's the bookstore?"

"Great. Helen's awesome, and the store's so much fun," I said as I paid the bill. "How's life on your end?"

"Looking forward to Christmas break. Been studying like crazy for exams. It's exhausting." The bags under Sam's eyes agreed with her statement.

"I remember those days. Hang in there. You can do it."

Sam smiled and handed me my drinks in a cardboard carrier. "Have a great day."

I had become a regular at the coffee shop and learned that Sam was a student at UNC Wilmington, working on her degree in hospitality. I offered to pass her résumé on to friends in the business when she graduated.

"Brrr, it's getting chilly out there," I said to Helen as I entered the bookstore. "I brought you a hot chocolate and a doughnut."

"Yummy," Helen said from behind the counter. "Exactly what I needed."

I set the food and drinks onto the counter and removed my coat. Feeling a chill race up my back, I shivered and rubbed my hands together.

"We have the electric fireplace we purchased for Stories with Santa. Let's go sit," Helen said as she grabbed her drink and walked toward the chairs positioned by the fireplace. I followed behind her, sat in the chair, and cozied up to the fire.

"This is nice," I said.

"I don't think we'll be too busy this morning. We have at least an hour before the regulars show up. So, it's the perfect time for you to tell me more about Gray." She was holding her hot chocolate as if it were a precious gem.

"Oh, I see. You bring me to the fire to warm me up so I'll spill more beans."

Helen barked out a laugh. "That's the plan." She winked. "I haven't asked in a while, after all."

"Today's perfect," I said. "Before I get into Gray, Josh brought me flowers."

Helen whooped. "He did?"

"I want to give him a chance, but I'm not sure I'm ready." I remembered the grin on his face when I said I'd have coffee with him, and I couldn't help feeling lighter, somehow.

"When you're ready, you'll know."

"You're right. I don't need to stress about Josh." His grin was still front and center in my mind, but I shook it off.

"Right. Now tell me more about Gray." Helen steepled her hands on her hot chocolate like her fingers had been bitten by frost.

I snorted. "You're relentless, you know."

"Your mysterious past is my new pastime. Better than any novel on my shelves. Plus, you and I both know you need to talk about him and get him out of your system."

I almost choked on my coffee. She wasn't wrong. "I'm going to start by saying I was head over heels in love with Gray. I loved his brain. I loved his body. He made me feel good, and I loved every single thing about him. Our relationship was fulfilling in ways I can't describe. I thought I knew him completely. I thought we'd spend the rest of our lives together. For two years, Helen, I thought my life with him was sheer perfection. I had the career I wanted, and I was killing it. I had the man of my dreams who treated me like a queen, and everything was falling into place."

"I've been waiting for the catch because he sounds too good to be true."

"The day was a Tuesday, and that's when everything changed. I'll never forget that day. I woke in Gray's bed like any other day, and he'd already left the house. He liked getting up early and working out before going into the office. I wandered into the kitchen to make coffee and noticed his text message about a meeting."

The text message flashed through my mind like it was yesterday, "Don't forget the big pitch meeting. Got to plan for Dunkin' Donuts. I'm going to the office after my workout. See you there. Love you, heart emoji, kiss emoji."

I clicked on my calendar to locate the meeting time, but instead, panic had pulsated through every pore in my skin like prickly needles sticking me from head to toe. I remembered thinking *I should've gotten my period three weeks ago.*

At the time, I had refused to believe I was pregnant and told myself something else had to be going on. I was taking birth control. On my way to work, I had stopped at the drugstore and purchased three different brands of pregnancy tests. I'd asked the lady at the counter to point me toward the bathroom. I had taken the bag and my receipt and swiftly walked in the direction she'd pointed.

In the bathroom, I'd ripped open all three packages, pulled one test from each, and peed on all three. I'd replaced the caps, set them on the bathroom floor, and waited for my results.

I had sat quietly on the toilet and looked down toward the ground, staring at the sticks, expecting to wait the full three minutes. Instead, in mere seconds, a pregnant confirmation plus sign appeared on the first stick, then two pink lines appeared on the second, and finally, the third stick, taking a few seconds longer, displayed the word pregnant.

"Checking my calendar that day made me realize my period was late, and I soon found out I was pregnant. I had a teeny tiny baby growing inside my belly." My eyes instantly blurred with tears that trickled down my cheeks.

Helen took my hand in hers, and I noticed her eyes were shining with tears, too. "You were pregnant?"

I nodded. "I hadn't been ready to be a mother. I didn't even know if Gray wanted to be a father. We'd never discussed it, but I knew he didn't have children with Catalina. How could I manage my career and a baby? I had worked so hard. I had a perfect life. Motherhood was not part of my plan. I didn't know what to do. I needed time to process the news. Finally, I picked up the tests, wrapped them in a paper towel, threw them into the trash, and went to work.

"I went about my day, doing my best to act normally. Inside, I was a disaster. Several days had passed before I finally called the doctor to make an appointment. The first available appointment was five weeks away."

Helen took my hand in hers again and gently squeezed. I was grateful for the comfort.

"I decided I wouldn't say anything to Gray until after the visit with the doctor. Anything could happen, right? I wasn't even sure

I wanted to keep the baby. As much as I loved him, we weren't married. He didn't need to know right away. I pretended I wasn't pregnant, and life went on as usual." My voice cracked as the emotions I'd buried rose like a volcano about to explode.

"My relationship was getting a little difficult, especially with morning sickness. I convinced Gray that I had an irritable stomach and promised to make an appointment with the doctor to evaluate my allergies and determine what foods might be making me sick."

"That's tough," Helen said. She took a sip of her drink and looked at me. Her expressive eyes were filled with empathy.

"I stayed at my apartment a few nights a week to make hiding the pregnancy easier. Nights alone in my apartment gave me time to consider my options and ponder life with a child. I thought about adoption and wondered how that'd look at work. How could I go to work with a pregnant belly? People knew that Gray and I were together. What would people think of me if I gave birth and didn't return to work with a baby? What would they think of him? Perhaps I could work from home when I started to show and blame my absence on some mysterious disease."

Helen's tone was kind. "Having a baby is life altering. You were doing the best you could."

"I considered having an abortion. I wouldn't have to tell anyone if I chose that route. I'd take some time off work to recover and return to my life. Abortion would be simple, I thought. Except, abortion is never simple. This was a heavy choice, but I didn't completely rule abortion out as an option. I thought I loved Gray unconditionally, and that he loved me the same. However, I was terrified that a baby would ruin our perfect relationship."

"Oh, honey," Helen said without an ounce of judgment. I breathed a sigh of relief as I white knuckled the armrests of the chair I was sitting on. The memories washed through me like a hurricane swirling and kicking me on the inside.

A few weeks later, I found myself sitting in my ob-gyn's ultrasound chair with my legs spread and my feet nestled in the stirrups as I waited impatiently for the tech to begin. I'd clenched the paper sheet draped over my legs as she placed a condom and gel on the wand.

The technician had said, "This will be a little cold, and you may feel some pressure." She reached under the sheet, inserted the wand, and an image of my uterus flashed onto the screen before me. She moved the wand around, clicked the keys on her keyboard, and took measurements.

A whooshing sound, like being submerged underwater, rushed through the room. Then, a sound like a washing machine swishing clothes back and forth graced my ears.

I hadn't realized what I was hearing, but the tech had said, "That's the sound of your baby's heartbeat. Good and strong, the heartbeat's about 150 beats per minute. The baby appears to be approximately thirteen weeks. Congratulations."

"When I heard my baby's heartbeat for the first time at that appointment, I almost blacked out. I was so overwhelmed."

Every emotion had simultaneously flooded my body like a dam breaking. The swishing, swishing, swishing sounds seemed to get louder and penetrated my eardrums straight through to my heart. I had felt an overwhelming need to protect the innocent life growing inside me.

Helen tenderly squeezed my hand.

I looked up at her; tears continued to fill both our eyes. "I left the doctor's office with a healthy baby in my tummy, a prescription for prenatal vitamins, and an approximate due date of June twentieth."

"As in this past June?" Helen asked. "Like a few months ago, June?"

The concern in her voice almost made my volcano of tears erupt into a crying mess.

Chewing my bottom lip nervously, I said, "Yes. June. A few months ago." I lowered my head and let out a sigh. "Helen, I haven't told anyone this. Randy and Renee didn't even know I was pregnant. This needs to stay between us, for now. I'll tell them, but it'll break my brother's heart."

"I won't say a word. Did you tell Gray?"

I nodded.

Working up the courage to tell Gray about the baby had been difficult. I'd wanted to tell him. I'd wanted us to be a happy family. But something deep inside my gut knew it wouldn't turn out that way.

"Whenever I thought I'd tell him the truth, I'd chicken out. Carrying on like usual was more challenging by the day. My naked body was changing, making the pregnancy difficult to hide. I avoided walking around naked, worried Gray might notice my little bump. Sex had become more painful, too, and it had become obvious to him I was hiding something."

"That must have been difficult. I can only imagine."

"He'd asked me if I was having an affair. I was sixteen weeks pregnant, and I knew it was time to tell him. So I ended up blurting out, 'I'm pregnant.'"

"What'd he say?"

"He said, 'So, you are having an affair?'"

Helen inhaled sharply.

I remembered him shouting at me, his eyes filling with an intense rage I had never seen before. I had been so stunned and confused. Backing away from him, I'd said, *"What? No. I'm not having an affair. Didn't you hear me? I'm pregnant. I'm sixteen weeks pregnant with your baby."*

"Helen," I whispered. "He was so angry. He didn't believe the baby was his." Tears slid down my cheeks.

Helen gripped my hand tightly in hers.

In my mind, I could still see him, seething with anger and moving toward me. His words echoed inside my head, *"That's fucking impossible, you cheating, lying whore. I've given you everything. I've treated you like royalty. I was married for fifteen years, and all my wife wanted was a baby. We couldn't have children. So, I know you're lying. I won't have a whore in my bed. Get out. Get out right now, and don't come back."*

"He called me a lying whore and told me to leave."

Helen inhaled sharply again.

His words had come down on me like a sledgehammer that cracked me into pieces bit-by-bit. I remembered standing there in shock with my mouth open. Tears had gushed down my face, and I'd begged and pleaded with him to hear me. I repeatedly swore to him that I loved only him and had only been with him.

Between sobs, I'd told him that I loved him. I'd told him that I loved our baby—that the baby inside me was ours, his and mine. My heart ached as I'd tried to hug and kiss his face and assure him that I was faithful. He'd grabbed my wrists and pried them off his body. He'd looked at me, expressionless. *"Lizzie, it doesn't matter. We're through. Get out. I don't want a child. Therefore, it isn't mine. Do you get it?"*

I took a deep breath and continued. "When I finally forced myself to leave and return to my own apartment, I'd stayed in bed for two days, crying. Deep down, I'd known he wouldn't want the baby. I believed he loved me because he made me feel special. He made me feel desired, but now I know it was all bullshit. I'd felt alone and used. How could someone who claimed to love me call me a whore and toss me away like yesterday's garbage? I was so naive and stupid. He didn't love me. He probably never did."

Helen sat up straight and said, "He's clearly an ass, Lizzie. I can't believe he said those things to you." She brushed a tear off my cheek. "What about your job? What happened with work?"

"I'd be damned if Gray Stone was going to ruin my career. He was waiting for me in my office when I arrived. I hoped he was there to apologize, and we'd get back together and live happily ever after, like the fairy tale I thought our relationship had been. Instead, Gray was waiting to tell me I wouldn't ruin *his* career. He said, 'No one at work can know you're pregnant. If the baby's mine, and I don't think it is, I won't acknowledge I'm the father.'"

"I'm so sorry you had to deal with a man like that, Lizzie."

Me too. "He'd said, 'Either way, Lizzie, you can't be here.'" My hands shook as I remembered being consumed by hatred. *His career? What about my career?*

"I told him, 'The baby's yours, Gray. You can deny it all you want, but you and I created this baby. I've always been faithful. The fact that you'd even insinuate otherwise is disgusting and hurtful. I've worked hard for my career.' Why should I have to compromise anything because he got me pregnant?"

"Damn right."

"Cool as a cucumber and as snide as ever. Do you know what he said to me?"

"What did that asshole say?"

"He said, 'Because I'll crush you, Lizzie. I'll make your life here a living hell. I have vast resources and plenty of people who'll believe my side. You'll lose this battle.'" He had reached out and stroked my hair tenderly, a cruel kind of gentleness in his eyes."

"Ugh, he's such a prick."

"Then, he said to me, 'You foolish girl. I didn't love my wife. What makes you think I loved you? What makes you think I was faithful to you? I expected you to be faithful to me, but I'm Gray Stone. I can have any woman I want. You were fun, but it's time for things to end and for you to be on your way. Women are all the same. Easy. If you go quietly, I'll ensure the board provides a great reference for a different firm.'"

Helen jumped up off her chair. "What a dick!"

I had been enraged, consumed with hatred for him. I hadn't understood until that moment how you could love and hate someone so much at the same time. I'd wanted to kill him. I'd had dreams of choking the life out of him, but I still loved him.

"I continued going to work, using clothes to hide my bump, and heard whispers about my weight gain. And Gray was true to his word. He did everything he could to make my life miserable. He left me off meeting appointments. He didn't tell me about the correct deadlines for upcoming pitches, making me look incompetent at my job. He had all the power, money, and control, and I had his baby. A growing life inside my body that I couldn't hide and couldn't explain. Our relationship was public, so naturally, everyone would assume it was his, or they'd think I cheated. Either way, I was screwed."

Helen was pacing now. "What's his address?"

"Sit down, Helen. I'm not giving you his address."

"Why not? I know how to fight."

"I'm sure you do. Do you want me to finish before you commit first-degree murder?"

She sat back down. "Fine."

Despite all the emotions rolling through me, I almost laughed and realized how grateful I was for Helen.

"I'd made it to December twenty-third and did not return after Christmas. I'd had some money left in the trust, plus the money I'd saved. I figured I would work on my résumé and apply for jobs that started after I had the baby. I didn't quit or officially resign. I just stopped going into the office and did my work from home. In February, I received a letter from the board stating that my position had been cut. The letter said I had used all my personal and sick days, and they would pay me four weeks of unused vacation plus a three-month severance for my exceptional service to the firm. It also explained that my insurance would lapse at the end of the month, but I would receive information to sign up for Cobra should I want to continue my insurance coverage until I found a new job. Gray Stone Marketing appreciated my service, and I was welcome to reapply anytime."

"Vomit," Helen said, sticking her finger in her mouth and pretending to retch.

"I don't know what I thought would happen. I hadn't been to work in over a month." That letter cut deep, and it still pained me that I was tossed aside so easily. "The letter, the vacation pay, and the severance weren't because they cared. They wanted to cover their asses and ensure I didn't sue them. The board wasn't stupid. This was a human resources cover-up. Dot the i's, cross the t's, and pray I didn't go public. I probably could have insisted that I needed more severance, and they would have agreed to make me go away, but I just wanted to be done and put Gray Stone and his marketing firm behind me. I had to sign a document that I agreed to the terms and that everything I learned at the firm, including my relationship with Gray, would be confidential. Should I share company proprietary information, I could be sued. It all but flat out said that since I was sleeping with the president, our relationship was part of the agreement because I could've been given secret information while in his bed."

I looked at Helen, whose eyes were fierce. "Now, I'm working to regain my confidence and trust my decisions."

"Sweetie, you didn't do anything wrong," Helen said compassionately. "You fell for the wrong man. How could you know? He sounded like a dream. He manipulated you. That's not your fault."

"Somewhere deep down inside, I know that, but it doesn't make it easier to forgive myself for my bad choices."

"Forgive yourself for what, Lizzie? There's nothing to forgive," Helen said as she stood up and opened her arms. "Come here. We both need a hug."

Standing, I hugged her and cried into her shoulder, "But I lost the baby. My baby girl's gone."

SIXTEEN

Christmas was only five days away, and the town had gone all out. Every house was decorated with garland and lights. The Moore Street shops were bedazzled in a blaze of lights, with holiday figurines standing on doorsteps, entryways, and sidewalks. There wasn't a tree in Southport that wasn't covered with lights and glistening in the night. Today was a big day. Stories with Santa started at noon, and the Sights and Sounds of the Christmas Golf Cart Parade started at dusk.

Randy and Renee spent most of the day before decorating their golf cart for the big night. Multicolored lights lined the roof with large silver, green, and red ornaments hanging every few feet. Garland and lights dressed the front window rails, and snowmen holding palm trees were hooked to the center of each wheel. A large, illuminated, inflatable palm tree with a pink flamingo sat atop the roof.

"Ho, Ho, Ho," Randy called from the kitchen as I entered the room. "I'm practicing my Santa laugh for today."

He wore the white beard and tiny spectacles Helen had purchased for the event. I belly laughed.

"Have you been a good girl this Christmas?" he asked in his best old-person Santa voice. "I only give gifts to good little boys and girls."

Shaking my head at his antics, I said, "You're crazy."

"Hello, deary," said a high-pitched elderly voice behind me. "What do you want from Santa this year?" Renee was dressed as Mrs. Claus in a red velvet top with a fluffy white V-neck trim around the neck and a red velvet skirt with matching fluffy white trim around the bottom. She wore silver spectacles and had given herself rosy, red cheeks and subtle pink lips. Her long hair was tightly braided in a circle so it could be hidden under her wig.

"The wig's too hot. I'll throw it on when we get there," she said in her normal voice, holding a white curly wig adorned with a crown of holly and berries.

"You guys crack me up. You're going to have too much fun today, aren't you?" I said, laughing at both of them practicing their characters.

"It's Christmas, Lizzie. And we get to share the magic today. Hell yeah, we're gonna have fun," Randy said, adjusting his beard. "Where's your elf costume?"

"It's at the bookstore. I'll get dressed there. I've packed my snowman costume for the parade tonight. I'll be ready," I said, zipping up my duffle bag. "Random question. Are the workers done out back? I haven't seen them in a while."

Renee raised an eyebrow and asked, "Do you mean has Josh been around? Randy told me he brought you flowers."

I could feel the redness filling my cheeks as I blushed. "I was just curious when they might be finished." I acted low-key and unfazed by her question.

"Do you have a minute before you have to go?" Randy asked.

"Sure, I have a few minutes."

"Ren and I've been talking. We want to offer you the Airbnb." Randy grinned.

"But you guys will lose money if you don't rent it. I can't do that to you. You've done so much for me already."

"We've decided not to rent it out. We don't want strangers coming and going all the time. You'd be helping us out if you stayed. The guys haven't come in a while because of the holidays, and I told Josh he didn't need to rush our job. It should only take a few weeks when they start again after the New Year. The place is yours if you want it."

"I don't know what to say," I said, shocked.

"You're welcome to stay in the house. I don't want you to feel like we're asking you to leave, but it seems you'll be here for a while. We figured you might want your own space. It'd be a shame to let all the work go to waste. All you need to do is say yes," Randy said as he pulled the Santa coat over his white T-shirt.

I felt overwhelmed by his offer. I stared at him for what seemed like an eternity. Finally, I choked back my emotions, and said, "Yes. But with two conditions. First, I'll pay you rent. You and Renee can decide how much and let me know. Second, I'm still coming over for dinner." I hugged him. "Thank you, Santa."

"I'm glad. Now get going. You don't want to be late." He lifted his arm and waved for me to go out the door. "We can work out the details later. See you at the store in a little while."

Helen and I had prepared everything for Stories with Santa the day before. She'd decided that she wanted to be an elf instead of Mrs. Claus so she could be more involved in the event. Helen held the checklist in her hand and started calling the list out. "Reindeer food table, check. Fireplace, check. Cookie decorating station, 'Twas The Night Before Christmas, and Santa's chair is set up, check, check, and check. Snacks and hot chocolate stand, check. I think we're ready."

"It looks great. I'm going to get dressed." I walked toward the back room where I had hung my costume and dug out the striped red and green tights from my bag. I put those on first. Next, I pulled the green long-sleeve dress over my head. The scooped collar was white and furry with a holly pin. I fastened the red belt around my waist, which made the skirt bell out. The bottom of the dress had a red sequin stripe, followed by a thick strip of white fur and red tulle showing out from under the dress. My elf shoes curled up to a point with a red bell at the tip. I tied my hair into a French braid, and placed the green elf hat on my head, finishing off the ensemble with my makeup and red lipstick.

"I'm ready." Jingling with every step as I walked toward the counter. "We need to take a picture," I said, grabbing my phone. Helen and I squeezed together as I extended my arm to snap a selfie. "Say Stories with Santa." I clicked the button to snap the photo. I thumbed through the apps on my phone and opened the Instagram app. I hit the plus sign, chose the picture, and posted the image with the caption #twinning #storieswithsanta #bayviewbooks #southport.

Randy and Renee arrived, and Helen's neighbor Tess showed up dressed as Rudolph.

"Thank you for coming," Helen said to the group. "I appreciate you."

Helen had extended Stories with Santa for over an hour to allow everyone to have their picture taken with Jolly Old Saint Nick. Randy and Renee agreed to stay the extra time but left immediately following the last picture on Santa's lap because they had to change and get the golf cart. I barely had enough time to clean up and prepare myself for the parade.

Finally, sitting in their golf cart, I waited for the parade to start. I was drinking a hot gingerbread latte and fighting my exhaustion. Randy wore a red Christmas sweater, a multicolored light bulb necklace, and a black top hat. Renee, wearing a light-up Christmas tree headband, a green sweater with dangling ornaments, and green jeans, was sitting next to him in the passenger seat.

My Frosty the Snowman costume was a little less obnoxious, but not by much. I wore a white sweater and pinned large buttons down the center, a red scarf, white jeggings, and white fur boots. I painted my face white with an orange circle on the tip of my nose and wore a red top hat with a black sash around the rim.

"We look ridiculous," I said to Randy and Renee.

"Nah, it's fun," Randy said as the light bulbs around his neck flashed.

"There must be over a hundred golf carts here," I said as I stood on the back of the golf cart to get a better look.

"At least that many," Renee said. "We do Christmas right around here."

There were golf carts as far as my eyes could see. Each cart was decorated with extravagant Christmas décor, each more outlandish than the next. The sky was dark, but the street looked like the Las Vegas strip. Blinking and flashing lights were everywhere. The sidewalks were lined with people sitting and standing in anticipation of the parade.

"I thought there were loads of people on the streets for the Halloween parade, but this is insane. I think there might be twice as many people out tonight," I said.

Renee beamed. "What can I say? Southport loves Christmas."

Suddenly, Mariah Carey's *All I Want For Christmas* blared over the speaker, and fire truck sirens switched on and off in quick bursts.

Randy's eyes lit up as bright as the lights hanging around his neck. "It's time. Here we go." The golf cart jumped out of park as Randy popped the brake. He pressed his foot on the gas, and I jolted forward as he drove into line with the other golf carts.

We drove one block and stopped while waiting for the lead cart to move again. Over the blaring Christmas music, I could hear a faint bark. I looked around to see where the noise came from, but saw nothing. I continued to wave at the children in the crowd and danced to the music in the back of the golf cart.

"Sis, you ready?" Randy asked. "It's almost time for Frosty. We'll slow down around the bend, and you hop off when the song starts."

"Do I have a choice?" I said, laughing. "Yeah. I'm as ready as I'll ever be."

We turned the corner, and Randy slowed down. I hopped off the back of the golf cart and formed a line with the other thirty snowmen emerging from their souped-up Christmas rides. A few seconds later, the Hype Trap Remix of Frosty the Snowman bellowed through the loudspeaker, and we danced. Step together, step, jump, cross, turn, and slide, shimmy-shimmy, shake-shake, scoop-touch, hop, hop, bounce.

Front and center of the Frosties, I danced my heart out, giving it my all. Behind the crowd of people sitting on the curb, I could see a tail wagging. The song was halfway over, and I noticed the adorable Goldendoodle excitedly pushing between the row of people and barking loudly. He made his way to the street and sat directly in front of me with his tongue hanging out of his mouth.

Suddenly embarrassed, I searched the crowd for Cooper's owner. I could barely see his head of dark hair tucked under a Santa hat, bobbing up and down through the throng of parade watchers. My heart did a flip-flop in my chest.

Weeks had passed since the flowers, and I had not texted Josh because I chickened out.

Of course, I chickened out. My judgment sucks.

Helen was dancing off my right shoulder and said, "When this song's over, you better pet that dog. See where it leads, Lizzie. You've got this."

Step, touch, step, clap, turn, and pose. The music ended, and Cooper charged toward me, wagging his tail and panting. I leaned over to kiss him.

"Come on, boy. Let's go find your daddy," I said in my best talk-to-doggy voice. I hollered to Randy that I'd return the dog to its owner and catch up with them later.

Renee chased after me and said, "You've got this. Go for it."

Josh worked his way through the crowd as Cooper and I stepped onto the sidewalk. He was wearing a green Christmas sweater with various-sized red and white candy canes scattered on the sleeves and a giant candy cane on the chest. His head was sporting a traditional red Santa hat, and he wore his perfectly fitting jeans.

"He spotted you dancing in the street and took off," Josh said as he attached the leash to Cooper's collar. "I think he likes you."

Petting the top of Cooper's head, I said, "I like him too."

"You never did text me about that coffee." He rocked back on his heels, his tone cautious. "Southport Coffee Co.'s open. How does hot chocolate sound?" I must have looked shocked because he raised his hands and said, "No strings. Just two people having a cup of hot chocolate."

"Hot chocolate sounds great, but I'm not sure I'm dressed for the occasion." Frowning, I looked down at my snowman getup.

"You're the cutest snowman I've ever seen. Your outfit doesn't bother me if it doesn't bother you." Smiling, he pointed to his sweater and said, "I mean, I'm wearing candy canes and a Santa hat. I think it'll be fine."

You can do this, Lizzie. "A hot drink sounds amazing right now."

"Great," he said.

We strolled through the crowd, occasionally stopping to watch the passing golf carts in the parade. I texted Randy and Renee to tell them I had found Cooper's owner and that the owner was Josh. I told them we were getting hot chocolate at the coffee shop and that I would be home later. Randy replied with a thumbs-up, and

Renee replied with a heart eyes emoji. I giggled at her response and tucked my phone back into my bag.

I waited on the porch with Cooper while Josh went inside to order our drinks. Seating was plentiful since most of the town was watching the parade. I chose a small table in the corner with a good view of the parade and was close to a railing for Josh to tie Cooper's leash.

Jingle Bell Rock was blaring over the speakers. Carolers in choral robes walked between the golf carts, patiently waiting for their cue to sing. I sat observing the aura of the town, quaint and peaceful. The vibes filled my heart with happiness, and I had let my guard down bit-by-bit each day. If a Hallmark greeting card were a town, this would be it.

"Hot chocolate for the lady," Josh said in a British accent as he set the large mug on the table in front of me. Steam radiated from the top, and little marshmallows floated around inside. "I wasn't sure if you were hungry, so I got a few doughnuts and croissants."

"Thank you," I said, wrapping my hands around the mug to warm them. "I'm sorry I didn't call or text sooner. Work's been crazy."

"I understand."

"No. That's not true. If we're going to be friends, I shouldn't lie to you. I thought about reaching out several times, but I didn't." A flicker of worry flashed across his face.

"Wait, I didn't mean it like that." Trying to explain, I said, "Ugh, I'm doing a poor job of getting this out. Basically, I'm a disaster."

I threw my hands up in a huff. "I've got things I need to work through. As much as I wanted to have coffee with you, I wasn't sure it was a good idea."

"Lizzie, we can take this at your pace," he said as he reached across the table for my hand. "For tonight, it's hot chocolate and doughnuts. Nothing more, nothing less." I felt my nerves settle, but I refused to let my guard down completely.

"Friends," I said. Although internally, my senses sang like a choir of angels telling me to follow my heart.

"I'll take friends for now," he said. "You seem like you prefer honesty. Here's the truth, though. I don't want to be your friend forever."

Afraid I would give in to him too quickly, I changed the subject and said, "Let's play a game."

Confused, Josh said, "Um, okay, sure. What'd you have in mind?"

"Twenty questions. We ask each other questions, and we must answer honestly. We each get one pass on a question we don't want to answer." I pulled off a piece of croissant and popped it into my mouth. "I'll go first. Did you grow up in Southport?"

Crossing his arms behind his head, Josh leaned back in his chair. "Yep. Born and raised. My parents met in Georgia, but my grandparents are from here. So, my mom and dad moved back a few years after they got married. Okay, my turn." He pressed himself against the table, inching closer to me. "What brought you here?"

I hesitated. Biting my bottom lip, I considered my answer. I couldn't pass on Josh's first question, but I didn't want to get into the history of my past with him. I let out a small sigh and said, "I was tired of New York City. My job was demanding. I needed a change of pace and wanted to be closer to my brother."

I ran my fingers along the rim of my mug as I thought about my next question. "Tell me about your sister. What's her name?"

Josh looked puzzled. "My sister?"

"Um ... don't you have a sister? Well, I guess it could be a brother. Back in October, you said you had a niece at the Haunted Read."

Josh started laughing. "Damn, I'm sorry. I lied."

"You lied?"

"I wanted an excuse to visit you at the bookstore, so I said my niece was at your event. But I shouldn't have lied about that. It was stupid."

Raising an eyebrow at him, I said, "Well, that question doesn't count, then. I get a do-over because you tricked me."

Josh smiled. "It was a white lie, and for a good reason." Puffing out his lower lip and looking sad, he said, "Can you forgive me?"

"Yeah, yeah. I forgive you."

Damn him; he's so cute. That face, ugh, what's not to forgive? He lied to come and see me, so he gets bonus points for that.

"All right, Mr. Pouty Face, next question. How'd you get into construction?" I crossed my legs and tried to relax. I evaded his first question with an honest answer. He seemed satisfied with my response.

"My grandfather was in construction, my dad was in construction, and now I'm in construction. It's a family business. My grandfather built many of the homes that you see today. He passed the business to my father, and my father passed it down to me." He reached down to pet Cooper's head. "What was your job in New York? Do you currently have a boyfriend? Fiancé? Husband?"

"That's two questions. I'll answer the first one." I couldn't help but flirt with him. He was incredibly handsome and sweet. "I was the Chief Operating Officer for a marketing firm. I started as an executive marketing assistant and worked my way up."

He raised an eyebrow at me and smirked. "I'm picturing you bossing all the men around in a business suit with a short skirt and heels." His tone was smooth with a hint of sexy. "Did you boss them around?"

Tilting my head with squinted eyes, I asked, "Is that an official question?"

"No. Forget it. My official question. Are you in a relationship with anyone?"

"No," I said flatly.

"Were you in a relationship with someone back in New York?" The coffee shop porch light caused his bright blue eyes to sparkle in the darkness. I felt like they were tiny portals into his soul. Despite his robust and solid exterior, I could see gentleness in his eyes. I could see the eagerness in his heart for an answer to that question.

I took a deep breath and exhaled through my nose, causing the cool air to sting my nostrils. I reached for my mug and took a sip of my hot chocolate. "Yes. There was someone. His name was Gray. I thought we were in love. I thought I'd spend the rest of my life with him, but we had a nasty breakup. I feel like a fool, and I am not ready to open those wounds. Is that honest enough for you?" *Why am I annoyed?* It's not like I didn't know he wanted to be more than friends.

He reached his hand across the table and rested it on mine. I could feel his energy pulsating through my skin. Butterflies swirled around my stomach, and my toes curled in my shoes. *Steady Lizzie. Don't give in to this feeling. No matter how much Josh may seem to be a perfectly nice guy, you have to get your head right.*

Gently caressing my skin, he said, "I would never hurt you, Lizzie." He raised his hands, waving them in surrender. "I know, I know. Friends. We're just friends. I can't explain it, but I feel something for you. I need to get to know you better. I want to make you happy. If I can't do those things, I think I'll go crazy."

I wanted to believe him. My body wanted to be consumed by him; there was no denying that. I felt my desire for him boiling as blood pumped from my heart and flowed through my veins. My head screamed no, warning me to be cautious. It's like all my senses were in overdrive, fighting for control of the wheel. My chest felt heavy, and my breath quickened.

"I think I should get home." I pulled my hand away from his and stood from the table.

"Wait."

Was that desperation in his voice?

"I didn't mean to push. I won't deny my feelings for you, but I can and do want to be your friend. I'm a good listener." He ran his finger along the rim of his mug. "I'm here if you ever want to talk."

"Thanks, Josh. You seem nice, but I'm not ready. I don't know if I'll ever be ready. Thank you for tonight."

I had to get away before he saw me break down. *Or worse, before I let him kiss me.*

"Please, at least let me walk you home. It's dark. What kind of gentlemen would I be if I let you walk home alone?"

I didn't want to walk home alone, but I was sure I couldn't control myself. If he kissed me, I'd be done. Toast. Melted. No longer able to stand my ground.

"That'd be nice," I found myself saying. "Thank you."

I took the hot chocolate mugs inside, and Josh untied Cooper. He was waiting on the stairs with Cooper in tow when I returned. He reached out a hand to guide me down the steps and said, "My lady," as he bowed.

I laughed. A smirk growing on my face, I said, "Really? My lady. You're a dork."

"It was worth a shot. You lead the way."

"What about you? Tell me about your past girlfriends."

"Which one?"

"Oh, wow. That many, huh? I don't know. Pick one." I shrugged my shoulders and tried not to let his comment bother me. *Because it absolutely did bother me.*

"Nah, I'm kidding. I was engaged a few years back. Her name was Jess, but she broke it off. She wanted to travel and see the world. Apparently, she wanted to travel and see the world with Gustavo, the guy she was seeing behind my back. She left her engagement ring and a note on my kitchen table one day. I don't cheat—it hurts too bad." I could hear the sadness in his voice as he shared the memory with me.

"I'm sorry. What a horrible thing to do." I didn't know Jess, but I wanted to throw something at her. Maybe my fist. *How could she do that to him?*

"It's okay. It was a long time ago. I'm glad she broke it off before we got married."

I saw the hurt flash across his face as he said the words. In a weird way, that made me feel connected to him. Enough sad questions. "Here's an easy one. What kind of music do you like?" he asked.

Right in the middle of the street, I started doing the Running Man and Roger Rabbit. "I enjoy most types of music, but my favorite is nineties hip-hop. I keep that fact on the down low, though, so don't tell anyone."

"Your secret's safe with me." His eyes shined with amusement.

"What's your favorite movie?"

"No brainer. *Top Gun.* What about you."

"*Harry Potter.* I've watched them all at least ten times."

We went back and forth, asking each other question after question. We laughed, and then laughed some more. For a moment, I forgot the ache that had taken up residence in my heart. The walk was easy. Fun. Josh was straightforward and honest. If I trusted my instincts, I would be convinced he was genuine, but that was the problem. I didn't trust my intuition. I had been disgusted with my inner decision-maker for some time now.

How could I be sure that my instincts are correct about Josh?

"Looks like we're here," he said. I was having so much fun that I didn't even realize we were already at my house. Part of me felt sad. I didn't want the night to end.

"Is that Santa on the front porch?" He pointed at a life-size, light-up statue of Santa Claus. The figure moved slowly from side to side with one arm up like he was waving at us. As we approached the mechanical Santa, it stopped moving and said, 'Ho Ho Ho. Merry Christmas.'"

"Good Lord. He wasn't there when I left this morning. Not sure where he came from. It must have been a sale at Lowe's or something. Who knows? Renee and Randy are always looking for an excuse to buy more Christmas decorations. I give them a hard time, but honestly, I love it. Their Christmas spirit makes the holiday fun."

"Well, that Santa sure is something," he said with wide eyes. He stood at the bottom of the steps holding Cooper's leash in one hand while his other hand was propped on the railing. His square jaw was relaxed into a gentle smile. "I had a good time tonight."

"I did too. Thank you." I bent down on one knee to steal some kisses from Cooper and pet him behind the ears. Josh stepped in closer as I stood up. He dropped the leash and wrapped his arms around my waist. For a moment, my mind urged me to pull away, but my body enjoyed his warmth. I slid my arms around his neck and hugged him back. The hug lasted longer than it should have, but his embrace felt pure. His warmth flowed through me like rays of sunshine on a hot summer day. I slowly pulled away, and Josh leaned in and pressed his lips to my cheek.

"I'd love to take you out again, Lizzie."

The touch of his lips sent a ripple of tiny electrical shocks down my spine. *Just friends. We're just friends. Yeah, I'm definitely in trouble. Say good night and go inside.*

"Good night, Josh." I grabbed his hand in mine and squeezed it gently. I slowly slid my hand away to walk up the stairs and go inside when his grip tightened and pulled me back into him.

He cupped my face with his hands. His beautiful, honest blue eyes stared down at me, causing my self-control to melt away like candle wax dripping beneath a flame. He brought his lips to mine and kissed me. The way his lips lingered told me how much he'd wanted this kiss. I'd wanted this kiss, too. I needed it, like a human being needed oxygen. I tingled in places I didn't even know existed.

He slowly peeled his lips away, and our eyes met again. Part of me wanted every ounce of him, but the other part was terrified of his intensity and wanted to run away and never look back. I took a small step back and said, "Is that how friends kiss these days?" His eyes twinkled in the moonlight, causing my desire for him to burn deeper.

He pulled me back into him, never breaking eye contact, and whispered, "Wait until we're more than friends." The sound of his words made my insides quiver. "Until next time. I'll text you."

SEVENTEEN

January

I stood quietly as I placed new inventory on the bookshelves. A few weeks had passed since my hot chocolate with Josh. He had texted me every day since. We flirted when he worked on my soon-to-be apartment, and he had brought me croissants from Burney's twice that included a sweet note to brighten my day.

Josh was nice. His kiss from that night lingered on my lips, but whenever I thought I might allow myself to fall for him, the pain of my relationship with Gray rushed through me like a kayak on a white water rapid. I wanted to give Josh a chance, but my wounds were still fresh.

"You're awfully quiet today," Helen said as she opened another box of books. "What's on your mind?"

"Nothing." I continued to organize the shelves and worked my way down the bookcase, dusting and cleaning as I went. When I reached the end of the case, I saw myself in the pirate book armoire out of the corner of my eye. That's what I started calling it. I turned toward the glass mirrored door and stared back at my reflection. Lost in thought, I could hear Helen's faint voice. "Lizzie? Yoo-hoo, Lizzie. Earth to Lizzie."

I could see Helen's reflection in the glass as she stopped taking books out of the box, looked straight into my eyes, and said, "You don't have to tell me, but clearly, you have plenty on your mind."

"I'm thinking about Josh."

She frowned. "Well, those should be good thoughts, right?"

"It's complicated."

"Then uncomplicate it. Josh's a nice guy. He seems to be into you. What's the problem?"

"I wish it could be that simple. I don't know what I want anymore after Gray," I said, louder and whinier than I wanted.

"Man, Gray really did a number on you, huh?" Her tone was apologetic. "I'm always here for you anytime you want to unload."

"You're a good friend," I said and let out a sigh. "I hate myself for believing that what he and I had was real. Sometimes, I wish it *was* real. And the worst part of all is that I still miss him. I'm stupid. Stupid, stupid, stupid."

"You're *not* stupid!"

"He seemed genuine, or maybe I only saw what I wanted to see. That's the problem. I don't know. I feel like his fancy dates and expensive gifts swept me off my feet. I had a key to his apartment, and he treated me like I lived there. I thought we were building a life together. I suppose that's how he treated all his girlfriends, and I wasn't anything special." Turning away from the glass, I kneeled down and pulled another box toward me. I pulled out my utility knife and cut down the center to find a set of romance novels. I wanted to throw the box out the window. I glanced at Helen. She was watching me with heartbreak in her expression as she slowly stacked books on the floor.

"I swore I'd never be the girl who slept her way to the top. I didn't sleep my way there. I was already there, but I couldn't help but feel I was just another notch in his belt. Most days, I feel so stupid for allowing the relationship to happen. We made a baby together, Gray and me. I felt her move, and I loved her more than I loved myself. I can't help but think that my choices caused me to lose her because I wasn't good enough to be a mom and didn't deserve her."

A tear trickled from the corner of my eye. I had slept with a married man. I compromised my integrity by sleeping with my boss. I fell in love with a man who pretended to love me back. He shut me out the second he found out I was pregnant. Despite that, I loved him and wanted to win him back. Part of me still loved him, and I hated myself for that.

"I was eight months pregnant, and the only baby item I had was a pink baby blanket that I purchased from a kiosk in the mall. It had a white satin elephant stitched in the corner. I hadn't even started the nursery. I had no job, yet I couldn't stop envisioning a life together with Gray and our baby, even after everything he said and did to me. I was determined to make a life with him. I had to try again." As I thought about that day, I sliced open another box filled with cookbooks. Delicious recipes filled their pages and I couldn't help but feel like I was a recipe for disaster. "Sometimes, I still envision the possibility of that former life."

I'd woken up early in the morning, took a long hot shower, and slathered my skin with Cherry Blossom lotion. The scent had been Gray's favorite. I had dried and fixed my hair, applied my makeup, and put on the nicest maternity clothes I'd owned: black leggings and an off-the-shoulder red blouse. I topped off my outfit with high-heeled boots and red lipstick.

I'd been confident that I could win Gray back. The baby would arrive soon; surely, he'd want to meet his daughter, the beautiful baby girl that he'd helped create. I'd taken an Uber to Gray Stone Marketing and traveled the twenty flights up the elevator. Alone in the small square box, I'd tossed my words around and tried thinking through every possible scenario.

I'd stepped off the elevator and marched straight to Gray's office. His assistant, Claudia, had hopped up from her chair and shouted nervously, "*You can't go in there. He's in a meet—*"

"I'd barged right into his office, Helen." I'd done my best to look desirable with gigantic pregnant boobs and a round belly. "But that asshole made me wait until he was off the phone."

He'd lifted a finger and waved it back and forth, motioning that he'd be a minute. I'd waited and waited and waited. After several minutes of him pretending I wasn't in the room, I grew angry.

"So, I ended his call." Hitting disconnect on that phone had felt so good.

"Then I said, 'The baby's almost here. I'm giving you one last chance to be a part of this child's life. Our child's life.' Who was I kidding? He didn't care. But I pretended that the life we created mattered to him. I wanted to believe he could love our baby and me."

His nostrils flared as he slammed the phone into the receiver. "God, if I'd known how crazy you were, I wouldn't have slept with you." Then he shouted, "I've told you repeatedly I don't want to be with you. I want nothing to do with you. I don't even believe that it's my child. You need to leave. Now." His words brought back a rush of pain.

"He'd told me I was crazy and to leave. That the baby was not his child." I'd felt my embarrassment mix with desperation as it filled my gut like an overpacked suitcase.

Gray had stood from his desk and moved toward me. His eyes had looked soulless. As he'd approached, the vibrant green glimmers faded to black, but I had refused to show any emotion.

I had choked back everything I felt. "I said to him, 'She's your daughter, and you'll never be a part of her life. I came here one last time to give you a chance to be a father to your daughter. I understand if you don't want to be with me. Don't you want the chance to know her? If I walk out that door, you'll never know her.'"

He had reached down and pressed a button on his phone. The line had rang once, and the man on the other end said, "Security."

"Yes, hello. This is Gray Stone. I have an unwanted visitor in my office. Please come now and remove her immediately."

"He called security. He fucking called security. Then he said, 'You have about one minute to get out of here, or they will escort you out. We had fun, Lizzie, I'll give you that. I enjoyed sleeping with you, but that is where it ended for me. I don't want you or your baby.'"

"Oh, my." Helen covered her mouth with her hand. Her eyes were enormous.

"I ended up screaming at him. 'Fuck you, Gray Stone. Fuck you.'"

Then, turning on my heel, I'd walked as fast as my legs could carry me. Tears had instantly flooded my eyes and poured down my face.

I'd done this to myself.

How could I continue to love him? What was wrong with me? Never in my life had I behaved that way. He had been intoxicating, like a drug that I couldn't quit. A natural high.

"When I got to the elevator, I could see a crowd waiting for the doors to open, and I panicked." I'd felt like a rat trapped in a cage; all I wanted to do was escape.

"So, I went for the stairs. I have no idea how I expected my pregnant legs to make it down twenty flights of stairs. But at that moment, I didn't care. I needed to get out. I needed to get away from Gray, his business, his building, and his city."

My hands shook as I lifted the utility knife once more to open another box. "The next thing I knew, I was waking up in the hospital."

Helen reached out and took my hand in hers, steadying me. "Honey …"

"I pushed open the stairwell door, and the world went black."

Squeezing my hand, Helen said, "He was not the man you thought he was. He made you believe he loved you. It's not your fault, Lizzie."

"Except, he didn't love me." I dropped my shoulders and hung my head. "I threw myself at him like a groupie. I tossed my self-worth aside for the possibility of being with him again. And because of that, I lost my baby."

I leaned against the bookcase, hugged my knees to my chest, and cried. "My baby, Helen. She's gone. Why? Why'd I have to lose my baby?" I said in between sobs.

Helen sat beside me and gently rubbed my shoulder. "Let it out, Lizzie. It's okay to let it out."

"I haven't even told my brother. He doesn't even know he had a niece. My heart aches for her every day. The pain's like a giant void inside my heart, and nothing will ever fill it. And Josh—poor Josh. He thinks I'm the woman of his dreams. I'm broken and shattered. He shouldn't have to pick up my pieces."

I cried so hard that I could barely breathe, and I'm not sure if Helen could understand the words coming out of my mouth. "It's likely I can't have children, Helen. The doctor said I'd suffered a great deal of trauma. He told me he wasn't sure I'd survive another pregnancy. They weren't even sure I'd live."

My head fell between my knees, and I sat there, letting my body feel every emotion for the first time since that day in Gray's office. Feelings of regret, anger, and despair crashed down on me like a tidal wave slapping the shore.

Helen walked to the huge wooden front door and hung the closed sign. Then she shut the door and turned the inside lock. When she returned to my side, she said, "I'm sorry you've had to endure this pain alone. No mother should experience the loss of a child."

"I don't even remember what happened." I took a slow breath and collected myself in an attempt to stall the tears that fell down my face. Then, using the bottom of my shirt to dry my eyes, I said, "I was in a coma. I don't remember anything after opening the stairwell door. That day plays on repeat in my head. Did I trip? Did I pass out and fall? Why did I have to take the fucking stairs?"

I started sobbing again. "The hospital said I was in bad shape when I arrived. I was hemorrhaging and going in and out of consciousness. The doctor said he couldn't believe I was awake at all. He'd said the pain alone should've been too much to bear. They performed an emergency c-section, but the fall had caused too much trauma to the baby. They couldn't save her."

As I shared the story with Helen, my wounds cracked open like an egg. The memories I had bottled up oozed out, and my tears flowed endlessly like a broken dam. I remember that day like it was yesterday. I'd woken up alone, feeling empty and broken. The pain in my chest had been insurmountable. I never got to meet her, hold her, kiss her, or say goodbye. The gaping hole in my heart felt like the Grand Canyon. I had spent every day since, dreaming about my beautiful baby girl. What did she look like? Did she have a head full of hair? I dreamed of rocking her to sleep at night and reading to her. My nightmares' were filled with guilt. Guilt that my choices had caused my daughter's death. Why should I deserve love and happiness when my daughter never would? Why should I deserve anything at all?

EIGHTEEN

Josh asked me to dinner, and I looked forward to spending more time with him. My emotional walls were tall and thick, but he was growing on me, and I wanted to get to know him better. He was pretty damn hot too, which didn't hurt. Twirling around, I glanced at myself in the mirror. I wore a short floral maxi dress with spaghetti straps and high black boots with wedge heels.

Downstairs, Randy and Renee were on the couch watching football, their favorite Sunday afternoon pastime. "Don't wait up. I don't know when I'll be home."

Renee muted the game and looked at me. "Where you off to?"

"I'm going to grab a bite with Josh."

Randy stood up from the couch and peered at me. "Josh, huh?"

I rolled my eyes. "We're friends."

"It might get cold. You should probably grab a sweater," Randy said.

Holding up my jean jacket I had just retrieved from the hook, I said, "I'm wearing this. I'll be good."

A gentle knock rapped on the door, and I quickly moved to open it. "Okay, see you guys later."

"Whoa, you don't even want me to come inside and say hello," Josh said with a confused look on his face.

"No. I'm ready to go." I smiled.

"It's a beautiful night. Do you want to walk?"

"Sure." I looped my arm inside his and allowed him to guide me down the street. The bright rays of the setting sun gave way to beautiful hues of orange and yellow in the sky. The evening was cool, and a gentle breeze rustled the air around us as we walked.

As usual, Josh wore jeans that highlighted his positive attributes, and a button-down shirt with little sailboats stitched here and there. He looked even more handsome in the glow of the setting sun. My hands were getting moist from my nerves. Josh made it easy to let my guard down, but a flashing red warning light circled in my head. *Male, Danger. Male, Danger.*

I didn't trust myself with him, or maybe I didn't trust him with my heart. I wasn't sure I could trust anyone with my heart. *Damn you, Gray.*

"What's on your mind, Lizzie."

A little caught off guard by his question, I tensed slightly. "Not much. I'm enjoying the colors in the sky."

"The colors are spectacular tonight." He stopped. Turning toward me, he put my hands in his and said, "Friends?"

"Friends."

"I promise we'll go at your pace. Relax, and let's have a good time."

My shoulders fell a few inches, and relief washed over me. His understanding and gentleness made me want to wrap my arms around him and never let go. I leaned in and placed a kiss on his cheek. Resting my head gently on his shoulder, I wrapped my arms around his waist and said, "Thank you." Warmth filled my heart, and my anxiety began to melt away in his arms like an ice sculpture in the blazing sun.

A dog barked across the street. Startled, I jumped, and bumped my head into Josh's chin. I pulled away from him, and we laughed. He took my hand, weaved his fingers in between mine and smiling, we walked in silence, to Oliver's Restaurant on Bay Street.

We sat at a table overlooking the water and ordered wine while reading over the menu.

"Everything sounds delicious," I said, practically drooling over the descriptions of each dish on the menu.

"Yeah, I haven't had a meal I didn't like here."

Josh peered over the menu, his eyes drinking me in like I was the main course. His soulful gaze made my insides tingle. *He's so intense. Friends, my ass. He can hardly control himself.* I secretly loved his passion, determination, and willingness to go after what he wanted. Unfortunately, it's also what attracted me to Gray.

"So, how do you like working at the bookstore?"

"I love it. Helen's the best, and I enjoy creating new ways to draw people to the store."

Unfolding his napkin, he said, "Yeah, I can't imagine a small-town bookstore is crawling with people all the time."

"It depends on the day. Our events are usually packed, so that's good." I took a sip of wine and gazed out at the water. "What an incredible place to grow up."

"Small towns have their perks. I appreciate it more now than I did when I was a kid. As a kid, I felt like I was missing out on something."

"I get that."

"I'd love to raise my children here."

I raised an eyebrow as I took another sip of wine. "Kids?"

"Sure, someday. Don't you want to have kids?"

My stomach felt sick. I didn't know what to say. My body tensed. I wasn't ready for this conversation. "I guess I haven't given it much thought." I lied. "I've been busy working on my career most of my adult life."

He raised his wineglass in affirmation. "Well, it's a great place to raise a family. Peaceful and innocent."

We laughed and talked through dinner, and with each passing second, I felt more comfortable with him. He paid the bill, and we walked along the water, finally stopping to sit on a bench to watch the ships pass by. Josh held me in his arms, and I nestled into him.

I looked into his eyes and said, "I had a great time tonight. Thank you." Before I could react, he placed his hand gently on my face and kissed me. His lips were soft and tender. I closed my eyes and kissed him back, tasting his red wine from dinner on my lips. His kiss felt right, but I was afraid. Wanting more, so much more, I resisted the urge and pulled back.

"I know, friends," he said softly. I could see a glimpse of sadness in his eyes, and it broke my heart, but I wasn't ready to fully let my guard down.

For hours, we sat on the bench talking. We talked about everything from our childhood to our jobs, to our pets. He wanted me to tell him about living in the Big Apple. I wanted to know all about his construction business and his life before we met. We laughed and joked, and he teased me for my lack of a Southern accent. The moon sparkled against the dark sky, and the twinkling stars danced brightly. One by one, the people drifted back to their homes, and before we knew it, the time was 1:30 a.m. We were alone. Two friends, hanging out under the moonlight by the water.

"I didn't realize the time," I said as I stood up from the bench. "I think the whole town's gone to bed." Josh laughed at my observation.

God, he's even cuter when he laughs.

"Time flies when you're having fun," he said. I turned to start walking home, but Josh grabbed my waist and pulled me to face him. Standing before him, he looked up at me, and said, "You intrigue me, Lizzie. I could talk to you all night."

I placed my hand on the top of his head and ran my fingers through his hair. He exhaled deeply and pulled me closer. His head rested against my chest. My heartbeat fluttered and my arms tingled. He gently ran his fingers up my thighs. The sensation of his touch on my skin sent my senses into overdrive. I could feel his breath as he placed gentle kisses on my neck. Leaning my head back, I granted him full access. My body commanded him as my mind and heart screamed no. The constant struggle was exhausting, an internal boxing match and Josh's gentle caress made it impossible for my mind and heart to win.

Josh firmly, yet gently, gripped my waist and lifted me to straddle him. I clamped my fingers along the back of the bench and smiled at him. "You're not a good friend," I said. He frowned.

"Cut me some slack." He smirked as he tilted his head to the side. "You make it tough."

"*I* make it tough."

He slid his arms up my back and squeezed tightly. "You're beautiful, Lizzie. In every way. You've got to forgive a guy. I'm weak." He flashed his puppy dog eyes, and my heart completely melted. Point Josh. All that was left of my defenses was my brain telling me to keep my guard up.

"I make it tough," I said again. "You make it impossible." Wrapping my hands around his neck and caressing the back of his head, I leaned down and pressed my lips into his. Hundreds of miniature explosions erupted in my body and I lost myself in his arms.

He pulled away to look at me, and teased, "Can we still be friends?"

"Friends is all I'm capable of right now."

He whispered into my ear, "I'll take it." Then, gently kissed my cheek.

NINETEEN

Early March

I stood in the middle of my bedroom and stared at myself in the full-length mirror. My ribs were not as visible since I had gained a little weight. *What does one wear to go fishing?*

Josh and I had been spending a lot of time together over the last few months, during which he had been the perfect gentleman. We had managed to be friends who kissed each other good night, but he hadn't pushed me further than that. He let me take things at my pace and let me know he would be here when I was ready to open my heart. It had been easy hanging out with him. We'd grown to know each other without the pressure of a typical relationship. *Who am I kidding? I'm totally falling for him.*

Today, he wanted to take me fishing. I hadn't fished in years. My dad took Randy and me when we were little, but that seemed like a lifetime ago. As kids, we fished in a lake from the water's edge or in a small rowboat.

Josh wanted to take us into the ocean on his fishing boat. I'd never fished in the ocean, but I would go anywhere with him. I rifled through my drawers and pulled out my sparkly black bikini. The top was tied in the back and around my neck, and triangle pieces adorned with clusters of glitter covered my chest. The bottoms were also black, and the thin straps on my hips were covered in matching sparkly glitter bursts.

The day wasn't bikini weather, but I thought perhaps in the afternoon, it might warm up enough that I could sunbathe on the boat. I found a black pair of loosely fitted linen pants and pulled those on over my bikini bottoms. I walked over to my closet and searched for a top. Hanging right in front was a black short-sleeve crop T-shirt with a blue smiley face in the center. *Perfect.* I grabbed my blue cardigan sweater to throw over the top because the morning would be chilly. I ran a brush through my hair and braided it. Looking cute was important to me, but I also wanted to look like I was ready for a day of fishing. *Why am I so nervous about this date? We've been out before.*

I packed a beach towel, sunscreen, lip balm, and a book into my beach bag and walked downstairs to the kitchen. "Good morning," I said to Renee, who was standing in the kitchen reading the newspaper. "Do you happen to have a sun hat?" Then, turning my gaze to Randy sitting at the kitchen table, I said, "Or maybe you have a fishing hat that doesn't look ridiculous I could borrow."

Renee peered over the newspaper. "I have a black sun hat that would look great with your outfit. Let me grab it for you." When she returned from the laundry room with the hat in her hand, she asked, "Are you going to the beach today? It's Saturday. You don't have to work?"

"I took the day off. Josh's coming to pick me up in a few minutes. We're going fishing on his boat." I reached into the cabinet for a coffee mug, grabbed the pot, and poured a full cup.

"You two have been spending quite a bit of time together," Randy said. "Is this getting serious?"

"Nah. We're just friends. He's a nice guy, and I like spending time with him." *And kissing him. And maybe I'm totally into him.* But I wasn't saying that out loud.

Wrinkling his face into a smirk, Randy said, "Maybe I can come then, since you're just friends." He air-quoted the just friends part of his sentence.

"Sure, you want to come? Come on, then." I prayed he wouldn't take me up on my offer. Josh and I hadn't defined what we were, but I wanted to be alone with him. He had been patient with me and allowed me to take our relationship at my pace. I wanted to feel his arms wrapped around my body in the sunshine. I wanted his tender kisses on my skin. He made me feel like I could love myself again, like I was capable of anything.

Renee laughed. "Randolph, you have a honey-do list for today. There's no fishing with your sister and her boy, who's just a friend that she sees almost every day."

Thank you, Renee. I didn't think Randy would come, but I wasn't ready to admit that this was a date and Josh was more than a friend. I could hear the tires crunching over the rocks in the driveway. "That's my ride." I grabbed my beach bag and walked toward the door. "I'm not sure when I'll be home, so don't plan on me for dinner."

"Sounds good, sis," Randy said. "Have fun." He followed me to the door and held it open as I walked over the threshold.

Josh was getting out of his truck as I stepped onto the porch. Randy rushed outside and hollered, "You guys almost done out back?"

"Yes, sir. We'll be finished on Monday," Josh replied and gave a little wave.

"You hear that, Lizzie. Your apartment will be ready on Monday."

"That's exciting," I said. "Thank you both." Josh had opened the passenger door and was waiting for me to get situated inside the truck before closing it.

Waving goodbye to Randy, Josh said, "See ya later."

"I grabbed you an extra-large caramel latte and a glazed croissant." Josh handed me the coffee and placed the baggie with the croissant into my lap once he was back in the truck. "You look absolutely beautiful this morning. You're beautiful every time I see you, but today you look even more beautiful than yesterday."

I could feel my cheeks getting hot. I nudged his arm with my hand and said, "Joooshh. You're making me blush."

"It needed to be said. You're beautiful. Inside and out, Lizzie Levine."

"You aren't so bad yourself." I leaned over and kissed him on the cheek.

We arrived at the dock a few minutes later, and Josh grabbed my bag.

"This way," he said. We walked down a short sidewalk and stepped onto a dock with hundreds of boats floating in their slips. "I came out early. Everything's ready and in the boat except you."

"Which one's yours?"

"Almost there, just a few more steps."

As we made our way through the docks, the boats kept growing in size. The only boats left were gigantic, some of the biggest I had ever seen.

"We're here." He stepped onto the deck and reached out his hand. On the side of the white, massive iridescent boat were the words Hammer of the Sea in red block letters.

"This is your boat?" I asked in wonder. It was more like a yacht.

"Yep. She's all mine. Most people have a mortgage. I have a boat." He laughed. "Come on board."

The boat had two decks. Benches with soft white cushions lined the back, glass sliding doors covered the entryway to the cabin inside, and a narrow walkway led us to the bow with more seating. Fishing poles sat inside white cylinders, and a tackle box was nestled in the boat's point.

We walked around the other side and took the stairs to the upper deck. Four soft white lounge chairs lined the back, and several captain's chairs were stationed at the front of the upper deck. Josh motioned for me to sit in one of the captain's chairs. He reached into the Yeti cooler affixed to the boat and pulled out two champagne glasses, a plastic container of orange juice, and a bottle of champagne.

"Mimosa," he said and raised the two glasses that dangled between his fingers.

Panic crept into my gut. *This is Gray all over again.* I don't want a wealthy man who spoils me with lavish things. I want a man who will truly love me and share his soul with me. Grandiose gestures do not mean love.

Josh isn't Gray, and you're just friends. Enjoy the moment.

Sensing a shift in my energy, Josh said, "What's wrong?"

"Everything's fine. The boat's amazing. What kind of girl would I be if I didn't like a mimosa?" I tried to reassure him I was okay.

"We're friends, right?" Josh poured champagne nearly to the top of each glass.

"Yes. We're friends." *Where's he going with this line of questioning?*

"I'm a friend you can trust, Lizzie. I swear." He shifted his weight and continued, "I thought we agreed to be honest with each other. I can tell something has bothered you. You can tell me." He reached out and brushed a strand of my hair behind my ear.

I don't know why, but I decided to tell him. Josh hadn't given me any reason to believe that I shouldn't trust him, and if I'm going to let him into my heart, I needed to be honest. So, to gather my courage, I accepted a glass of mimosa from him and took a large sip.

"You asked me if I had a boyfriend on our first date at the coffee shop."

He cut me off and said, "You have a boyfriend?"

"No, no. I *had* a boyfriend. His name was Gray." I took another gulp from my flute glass. "He was the owner and current president of Gray Stone Marketing, where I worked."

"You dated your boss." His tone was more surprised than judgmental.

"I deeply regret that decision. Gray was disgustingly wealthy, and I think I got swept up in all the extravagance. He broke my heart, and I can't go through that again. I moved here to live a simpler life. As I've gotten to know you, I thought you were a simple man. A man that I could live a simple life with."

His grin widened and filled his entire face. "You think you could live a life with me? As more than just friends?"

Shit. I didn't intend to tell him I actually had genuine feelings for him.

"That's not ... I don't ... Ahh shit ... Yes, I've thought about a relationship with you, but I'm broken. My wounds are so deep, I don't know if I'll ever be ready. But your boat made me pause."

"My boat? What? Why?" he said, chugging the last sip left in his glass. He reached for the bottle and poured another. I tipped my glass in his direction, signaling that if this conversation was going to continue, I needed a full glass too.

"I don't want another rich guy who will buy my affection and trick me into loving him. I want simple."

"I'm a simple man," Josh said, handing me my glass. "Most of what I have has been passed down from generation to generation. My house, for example. Well, it will be my house—it's been in our family for generations. I love to fish and be on the water, so I took what money I had and bought this boat. It's the only expensive thing I own."

He walked toward me and placed his hand on my cheek. "If it makes you uncomfortable, I'll sell it tomorrow. All I want is for you to be happy and for me to be a part of your happiness." He cleared his throat. "As friends, of course."

He looked beautiful, with his skin glistening in the sunlight. I was falling for Josh Miller. I was falling so hard that I was terrified I might shatter into a million pieces when I landed. I placed my hand on his and said, "Thank you." Gratitude filled my heart as I gazed into his eyes. "Thank you for being patient with me."

"Whatever you need, Lizzie. When you're ready, let me know. In the meantime, we can fish." He laughed.

Together, we climbed down the stairs and walked to the front of the boat. Josh lifted the lid to the tackle box and pulled out a bucket of shrimp. He scooped a few out of the bucket and baited them to our hooks. After we dropped our lines out into the water, Josh said, "Now we wait. When you feel a little tug, reel in your line." He looked over at me and smiled. "The goal's to catch some small fish, and then we use those to catch the big fish. With any luck, we'll catch dinner."

I raised my eyebrow. "Dinner?"

"Yep. If we catch dinner, you have to promise to eat with me tonight at my house. I want you to meet my dad." Josh reached out his hand for me to shake it.

Gripping his hand firmly, I said, "Deal." He pulled me into him and planted his lips firmly onto mine. I felt his arms wrapping around the small of my back and sliding down to gently pat my ass. My insides turned warm, and I felt at peace in his arms—no hesitation, no regret, and no doubt that I could trust him with my heart.

"Look," he exclaimed, pointing to my rod leaning against the boat's edge. "You caught one."

The tip of the rod bobbed gently up and down. My eyes shimmered with fascination as I picked up the rod and reeled in my fish.

"You caught the perfect bait fish," Josh exclaimed. He unhooked the fish and tossed it into the ice cooler. We continued catching small fish for over an hour. We talked and laughed, spending time with him was easy. Josh caught fifteen bait fish, and I managed to reel in ten.

"I'll tell the captain we're ready to move to our next spot. It's time to catch the big fish," he said, pumping his fist in the air.

"You have a captain?"

Sheepishly, he said, "Well, yeah. Who'd you think was driving the boat?"

I laughed. "I guess I didn't think about it."

"Usually, I drive the boat, but I wanted to spend all my time with you today, so I hired a captain."

The air was warmer now, and the sun was shining brightly.

"Do I have time to catch some rays and read before our next destination?" I said.

"You sure do." He disappeared inside. Realizing I had not been inside yet, I chased after him.

"Wait," I said. "You haven't given me a tour."

The glass doors opened into a beautiful sitting area with a plush tan couch and coffee table and windows overlooking the ocean on all sides. Two captain's chairs sat at the front of the boat by the steering wheel and a set of fancy gauges I didn't recognize. I waved to the captain sitting in one of the chairs. His smile widened, which added to the wrinkles on his face.

A narrow staircase took us below deck and opened to a small kitchen with a refrigerator, stove, and microwave. A few cabinets lined the wall. Off the kitchen was a doorway to the bedroom. Josh held open the door to the bedroom for me to step inside. A king-size bed filled the room. There was a small closet, one dresser with a few drawers, and small windows lining the ceiling.

I gasped. "You could live on this boat."

"I could, and I have. Now, I stay in the house to care for my dad, but occasionally I'll take the boat out overnight."

"Would you really sell this boat for me?"

"In a second, if that's what you wanted," he responded without hesitation.

"I'd never ask you to do that. Plus, I don't want you to sell it. In fact, I want you to teach me how to drive it someday." I winked and could see his shoulders relax. "What?"

Laughing, he said, "I'm glad you don't want me to sell it. I would've, but I really didn't want to."

Lunging forward, I threw my arms around his neck and squeezed him tightly. "I'm going to the upper deck to lie on the lounge chair and read," I said as I gave him a peck on the cheek.

Back on top, I removed my sweater and T-shirt, folded them neatly, and lay on one of the lounge chairs. Then I reached into my bag, took out my book, and read.

Josh appeared about thirty minutes later. "I brought you a sandwich if you're hungry." He set a tray on the small table beside my chair. "I also have wine and a bottle of water."

"Sounds great." I sat up and watched Josh pour me a glass of red wine. His dark hair glimmered in the sun, and beads of sweat trickled down his bare chest. His body was divine. I could not peel my eyes away from him. He didn't have a washboard stomach, but he had abs. He was beefy but in a good, strong way. His butt looked as good in his bathing suit as it did in his jeans.

"I like your bathing suit," he said. His soft gaze explored my body, and his lips parted. "You look comfortable." He cleared his throat and tied the string on his bathing suit as if he was doing his best to keep his swim trunks on. "Happy?"

"I am happy." I shocked myself as the words came out of my mouth. *I do feel happy. I can't remember the last time I felt pure joy.*

"It makes me happy to see you happy," Josh said, sitting beside me. "Would it be too much if I admitted that it's taking every ounce of strength I have to keep from carrying you to the lower deck and untying your top?"

I leaned forward, looked directly into his beautiful blue eyes, and whispered, "I know the feeling."

The intensity of his stare burrowed straight down into my soul. I took the wineglass from his hand and sat back in my chair. Josh made me feel safe, sexy, and loved. I wanted to cling to those feelings at this moment. I swirled the wine in my glass and sipped, never breaking eye contact with him. We said nothing as he took a step closer.

He looked over at the sandwich and said, "You should eat. You'll need energy for what's coming next." Was he talking about fishing or something else? *Get your mind out of his bedroom. Of course, he's talking about fishing.* I picked up one-half of the sandwich and took a bite.

"Turkey and cheese," I said. "My favorite."

TWENTY

Josh caught five red snappers and several fish we had to throw back. I, however, didn't catch any. The snappers were dinner, so I'd be meeting his father tonight. Oddly, I wasn't nervous. Instead, I was excited to meet the man who had raised Josh.

Just as I was about to sit down and call it quits, the tip of my rod started to bend.

"Josh," I screamed. "I think I've got a big one." The fish was wriggling and pulling hard on the line. The fishing rod was bending in a full U, and I was leaning back on the weight, reeling the line as fast as I could.

"Slow down. You don't need to reel that fast." He stepped behind me to provide leverage while I tugged, pulled, and reeled in the fish.

"This might be the biggest one yet." My voice was breathy. I had no idea how difficult reeling in an enormous fish could be.

When I thought I had almost reeled him up, the line released and pulled away. I yanked hard on the rod and reeled him in again. Josh helped.

Fighting against the fish, I pulled with all my might one last time. The line snapped, knocking me back into Josh and sending us both hurling to the floor. I landed on my back on top of his chest. Bursting into laughter, I dropped the rod beside us, rolled off Josh, and lay beside him.

"That must've been a huge fish." He reached over and wiped a hair off my face. His hand lingered for a moment, and I smiled at him. His touch was gentle. Before I could say or do anything, Josh rolled over and swaddled me in his arms. He continued to roll us both until I was on top of him. Brushing the hair out of my face again, he breathed out and whispered, "Damn, Lizzie. You're so beautiful." Wrapping his hands gently around the back of my head, he pulled my face closer to his and kissed me.

Oxytocin spread through my veins like a wildfire burning deep inside my body. I parted my lips, and his tongue entered my mouth. His kiss was slow and methodical. Taking his time, he tasted every ounce of me. Finally, I pulled away from him and sat up. Taking in the full view of me sitting on top of him, Josh let out a soft groan.

I leaned into his ear and whispered, "I don't want to be just friends anymore."

Josh groaned louder and said, "I don't want to push you." I stood up and reached for his hand. "We don't have to do this. Are you sure?"

"I'm sure. I want to be with you. I'm ready." I pulled him up to stand in front of me. He put his hands on my thighs and slid them under my butt. My body stiffened. He barely missed my scars. *What if he touches them? What if he sees them? Stop it, Lizzie. Commit or don't, but stop thinking. Just feel.*

He pulled me into him and lifted me as he kissed me again. The warmth of his embrace ignited a fire inside me that burned away my fears. I entangled my legs around his waist and allowed myself to be present in the moment. He walked us to the staircase that led to the lower deck. I slid down his body and placed my feet on the floor. He entwined his fingers between mine and held my hand as he escorted me down the stairs and into the bedroom.

Using my free hand, I untied the strap around my neck. Then, I turned to face Josh with my breasts exposed and said, "Oops."

Like a hungry animal in the wild, Josh kicked the door closed behind him and rushed at me, and both of us fell onto the bed. He kissed my face, then my cheeks, and down onto my neck. His kiss lingered on my collarbone.

Tensing again, I urged myself to feel. *Lizzie, be in the moment. Feel. Feel it all.*

He wrapped his arms around me and flipped us so I was on top. He reached behind my back, untied the last string on my bikini top, and sent it flying across the room. Pressing my body against his sent blood rushing to my core. He felt so right. *Safe.* At this moment, I knew that I wanted him, needed him. Unlike Gray, I wasn't addicted to Josh like a drug addict is addicted to heroin.

Josh completed me. I wanted to experience every minute of life with him.

Looking into his tender blue eyes as they glistened from the sunlight trickling into the room, I whispered, "I don't want this moment to end." Josh moaned softly and rolled me onto my back.

"Don't worry. I plan to take my time," he said as he slid me to the edge of the bed. He trailed soft kisses down my neck, pausing at my nipple, and flicked it with his tongue. I breathed out, feeling his tender, genuine love all over. He could kiss my body all day, every day, and I don't think I'd ever grow tired of it. His mouth traveled every inch of my curves, working his way down to my lower belly.

He slipped his fingers into the waist of my pants, slowly pulling them and the bikini bottoms off, and tossed them onto the floor.

Okay, well, there it is. All my mistakes, showing like glitter, sparkled on my flesh for him to see. *It doesn't matter.* If he noticed, he didn't act like it.

He lifted my right leg and massaged the ball of my foot. He worked his way from my ankle, kissing the lower part of my leg, then my thigh, back to my stomach, pausing once again at the sensitive peaks of my breasts. Biting my bottom lip, I moaned until his lips met mine again.

Josh was perfect in every way. Completely engrossed in the moment, I let my fears slip away. He stood to slip off his bathing suit, and I pulled him toward me. Never taking his eyes off mine, he slid his hands up my stomach, cupped my breasts, and leaned in for another kiss. Then he pushed himself inside me. I had fallen completely and utterly in love with this man. He fit inside of me like a perfectly fitted glove. I shuddered at the explosions of emotion and pleasure I felt with him, like bombs bursting in the air. He made sweet, tender love to me, a genuine love I had not experienced before.

Afterward, he held me in his arms and caressed my skin. He lifted my chin so I could look at him and said, "I love you, Lizzie. I understand if you're not ready to say it back. But I can't go another minute without you knowing that I love you."

I stared at him and said nothing. I could see the love in the way his eyes looked at me. I wanted to capture that look and freeze it in time. I climbed on top of him and pressed my lips to his. Sitting up, so he could fully see my face in the sunlight, I said, "I love you too."

He slipped back inside of me, and we made love all over again.

White siding covered the entire house. A beautiful two-story porch with white rocking chairs on both levels welcomed us to the home's entrance. The roof was bright cardinal red and shined like a beacon for all to see. On top of the roof was a cupola, or a "Widow's Walk." I hadn't seen anything like it. His home stretched along Bay Street overlooking the Cape Fear River.

"This is your house?" I said with wide eyes. Character oozed from every inch of the home. It was stunning. "You actually live here. So, like, this is not a joke, right?"

Josh laughed, took my hand, and escorted me toward the front door. "This house belonged to my great-grandfather's great-grandfather. The views are beautiful, and our family's worked hard for generations to restore it while keeping the history intact." A wooden placard screwed into the siding beside the entry door said, Waylen Miller House 1868.

"Wow, 1868." I gently ran the tips of my fingers along the edge of the sign like I could somehow transport myself to the past through the placard. "Josh, I don't have any words. I can't believe this house has been in your family for over one hundred and fifty years. It's incredible. So special."

The beauty and elegance took my breath away. I gazed around the porch and took in the wooden pieces creating the porch floor. Thick, sturdy railings stood between each column and held up the porch above. I ran my palm along the wood, and wondered what it must have been like to live here so many years ago. Josh's ancestors stood exactly where I was standing right now. The thought gave me chills, and the hairs on my bare arms stood erect.

I had showered on the boat and changed into the sundress I had brought in my backpack, just in case we went somewhere after fishing. Meeting Josh's father was something I was looking forward to, and I wanted to look nice. It was a simple jean sundress with wide straps and a navy blue belt with large brown buttons. Then I grabbed my blue cardigan, threw it over my shoulders, and joined Josh on the front porch swing.

Looking up, I noticed light blue paint on the porch's ceiling. I tilted my head sideways and asked, "Why blue? It looks nice, but doesn't match the rest of the house."

"The color's called haint blue. The Gullah Geechee people of the South believed that haints, restless spirits of the dead, would haunt a home. The haint blue paint is a superstition to keep the spirits from taking up residence."

"Interesting," I said as I considered the tradition. I wasn't really into spirits, but if the paint kept them away, I was all for it.

"My family never wanted to test the theory, so we've always kept the porch ceiling haint blue," Josh said, shrugging.

Beautiful pine wood floors covered the entire house. The windows were designed in the perfect locations to allow maximum sunlight to flow into the interior. I imagined generations before me building a home with a happy family inside the walls of this house. Rich with history, culture, and love, I could feel the presence of Waylen's past and their life in this home. The experience was surreal.

"You must be Lizzie," a gentle, old voice said as its owner entered the foyer. I reached out my hand to say hello, but he stepped closer and gave me a big bear hug.

"Handshakes are too formal. I want to hug the woman who's brought so much happiness to my son. I'm Waylen, but you can call me Len."

I could see where Josh got his good looks. His father was maybe seventy-five. His hair was gray with white highlights, but he still had a head full of it. He was shorter than Josh, but not by much, and his eyes were just as blue and beautiful.

"Come, let's sit in the kitchen. Would you like a glass of wine?" Josh's father asked and beckoned us to follow him.

Cooper came charging into the kitchen. His tail wagged eagerly, causing his hind end to wiggle back and forth. I leaned over to pet the dog and said, "I'd love some wine." Cooper jumped up and placed his paws on my chest. "Len, your home is beautiful."

"Thank you. It's our family heirloom, so to speak. It's great to finally meet you. I've heard so much about you."

Raising an eyebrow, I said, "You have? All good things, I hope." I took a sip of my wine and sat at the kitchen table. Josh sat across from me, leaving the seat at the head of the table empty.

"Only good things. According to Josh, you're quite the woman," Len said as he took his seat at the head of the table.

"Dad." Josh's neck and cheeks turned red. "You can't tell her all my secrets."

"You know, son, I've learned through my years. If you find a good woman, you tell her every day. You love her fiercely and hold on to her as tightly as you can."

"Listen to your dad, Josh. Those are excellent words of wisdom." I patted his hand from across the table.

"Yeah, yeah. I hear you," Josh teased.

"Dinner will be a few more minutes. Why don't you give Lizzie a tour of the house?" Len suggested.

Josh led me out of the kitchen into the living room. Built-in bookshelves lined the far wall. Books upon books rested on the shelves. I could tell from the bindings that some of the books were very old, and I pointed to one in particular on the shelf. I was terrified to touch them.

"Is this an original Farewell to Arms?"

"Yes indeed. Many of the older books are originals. Each generation adds to the books," Josh said proudly.

"Unbelievable. I could stay in this room and never come out."

"Well, I hate to disappoint, but there's more to see," Josh said and led me into the next room.

The space opened into a sitting room with two small blue couches and a shellacked pine coffee table in the middle. Off the sitting room was a beautiful sunroom with a few rocking chairs and a six-top table.

"I added the sunroom to the house about five years ago. My dad enjoys it."

I followed him upstairs, which opened into a loft with another set of bookshelves filled with more books. Past the loft were several bedrooms.

"My dad sleeps in the primary bedroom on the first floor so that he doesn't have to climb the stairs every day." He opened a door on his left. "This was my bedroom when I was a kid, but I sleep in the primary bedroom on this floor now."

The room was spacious, with a queen bed, one dresser, and a nightstand. "We've turned this room into a guest bedroom."

He led me down the hall and pushed open a door on the right. "This is my bedroom." The room was beautiful. In the center was a king-size bed with four wooden bedposts. Two large windows opened to a beautiful view of the bay. Off to the right of the bed was a doorway that led into a small sitting room connected to the second-story front porch.

"No wonder why you're so happy. This is your view every morning." It was a gorgeous view.

"You could wake up here every morning with me." He pulled me closer. Like a flint, his hug sparked my desire. His eyes were filled with a mix of passion and adoration. I think it was the first time anyone looked at me that way. He leaned down and gently kissed me. I could hear the gentle waves crashing onto the sand. He released me, and I pulled him back into a tight embrace. He released me again. This time he put his hands on the top button of my dress, pulled the fabric apart, and then used both hands to unfasten the second button.

"Josh! What're you doing?" I said, but I didn't ask him to stop. *I didn't want him to stop.*

"You're beautiful and wearing a dress that's literally only staying closed with these buttons. It's nearly impossible to keep my hands off you." He undid my third button to expose my purple lace bra. He laced his fingers between mine and pressed my back against the wall between the windows. Then, raising our interlocked hands over my head, he gazed once more into my eyes. The sparks that danced inside my body spread like wildfire. He kissed my cheeks and down my neck to the top of my breasts above my bra.

He released my hands, and I threaded my fingers through his hair as he unsnapped my belt and let it fall to the floor. He lifted my right leg and placed it around his waist as he caressed my thigh with his hands, sliding them under my dress until he reached the top of my panties. He ran his fingers gently along the lace trim, decorating the top of my underwear.

I whimpered as I placed my foot back on the floor. Tilting my head, I pressed my lips to his and savored every second of his kiss.

Pulling away, I whispered in his ear, "We can't do this right now. Your dad's waiting for us."

He ignored my words and released the final three buttons on my dress with one hard tug. His hands reached inside my open denim dress, and he sensually glided his arms around my back. I didn't want him to stop. Every single nerve in my body ached for his touch. My heart ached for his love, and my body demanded to have him.

He lifted me slowly and carried me toward the bed. "Your mind, your eyes, your dress, your face, your love. All of it makes me crazy.

I don't want to do anything but lie here with you," Josh whispered in between placing frantic, hungry kisses on my chest, stomach, and thighs.

I knew one of us had to be strong enough to end this moment. I couldn't skip the first dinner I was invited to with his dad because I was making love to his son.

I kissed his cheek. "Good things come to those who wait," I said. "Your dad's waiting for us. How about you let this moment live in your thoughts, and we'll pick up where we left off another time. I promise the wait will be worth it."

He moaned. "I'm not sure I can wait." He slipped his hand down my panties and suckled my breast. Once he freed my nipple from his tongue, he whispered sensually, "Are you absolutely certain you want to wait? I'm confident I can make it worth it right now."

And boy did he ever.

Red snapper cooked in butter, salt, and pepper with baked potatoes and corn on the cob was set out on the table.

"That was a long tour," Len said.

"Sorry, Dad. Lizzie was enjoying the books." Josh shot me a sideways glance. "She works at a bookstore, remember?" he said as he pulled out my chair. *Did Len know? Could he sense what had just happened one floor above him? Probably. The glow radiating from my skin gave us away.*

"Yes, sir. I'm sorry. I didn't mean to keep us that long. I love books, and I'm fascinated by the antique books you have. All the books, really." I lied. Well, it wasn't exactly a lie. Of course, I was fascinated by the books, but that wasn't what delayed us. "The food looks delicious."

"Let's hope it tastes as good as it looks. This old man can still cook. Eat up," Len said as he lifted the plate for me to take the fish. I scooped several small pieces onto my plate.

"Thank you," I said as I reached for the potatoes. I helped myself to a spoonful and passed the bowl to Josh. Then, looking at Len, I asked, "Where'd you learn to cook?"

"My father taught me. He learned in the Navy." He placed his napkin on his lap and smiled.

"Tell me about your family. There's so much history here."

"You don't want me to bore you with old stories," he said, waving his hand.

"I love history. I'd love to hear boring old stories."

His smile was warm. "My dad's great-grandmother Anna Miller was the first woman to register to vote in Brunswick County after women were allowed to vote."

"How cool's that?" Josh chimed in.

"That's super cool," I said.

Len ate a bite of his fish before continuing. "My family were either fishermen or builders. We built the Miller Hotel on the corner of Howe and Bay. The town loved to hang out and socialize in the refreshment parlor." He wiped his face with his napkin and continued. "That's what we called it back then. We used to host dance parties every Saturday night. It was a blast."

"You don't own the hotel anymore?" I asked.

"Sadly, it burned down in the sixties and was never rebuilt. The lot's still vacant to this day," Len said, and took a sip of his drink.

"I've thought about building a new hotel on the land, but so much has changed since then, and getting the permits has been more than difficult," Josh said.

"My great-great-great-grandfather, Leonard Waylen Miller built this house with his own two hands. He was a fisherman and a civil war blockade runner."

"How did you manage to keep all those books?"

"Leonard's wife, Mary, loved books. She made sure that he built her a bookcase in the living room. Since then, each generation has added to the collection. We still honor that tradition one hundred and fifty years later," Len said proudly. "You're welcome to read them anytime you like."

"Read them," I gasped. "I'm afraid to touch them."

Josh and I cleaned up the dishes after dinner while Len read in the sunroom.

"It's getting late, and I need to start packing for the move on Monday. So, I should head home soon," I said, drying the plate in my hand.

"You could stay here." His eyes were filled with hope.

"I should go home. Randy and Renee are expecting me. They don't even know about you and me yet. If I don't go home, they'll worry."

Clearly disappointed, he said, "All right, I understand."

I walked into the sunroom and gave Len a huge hug. "Thank you for dinner and for welcoming me to your lovely home."

"Thank you for making my son happy. I haven't seen him this happy in quite some time. You seem wonderful, Lizzie. But please be careful with his heart."

"I promise," I said and squeezed his hand.

TWENTY-ONE

My belongings were packed and ready to be carried to my new apartment in the backyard. I woke up early and met Renee downstairs in the kitchen. Hoping to find some decent furniture, we planned to hit some yard sales this morning. Randy wanted to replace the bed in the guest room, so he offered to let me have it, but I still needed furniture for every other room in my apartment.

"Good morning," I said to Renee as she poured coffee into to-go cups to take with us. I handed her an envelope with the words *Thank You* written on the front. "One month's rent, a security deposit, and a little extra for the bed."

"Lizzie, seriously. You don't have to do that."

"Yes, I do. I'm grateful for everything you both have done for me. Please take it."

I reached into the pantry and grabbed the bag of bagels. I popped two into the toaster and took the butter from the fridge.

"What's on the list for today?" Renee asked.

"I'd love to find a couch and chair to complement the coffee table Randy made for me. I also need a small kitchen table. I think a round shape would be best with at least two chairs, but hoping we can find four. Oh, and I'd love to find a bookshelf."

Ding.

The bagels popped from the toaster, and I buttered them. *Having my own space will be nice. I hope we can get everything done today.*

"Josh's coming over to help Randy move the bed and the rest of my things into the apartment while we hunt for treasures," I said. "I'm a little nervous leaving the two of them alone."

I'm afraid Randy will give Josh the third degree. What are your intentions with my sister? If you break her heart, I'll kill you. Do you think you'll be spending the night here?

My thoughts gave me pause. "Maybe it's not such a good idea for the two of them to be alone. Shit. Did I say that out loud?"

We burst out laughing, and Renee said, "Your brother will go easy on him. Don't worry." She covered her bagel in a paper towel and picked up her coffee. "He's all bark and no bite."

"I hope you're right."

Renee took the keys to the pickup truck off the hook, and we walked into the garage. We could hear the birds chirping love songs as we pulled out of the driveway. The sun was barely up, but we had to get an early start if we wanted to find anything good.

Renee suggested we go to Wilmington. We drove for thirty minutes and found a neighborhood with a yard sale sign by the entrance. The poster was bright yellow with the words 526 SUNNYDALE DRIVE 7 A.M. – 2 P.M. written in thick black marker.

Renee turned right into the subdivision, and we drove slowly until we found Sunnydale Drive. She turned the car left, and we could see vehicles lining the edge of the road a few houses down on the right.

"That must be the place," I said eagerly.

Renee pulled the truck behind the last car and parked beside the curb. We approached the house and saw numerous tables covered with dishes, glassware, and silverware. Racks of clothes lined the driveway, and furniture galore.

"We hit the mother lode," I said. With the plethora of household items in front of me, I grinned like a kid on Christmas morning.

"Hello. Welcome to Sunnydale. We host a block party yard sale with the entire street once a year," the lady said, standing by the sidewalk and greeting everyone as they walked by.

I didn't even notice that both houses on either side also had items for sale in their front yards. Renee and I did a lap of all three houses and made mental notes of potential purchases. I found a gray couch with a matching ottoman and a comfy red lounge chair. Haggling was not an option because I wanted them, so I offered fifty dollars more than their asking price to guarantee no one else could purchase them. The total for the three items, including the extra fifty dollars, was three hundred. *What a great deal. I'm so excited about decorating my new space.*

Next door, I found a round glass-top table.

"Renee, look at this," I called to her. She was looking at Christmas decorations in the neighboring driveway. "The base is so cool."

"Very cool. I've never seen anything like that."

A round, black wooden base about two feet wide sat on the ground, and two interwoven circular pieces of wood, also painted black, held the glass top in place.

"How much for this table?" I asked the homeowner. She wore a white T-shirt with an American flag on the front and the word freedom in all capitals.

"Fifty dollars," she said.

"I'll take it. Does it come with chairs?"

"No chairs. Just the table."

Renee and I loaded up the couch, chair, and table with the help of a guy named Bud. Apparently, that was Bud's job today. According to him, he was roped into helping people load furniture. I slipped him a twenty-dollar bill and thanked him.

Looking at Renee, I said, "I want to look at the dishes before we leave," as I pointed to the tables full of them.

"Take your time. I'll check out more Christmas stuff."

I found a set of six white dinner plates with a red gingham design decorating the edge and six red salad plates. I also bought eight Waterford Crystal water glasses, four red wine glasses, and a complete silverware set. The nice lady working the yard sale wrapped everything in tissue paper and neatly placed it in a large cardboard box.

My phone vibrated inside my purse, and I dug through my bag to find it. Glancing at the screen, I saw a text from Kit, my nurse back in New York. I clicked open the message.

Kit: I miss you. It's been too long. How's life?

Distracted, I didn't see Bud running over to scoop up the box and place it into the back of the truck.

"Thanks, Bud. Sorry, I wasn't paying attention."

Looking back at my phone, I typed my response and pressed send.

Me: So good to hear from you. You're a good friend, checking on me.

Me: Life's great. I'm moving into my own place. I met a guy. How are you? Heart eye emoji.

Three dots appeared, then disappeared.

A few seconds passed and then a beautiful picture appeared. Kit was smiling brightly. Standing next to her was a shorter woman with eyes darker than her hair, holding an adorable little girl. *This must be Kit's sister and her niece. So sweet.*

Punching in the letters on the text, I replied.

Me: Beautiful. So sweet.

I clicked send and dropped the phone back into my purse. I found Renee sorting through various garlands and told her about my epic finds.

"I'm ready when you are," I said. "I'd like to get a few decorative pillows, and I still need chairs for the kitchen table. Oh, and some pots and pans and cooking utensils. But I think I'll find those things at the store."

"We can swing by Target on the way home if you want," Renee said as she looked at an array of snowman figurines.

"Perfect."

Josh and Randy had finished putting the bed back together when we returned. They unloaded the furniture I had purchased and carried it into the apartment. I found four red chairs at Target that perfectly matched my kitchen decor and fit the table nicely. Next, I washed my new dishes and silverware and unpackaged the other items I had purchased from Target.

"Renee and I picked up lunchmeat and rolls while we were out if anyone's hungry."

Without hesitation, Randy said, "I'm starving. Where's the meat?"

"I'll get everything ready." I opened the fridge, removed the freshly cut turkey and ham packages, and set them on the counter. Then I grabbed the American cheese slices, mustard, mayonnaise, and ketchup. I spread everything out on the little island with paper plates and napkins.

"Here you go. Help yourself. I'll cut up some fresh tomato slices and lettuce in a sec."

Randy was the first to make a plate. Renee put potato chips in a bowl and placed them next to the meat. Josh stood beside me while I cut up the tomato. He leaned over and kissed the top of my head.

"Thank you all so much," I said. "Thank you for this apartment, and thank you for helping me today. I appreciate you so much."

"We're proud of you, Lizzie," Randy said as he squeezed mustard onto his bread. "Anyone up for some axe throwing tonight? I have a membership and can get a good deal for the four of us."

Hugging Josh, I said, "Like a double date? I know you guys have assumed it, but we're officially dating."

"No shit. It didn't take a rocket scientist to figure that out. I figured you'd tell us when you were ready," Randy said, and then took a gigantic bite of his sandwich.

"Axe throwing sounds fun," Josh said. He patted my ass and walked toward the island to make his sandwich.

"I need to finish some things here first, and I'd love a shower. Can we meet you on the front porch in about two hours?" I glanced at Randy.

He had a drip of mustard sliding down his chin. I picked up a napkin and handed it to him. "Here, you have something on your face. Unless you want to save that for later."

"That works," he said.

After lunch, I cleaned the kitchen and finished putting away my newly purchased pots and pans. Then, I organized my clothes upstairs in the loft bedroom and made my bed with new tan sheets and a checkered bedspread.

Josh was putting together the kitchen chairs, when I hollered down to him to let him know I was getting in the shower. We needed to meet Renee and Randy in about forty-five minutes.

It felt good to have my own space. I was proud of my little backyard apartment. Pulling my freshly laundered towels out of the dryer, I entered the bathroom to shower and get ready for date night. I turned the faucet on and brushed my teeth while the shower water got warm.

Standing in the shower, I tilted my head back and let the water wash over me. *I've come a long way. I still have a long way to go, but I feel good.* The void that filled my heart still existed, and I hadn't quite forgiven myself yet, but I was moving in the right direction—taking my growth and healing one day at a time. I reminded myself of the many things I was grateful for.

I'm grateful for the life that grew inside me.
I'm grateful to have Josh in my life.
I'm grateful for the way he makes me feel.
I'm grateful for Randy and Renee.
I'm grateful for Helen.
I'm grateful for my new apartment.

Grabbing the shampoo bottle, I squeezed a dollop onto my hand and slowly massaged the soap into my scalp with my eyes closed. A cold breeze hit my skin, and I shivered. When I opened my eyes, Josh was standing before me, naked, with the spray from the shower coating his beautifully sculpted torso. He ran his hands over my hair and rinsed out the rest of the shampoo.

I leaned forward, and our lips almost met, testing our resolve to see who would give in first. Our naked bodies pressed against each other, and sparks soared through my core like fireworks on the Fourth of July. He hugged me, then slid his hands downward to cup my butt cheeks. He squeezed and pulled me closer. "I love you," he whispered into my ear.

"I love you, too."

Giving in, I could feel the soft tickle of his breath beneath my nose as he finally kissed me. Pulling me into him with his hand on my head, I leaned back and moaned as he kissed my neck. Josh reached behind me to grab the soap from the shower caddy. He squirted body wash on my new loofah and scrubbed every square inch of my body. He alternated between massaging and kissing my shoulders. He massaged my lower back and hips, and then my calves and feet.

He spun me around to face him, and I looked up into his intense blue eyes and smiled. With his arms extended and his hands pressed against the wall behind me, he brought his mouth close to mine but didn't meet my lips. He gazed at me for several seconds before he fused his mouth to mine. I exhaled as his lips traveled to my breasts and down my stomach. He moved like a masterful surgeon, his hands sliding down my thighs as he took a knee on the shower floor. Lifting my leg and wrapping it around his shoulder, he looked up at me and said, "Tonight's all about you, babe."

TWENTY-TWO

Silence filled the room as Randy walked toward the target to verify the shot.

"Bullseye!" he yelled, and everyone erupted in cheers. Renee and I were on a team against the boys, and she needed to land a bullseye for us to win.

"Rematch," Randy said with a belly laugh.

Josh and Randy destroyed us in the next game. Game after game, we played, laughed, and drank. I couldn't understand the combination of axe throwing and alcohol. While I enjoyed doing both simultaneously, my arms turned to jelly after a few hours. The last three axes I had thrown hadn't come close to hitting the board. They went straight to the floor.

"You guys can stay and play, but I think I should go," I said as I pointed to my fourth axe that hit the floor.

"I'll go with you," Josh said as he put his arm around my waist.

"We're almost done. We'll be right behind you." Randy lifted his arm behind his head and hurled the axe toward the board for his fifth perfect bullseye. Renee cheered and gave him a high-five.

Josh paid for our playing time and drinks, and we said goodbye. Exiting the building, Josh took my hand in his as we crossed the street toward the bay and found a seat on a bench at the water's edge. Stars glistened throughout the sky. Swirls of purple, pink, and blue splashed across the horizon.

I leaned my head on Josh's shoulder and turned my gaze toward the sky. "The stars are beautiful tonight."

"Wow, that one's super bright," I said, pointing. "It looks like it's dancing."

Josh took out his phone and held it up toward the star. "It's Venus."

"That's nifty. Your app tells you what we're looking at in the sky?"

"Yep."

According to Josh's app, we found Orion, Taurus, and Canis Major, also known as the greatest dog. The universe has billions of stars, and I wondered if other beings were living in another galaxy somewhere else.

"What're you thinking about?" Josh asked as he placed a gentle kiss on my head.

"I wonder if there's a place in the vast universe where souls go after they die." I wiped a small tear from the corner of my eye. I hoped he didn't notice. "I like to believe that when a person dies, their soul lives another life somewhere else out there."

A chill ran down my back, and I shivered. Josh wrapped his arm around me and pulled me in to keep me warm. "That's a deep thought. Interesting though, I've never thought about that."

I let him in a little more and shared more truth about my past. I told him I had a little girl once, but she died during birth.

He squeezed me tighter and kissed my neck from behind. "I'm so sorry you went through that. You've been through a lot."

"It was my fault. I brought it on myself."

He turned me around to face him. His eyes were overflowing with compassion. "Lizzie, you can't possibly believe that? You didn't do *anything* to deserve the loss of a child." He kissed my forehead and hugged me tightly.

The warmth of his love once again engulfed my heart, and I felt safe with him. I looked down at the ground, and said, "Randy and Renee don't know."

"I won't say a word. It's not my story to tell."

"I'll tell them. I just haven't found the right words."

He kissed my head again and said, "Thanks for trusting me, Lizzie. It means a lot that you'd share this with me."

With tears spilling down my cheek, I turned to look at him and tenderly kissed his lips. It was a kiss full of all the undying love and trust I had for him. He kissed me back, and I fell in love with him all over again. I slowly pulled my lips from his, and looked intently into his eyes, and said, "I love you, Josh. I love you more than I've ever loved anyone."

He reached out and brushed a strand of my hair behind my ear, and with his palm, he cupped my cheek. "I see you, Lizzie. I understand you." He kissed my forehead. "You have a tough exterior, but you guard your heart." He kissed my forehead again. "I don't take that lightly. I vow always to protect your heart."

He used his thumbs to wipe away the tears from my cheeks and took me into his arms. He hugged me purposefully and didn't let go as if his embrace could wipe away the past, and I felt at peace. The peace that perhaps I might someday let go of my regrets and find a path toward self-forgiveness. I could feel his heart beating next to mine. *Two hearts beating as one.*

"We should probably get going. I need to get up early for work tomorrow," I said. Josh stood, pulled me to him, and kissed me. Under the stars, wrapped in each other's arms, and living in the moment, we danced to the beat of our own drum. We swayed side to side in perfect harmony to music that only we could hear.

"Did you move the chairs against the wall?" I asked Josh as he entered the apartment behind me.

"No, what're you talking about?"

"The chairs. The kitchen chairs. They were around the table when we left, and now they're against the wall."

"I don't know. Maybe you moved them before we left?"

Am I going crazy? Why would I do that? No. I know they were sitting around the table.

My heart pounded as I paced back and forth through the living room.

"The blanket on the couch. It's on the floor now." My words were coming out faster and louder as panic set in.

"I don't know. Maybe it fell off the couch when we closed the door. It's okay. Calm down. It's going to be okay," Josh said softly to reassure me.

"Someone's been in here. I know it. Look—" I pointed to the blank wall. "You hung that picture today. You have to remember that. Why would I take it down and lean it in front of the bathroom door?" My chest tightened. My fingers tingled, and I stretched my hands and balled them into fists, as I worked to shake off the pins and needles.

Already climbing the stairs, Josh said, "Go. Run to the main house. Check on Randy and Renee and call the police. I'm going to check upstairs, I'll be right behind you."

I sprinted across the backyard and flung open the door. Standing in the kitchen, I shouted, "My apartment was broken into. Are you guys okay?"

I punched 9-1-1 into the keypad on my phone. A woman answered on the other end.

"9-1-1, what's your emergency?"

I explained what had happened and gave her the address. I could hear Randy's feet clambering down the stairs, and he appeared seconds later in the kitchen, with Renee a few steps behind him. Randy stood listening, his eyebrows drawn together and his arms crossed over his chest.

"Did you guys notice anything out of place here?" I said, looking at Randy who was barely holding it together.

"No, everything seemed fine when we got home," Randy said and pulled me into a tight hug.

Josh burst through the back door panting, and said, "The apartment's clear. No one's inside."

"You searched alone? Are you crazy?" Randy said as he poured water into four glasses.

"Here. Drink some water." He handed the first glass to Josh and then one to me.

"I don't know what's going on. We walked into the apartment, and things were out of place," I said, between gulps of my water.

"Was anything missing?" Renee said as she picked up the last glass of water from the counter.

"Honestly, I didn't look hard enough. But nothing seemed to be missing. Things were more out of order than missing. My TV was there." I finished the water and refilled my glass. "If it was thieves, why not take the TV? It was still in the box. Would've been easy to steal."

Josh finished his second glass of water and pulled me into his arms. "It'll be okay."

"I don't want to sleep there tonight. I feel like they've invaded my home. Even if they didn't take anything, it doesn't matter. I feel violated."

Renee was sitting at the kitchen table and looked at me, her eyes filled with concern. "I completely understand. It's scary."

"You can stay here," Randy said.

"I think you need to stay in the apartment. Don't let some asshole make you uncomfortable in your new home," Josh said. He spun me around to look at my face. "I'll stay up and keep watch, so you feel safe."

Maybe he was right.

"I'll help, too," Randy said.

A knock at the door startled us; the police had arrived. They took a statement from each of us and walked through the apartment to ensure that no one was inside. Then, they walked through again with me so I could point out any missing items. Nothing was missing.

Who'd do this? I don't understand. Why enter my home just for the sake of breaking and entering? It doesn't make any sense.

Deputy Wilson took my contact information and said the police would be in touch. He handed me a business card. "If anything else comes up, or you find something's missing, give me a call."

I thanked him, said good night to Renee and Randy, and locked the door. I was exhausted but too scared to sleep. Josh stayed in the living room and hooked up my TV while I went to change into my pajamas. A few minutes later, he appeared in the doorway.

"I'll rub your head until you fall asleep," he said gingerly. I nestled under the covers, and Josh climbed in.

I scooted closer to him and tucked my head under his arm. My eyelids were heavy, but I was too anxious to fall asleep. My stomach was in knots, and I couldn't shake the feeling that someone had done this to me on purpose. Josh gently caressed my face with the tip of his fingers, and I finally drifted off to sleep.

TWENTY-THREE

As the sun's rays danced on my face, I walked down Moore Street toward the store. Last night was long, and I wanted more rest, but Helen had asked me to open the store. Skipping a shower was a good decision because I could get fifteen extra minutes of sleep. Josh decided to take the day off. He had stayed up all night watching me, protecting me. Before he'd left, he made a fresh pot of coffee and placed a note on the counter.

Lizzie,

You're even more beautiful in your sleep. Enjoy the coffee. I'm going home to rest. I love you more today than yesterday.

XOXO Josh

Thinking about his note made a smile stretch across my face as I walked up the stairs to the bookstore. I unlocked the heavy wooden front door, propped it open, and flicked on the lights. Setting my bag on the counter, I was ready to attack the day and put the events of last night behind me. I turned on the sound system and read the list Helen had left me. She said she'd be about an hour late.

Turning on the front desk computer, I checked to see if we had any orders come in yesterday. Betty Hilt and Thomas Lynch placed an order for pickup today. I pulled the books and stored them behind the counter.

Grabbing the cleaning supplies, I wiped down the bookshelves. Helen was insistent the shelves be dusted every day. *"No one wants to buy books from dusty bookshelves."* Her words played through my head like a broken record. *"The wood must be shiny."* With Lady Gaga blasting through the speaker, I barely heard the doorbell's beep.

Standing in the far corner of the room, I said, "Welcome to Bayview Books. I'll be right there."

I threw the Pledge and dust rag back into the supply closet and headed toward the front of the store.

I stopped dead in my tracks when I saw him.

"Hello, Lizzie," he said.

"How'd you find me?"

He looked incredible, as always. Seeing him turned my insides to a stew of butterflies, hatred, and anger.

"I knew your brother lived here, so I took a chance that you'd have come here. I found your picture from the bookstore on social media." He walked a few steps closer. "Do you work here?"

"Yes." I didn't want to engage in conversation with him. I wanted him to leave. "Why are you here?"

He moved closer, only a few feet away from me. "I needed to see you. Work isn't the same without you. The firm needs you to come back."

"Bullshit. The firm let me go. Having your pregnant fling around was too much office gossip for you, remember?" My tone was stern, but I maintained my composure.

"The board wants you back, but I need you, too."

I rolled my eyes and walked past him toward the front counter. I needed to put a barrier between us as quickly as possible. But he grabbed my arm and pulled me into him as I passed by.

"I miss you, Lizzie. I need you back in my life. I screwed up."

I yanked myself free from his grip. "I have nothing to say to you, Gray. Please leave and stop texting me, stop following me, and stop creeping into my apartment."

He blinked. "Huh?"

"Don't play dumb."

"I have no idea what you're talking about."

"Whatever. You came, and you said your piece. Now please leave."

Helen walked through the front door. She looked at me inquisitively. You could cut the tension in the room with a knife.

"Look, at least let me take you to dinner tonight. The firm has a proposal for you. You'll be able to work remotely from here if you'd like." He glanced at Helen. She stared back, and looked him up and down. "Meet me at that restaurant Fishy Fins tonight at seven, and I'll give you the details."

I didn't even bother to look up. Instead, I pretended to be busy with paperwork on the counter. Then I watched Gray's back as he left the store.

"What was that about?" Helen said, putting her purse behind the counter.

"That was Gray."

She froze. "*The* Gray, as in I'm not the baby daddy, asshole Gray?"

I didn't look up as I wiped the already spotless counter. "The very same."

"What the hell?"

I shook my head, I felt numb all over. "I don't know. He said the firm wants me to come back to work. He wants to go over the proposal with me tonight at dinner. Oh, and he said he screwed up and wants me back too."

"Um, no. You're not going, right?"

"I don't know. The money could be good. I feel like I should at least hear the offer." *Was I really considering this?*

"It's up to you. But I say hell no. Fuck him and his firm." Helen started to pace. "I knew I should've bought a gun for the store."

I snorted. "I'm happy, Helen. I finally feel like I've put the pieces of my life back together. This time around, I know he's an asshole. My eyes are wide open."

"You aren't considering taking him back, are you?"

"Oh, God no. I'm head over heels in love with Josh." I smiled and then scrunched up my lips. "I'd be lying though, if I didn't admit it felt a little good hearing Gray say he screwed up."

"Yay. I knew Josh would win you over. He's a good man. I'm so happy for you." Helen clapped her hands together as she spoke the words. Then, putting her hands on her hips she said, "Gray, though. You're playing with fire, Lizzie. I could feel his intoxication radiating from his skin when I entered the store. He's a powerful man in more ways than one."

"I can handle myself. I promise. If I go tonight, do you think I should tell Josh?"

Annoyed, Helen tilted her head. "Honesty is usually the best policy, I think you should probably tell him."

I blew out a breath of air and dropped my head. "I know Josh isn't going to like the idea of me going to dinner with Gray."

"You do what you want, but I say tell him," Helen said. "If you think it'll be too hard to tell him, maybe you shouldn't go at all."

I knew she was right. I was playing with fire by going to dinner with Gray, but I did miss some aspects of my job. If I was being completely honest with myself, I missed some aspects of my life with Gray too. A tiny bit of curiosity piqued my interest. I could try to call Gray and get him to tell me over the phone, but that wasn't his style, and I knew it. I needed to go to dinner if I wanted to hear about the job offer and find out why he really came. As usual, everything had to be his way on his terms.

Josh doesn't need to know. If I decide to take the job, I'll tell him then.

Fishy Fins was on the corner of Moore Street and Yacht Basin Drive. I did my best to wear the most conservative-looking attire I owned: a pair of ripped blue jeans and a T-shirt. I texted Josh that I was meeting an old coworker who was in town from New York for dinner and would swing by his house afterward.

I took a middle approach. I didn't lie. I am going to dinner with an old coworker, but I didn't tell him the entire truth. *Which was probably why I felt nauseous.* I went to the hostess stand and told the young, bubbly girl that I was meeting someone.

She looked about twenty years old, and her curly red hair was tied back in a ponytail at the nape of her neck. She wore a wrinkled blue polo shirt with the restaurant logo on the left chest and short black shorts.

"What's the name of your party?" she said, looking at the computer screen.

"Stone, I guess. I'm not sure if we had a reservation. He has sandy blond hair and may have arrived a few minutes ago."

"Yes. I see your reservation. Follow me."

We zigzagged through the restaurant to a small table in the far corner overlooking the water. All the surrounding tables were conveniently vacant. *I should've known he had connections here. Or he paid someone for a private table in the darkest corner of the place. Why did I come?*

"Who'd you pay to get this table?" I said as I sat down in my seat. A dozen red roses were stuffed into a beautiful crystal vase in the center of the table.

"These are for you," he said as he slid them to the side so he could have an unobstructed view of my face. "I stopped by after I saw you earlier and asked them how much I needed to pay for a reservation for the best table in the house and the surrounding tables."

"You're an asshole."

"I'm trying to be honest. I have money and use it to ensure I have the best table and quiet surroundings. So what?"

"You're still an asshole."

"You used to be impressed. I saw the way you looked at me back then."

Bile bubbled in my stomach like Old Faithful, and threatened to rise to my throat. I took a sip of water and choked down the rancid taste in my mouth caused by my immediate regret for coming.

"You're radiant," he said, reaching across the table and touching his fingertips to mine. I pulled my hands back and put them on my lap. His touch repulsed me.

"Gray. I came here to learn about the job offer. I might not even eat. If we could get to it, that'd be great."

"I've already ordered for both of us, and I have several things I want to say to you first."

Why did I come here? What am I doing?

"I should've known. Everything's always on your terms." The frustration in my voice was becoming harder to contain. I took a deep breath. *You're happy now. He's no longer a part of your life. Be calm. He's irrelevant.*

"Nothing has been the same without you. I admit, I'm a piece of shit. I've slept with many women. But you, Lizzie, I see you every night in my dreams."

"Is this supposed to be an apology?"

"Let me finish. Over the years, I've slept with lots of women. I am Gray Stone, I have money, power, and let's be honest, I'm gorgeous."

How did I not see how pretentious he was?

"The assistants from the office were always easy. So eager to please and climb the ladder, but not you. From the moment you started, you were focused and driven. You barely paid attention to me. Your resolve drove me wild."

"Seriously. Get to the point." I took a sip of my drink and looked out the window, my knee bouncing nervously up and down. Seagulls were swooping down into the water. I didn't resume eye contact, but Gray continued anyway.

"When you became an executive, I finally won you over. I had conquered Lizzie Levine, the unavailable. I didn't realize that I fell in love with you in the process."

I turned my head to face him. "Are you done?" I said coldly.

"I love you, Lizzie. I screwed up royally. I'm not sure I even knew love until now. This hole in my heart yearns for you. I miss you. I was horrible to you, and I'm truly sorry."

He reached into his pocket and pulled out a light blue box with a white ribbon that decorated the sides and tied into a bow on the top. He removed the ribbon, and I saw the words Tiffany & Co etched on the lid. He opened the box and revealed an exquisite pair of diamond studded earrings.

"I'm begging you to give me a chance to make it up to you. I know I don't deserve you. I don't deserve your forgiveness, but I had to try."

I placed my hand on the box and slammed the lid closed.

"You can't buy me, Gray. You're right—you don't deserve me. You had me, and now I'm gone. I'm happy. I've moved on. If you love me, then let me be happy." As I said the words, I felt free. I finally had the closure I didn't know I needed. But, I did need it.

"Josh, right? That's who you've moved on with." My brow furrowed, and confusion flashed across my face, quickly turning to concern.

"How did you ..."

He cut me off. "I saw him on your Instagram. You look happy. But I know that I can make you happier. I can give you more than he can."

"That's it. I'm done. I shouldn't have come." I stood up from my seat and tossed the napkin onto my chair. Before I could turn to leave, Gray leaped from his seat, grabbed me by the arms, leaned me back, and forced his lips to mine. Startled, I lost my balance long enough for the kiss to last longer than it should have. Finally, I gained my footing and shoved him off me.

Out of the corner of my eye, I saw Josh standing at a table near the bar, with a coldness in his eyes that sent dread coursing through my veins. His jaw hardened when our gazes locked, and he kicked a chair over, turned his back on me, and stormed out of the restaurant. The lady behind the bar stared after him with wide eyes.

Hot tears burned my cheeks. I turned back to Gray. "You saw him," I yelled. Heads from other tables turned to look at me, but I didn't care. "You knew he was there, and you kissed me on purpose. I hate you. Please don't ever come here again. Tell the board I said no."

I picked up my glass of water. "Oh, and Gray." I tossed the water in his face. "Go fuck yourself."

Running out of the restaurant, I tried to catch up to Josh. In the distance, I saw his golf cart, and I ran as fast as I could.

"Josh. Wait," I yelled at the top of my lungs. "Josh. Please. Let me explain."

He pulled the cart into a parking spot, and I ran toward him with painful urgency. He sat and waited for me. I slid into the passenger side, and his whole body stiffened. He wouldn't look at me. Knowing that I caused his pain made my heart ache, and I began to cry.

"I'm so sorry, Josh."

"Do you love him?" he said, his eyes guttered with sadness.

"No. I thought I loved him once upon a time."

"I saw roses on the table. You kissed him, Lizzie. I saw it with my own eyes."

"I know how it looked and what you must be thinking. I should've told you the whole truth from the beginning, but I don't love him. I love you."

He pulled away from me when I went to grab his hand.

"I don't want to touch you right now. I need some time to think." His voice quivered.

"He came here to offer me my job back. I didn't know that he'd try to get me back in the process. Please, Josh, you have to believe me. I love you. Only you."

"I need time," Josh said, his tone flat. He stood up from the golf cart.

"Where are you going?"

"I'm going home. I was getting food for my dad and me, which I left at the restaurant. I need to get us something to eat. You take the golf cart. It's late." His disappointment shined like a beacon in the streetlight's glow. I scooched over to the driver's side, dropped my head onto the steering wheel, and let the tears fall. "I have another golf cart that my dad rarely uses. I'll get this one back from you, eventually."

"Josh, can we please talk about this? I messed up, but I don't want anything to do with him. He knew you were standing there. I didn't want to kiss him."

"I need time, Lizzie. Please, give me that?"

I lifted my head off the steering wheel and looked at him with red, swollen eyes. Then, reluctantly, I said, "Yes."

Josh turned and walked away.

What else could I do? I wanted to jump off the cart and run after him. I wanted to kiss his face and tell him again how sorry I was. He's asking me for time. I should at least grant him that. *Screw it.*

I jumped off the golf cart and chased after him.

"Wait!" I called out, but he continued walking.

I raced to get in front of him, forcing him to stop. I flung my arms around his waist and pulled him close. He stiffened, but soon relaxed into me for several minutes.

Leaning into him, I pressed my lips to his. I kissed him like this would be the last time our lips touched. But he didn't kiss me back. Like a battering ram, Josh's resolve crushed my heart.

"Lizzie, I can't do this. I told you I don't do cheating. I'm hurt. I need to think."

He's hurt. I hurt him. My heart exploded, and sadness filled my entire body as if the world had collapsed in on me. I stood there alone, and watched him walk away. My legs must have moved on their own. Before I knew it, I was back in the golf cart, and weeping.

Yet another loss. I suppose it was inevitable. If they don't leave me, I self-destruct. Either way, the end result is the same. I screw shit up.

Later that evening, I made a hot cup of tea back in my apartment and brooded over my mistake. I wished I could rewind time and make a different choice, but it was too late for that. Still struggling with being in my apartment alone, I propped a chair under the front door handle and checked for the third time that the door was locked.

I roamed the house like a wounded dove, straightening up as I went.

A hot shower is exactly what I need.

After I turned on the hot water, steam filled the little bathroom. I placed toothpaste on my toothbrush, barely aware of my surroundings. I looked at myself in the mirror as I began to swirl the brush around my mouth. Condensation crept over the mirror, fogging the glass.

Etched onto the glass, the word *DIE* appeared before my eyes. I blinked. Then, blinked again.

Am I hallucinating?

Hoping it was a dream, I slammed my eyes shut. Slowly, I opened one eye, then the other. *DIE* was more prominently displayed on the glass now, and chills shot down my spine.

Okay. I'm not crazy; at least that's something.

I couldn't even think straight. Deciding against a shower, I turned the water off. My phone buzzed on the bathroom counter. A notification popped up showing the text was from "unknown." I tapped the screen to read the message, "Love the new space, wink emoji."

Rushing to the front door, I checked the lock for a fourth time. I climbed the stairs to my bedroom, fell onto the bedspread, and cried. I felt so alone, and the worst part was that I had done this to myself. Curled into a ball, and clinging to the pink baby blanket with the covers now pulled over my head, I cried and continued crying until sleep took me as its prisoner.

TWENTY-FOUR

My eyes were still puffy when I arrived at the bookstore. When I entered, Helen was sitting at the front counter reading. She paused and looked up at me.

"Good morning," I said flatly. There was nothing good about this morning, but I said it anyway. "I need to make a phone call really quick. I'll be right back."

Walking to the staff room, I dug Deputy Wilson's business card out of my purse. I punched the numbers into my phone and pressed the call button. A woman answered and said, "Brunswick County Sheriff's Department, how may I help you?"

"Hello. I need to speak with Deputy Wilson."

"He's out on a call right now. Can I send you to his voicemail?"

"Sure." I left him a message about last night and my phone number again, in case he didn't have it. I put my phone back in my purse and joined Helen behind the counter.

"So? How'd it go last night?" She lifted her head from her book and rested her elbows on the counter.

"I should've listened to you," I said, frustrated.

"Uh oh, not good. Huh?"

"I screwed everything up. I always screw everything up." My voice quivered as I spoke the words, and I fought hard to choke back my tears. I am not sure how it was possible that I had any tears left.

"You didn't tell Josh, I assume?" She raised an accusatory eyebrow.

"I told him I was meeting an old coworker for dinner. Except he happened to show up at the same restaurant, and he saw us kissing." I sniffled, and the tears started to gush like a dam breaking.

"You kissed him?"

"No. Well, yes, but I didn't want to, and I damn sure didn't initiate it. Gray must have recognized Josh from pictures I posted on social media. I was trying to leave. He planted one on me before my escape, in perfect time for Josh to see. He did it on purpose, I'm sure of it. It doesn't matter. I shouldn't have gone."

"Have you talked to Josh?"

"I tried. He was hurt and said he needed time." I used my hands to wipe away the tears covering my cheeks. "I can't lose him. I don't know what I'll do."

Changing the subject, Helen said, "Did you at least get a good offer for the job?"

"Hell no. We didn't even get that far. Gray was all roses, diamond earrings, and I love you's. I told him to tell the board no and then threw water in his face."

"Attagirl," Helen said, high-fiving me.

"I don't think he knows that I lost the baby. Actually, he didn't even ask. Ugh, he's such an asshole. What was I thinking?"

"Wait. Gray doesn't know? Didn't he visit you in the hospital?"

"Not even one time, and I was in there for months. My only friend was Kit, my nurse. She was a godsend."

"Are you sure you're okay, Lizzie? This must be a lot to process."

"My heart aches every day for my baby girl. I'm still working on forgiving myself for those mistakes. So, I guess we can add this latest mistake to the list of stupid shit I've done."

"Josh will come around. He loves you. Give it time."

"My physical scars from my accident have healed. My mental state is a completely different matter. I'm a complete mess."

"Physical scars? You mean the c-section?"

"Not just that. I broke my hip and shattered my femur when I fell down the stairs. I had three surgeries to put me back together. The doctor said that I'm lucky even to be walking again."

She took a step closer, her head tilted to the side, her lips pressed into a clenched half smile. "And you went through this all alone?"

"Don't feel sorry for me. Alone's what I do best. I'm starting to think I'm better off alone."

Lucinda, one of the book club regulars, came in, and I helped her find the Sci-Fi table she was looking for.

Meeting Helen at the counter, I said, "Plus, I wasn't totally alone. I had Kit. She was the nurse on duty the day I came in. She said that she had grown attached to me. She had lost a baby too. Kit told me she asked to continue my service during my recovery. When I woke up, we bonded instantly.

"For months during my recovery, she made special visits to my room and helped me with my physical therapy. We became friends. I don't know if I could've recovered without her." I fiddled with some bookmarks on the counter as I recalled my road to recovery, and my stomach clenched. The pain from my surgeries, the awful physical therapy, learning to walk again, and the endless pit of regret lingered in the air before me.

"I cried many times, expressing to her my grief for the loss of my baby. Kit could relate and shared with me her experience with loss. She said she and her husband had tried to have a baby for years but struggled. She finally got pregnant after their fifth round of IVF. She was pregnant with twins. During her sixth-month checkup, the doctor didn't find a heartbeat, and she had to give birth to two stillborn babies. I couldn't even imagine the pain."

"That's so sad. But she sounds like she's been through a lot and was the perfect person to help you."

"We shared each other's grief. She truly understood my pain and selflessly helped me through a tough time. I will always be grateful to her." A thin smile formed on my face as I thought about Kit. Her kindness and understanding helped me through an unimaginable time.

"What a blessing to have had such a compassionate nurse to help you," Helen said.

"She was." I stood up from my chair, walked over to the local author's table, and straightened a stack of books.

"I often think about telling Josh that I may not be able to have children. I've been afraid he'd break up with me. Doesn't matter now, I guess."

"Give him time."

Desperate to focus on work, I wandered around the store and collected my favorite springtime reads. "We should do a Helen and Lizzie's favorite spring reads table. What do you think?"

"I think that's a great idea," Helen said as she gathered some of her favorites to add to the pile. "Do you still talk to Kit?"

"We text. She checks up on me every once in a while. Making sure I'm doing okay."

"She sounds like a great friend."

Standing in the children's section, I straightened and organized the shelves. Today was Toddler Tuesday.

"What books should I read to the littles today?" I asked Helen while she organized the tables of children's games.

Every Tuesday, moms brought their toddlers to Bayview Books. We served coffee, juice, and doughnuts, and read a few books, and after reading, we provided a craft activity for the kids. Today's craft would be sand art. Messy fun.

She pursed her lips together as she thought. "Maybe one of the new *Winnie The Pooh* books that just came in."

"Perfect." I found the shelf with the new books and numbly searched through them for the best choice.

"You're a good friend, Helen." I chose a book and placed it in the children's sitting area. Then, picking up a box of checkers, I helped Helen organize the games. "I'm glad we met."

Her expression softened. "I'm glad we met too."

TWENTY-FIVE

By the time I got up, it was almost nine o'clock. I poured myself a cup of coffee and sat on the bench out front. Two weeks had passed since my horrible dinner with Gray, and my fight with Josh. His golf cart was still parked in front of my apartment. I texted and called him several times, with no response.

I curled my legs into my chest and rested my head on my knees as I watched the birds dance around the sky. Swooping down to rest on the bird feeder, they filled their mouths with seeds and flew away. I imagined them taking food to their babies and living happy little lives.

I miss him so much.

My aching heart caused physical pain through every inch of my body, and I was angry with myself. *Always making stupid choices.* If I had told him the truth to begin with, I'd be snuggled under his arm in bed right now. I had a hard time finding the motivation to do anything. No matter how hard I tried to move forward, the pain shackled me in place, rendering me useless. I knew I would eventually snap out of my funk, but self-destructing had become my cycle of life since my parents died.

Sipping my coffee, I watched as a male sparrow strutted along the edge of the white concrete birdbath. Fluttering about, a female sparrow was splashing around the water. Mr. Sparrow, whom I named Fred, stood perched along the rim, and watched the female sparrow as she flapped her tan-colored wings. Calling loudly, he beckoned her to join him. Fred spread his dark brown tail feathers and fluttered his wings, doing his best to attract her attention.

A second male sparrow attempted to land in the bath, but Fred squawked aggressively, pounced on the little guy, and made it clear that he should leave. The female sparrow fluttered out of the water and landed beside Fred on the edge of the birdbath. She arched her back, and he pressed himself against her from behind. Their organs rubbed together, and I presumed she would lay her eggs, and in ten or so days, Fred would have a sweet sparrow family.

I pulled my cell phone out of my pocket and opened a new message to Josh. I typed, "I'm watching Fred the sparrow attract his mate. I think they made baby birds right in front of me. Some sucker tried to swoop in and steal his lady, but Fred wasn't having it." I added three laughy face emojis. Then I pressed send.

I began a new message, "I miss you, Josh. I know you said you needed time. I want to give you all the time you need, but I need you to know how sorry I am. I'm begging you to give me another chance. Gray tried to swoop in on your territory, but I don't want him. I want you. Please give me a chance to explain. A chance to prove to you how sorry I am. Broken heart emoji. Sad face emoji."

Send.

I saw three dots pop up, and my heart skipped a beat.

...

He's responding.

Staring at the dots and holding my breath, I waited patiently.

...

...

...

...

...

No response. They were gone.

Enough of this. I love him. I love him more than I've ever loved any man. Get off your ass and go fight for him.

I raced toward my apartment, opened the door, and ran to the shower. I was undressing from the moment I stepped inside my house, and my clothes littered the floor along my path. I washed, and then shaved. My legs had to be silky smooth, I wanted to look and feel my best. Finally, I dried off and spread sunflower scented lotion on every inch of my skin.

Josh's favorite.

Excitement filled my heart, and I knew he missed me. How could he not? You don't just fall out of love with someone, and I knew he loved me with every fiber of his being.

I'll win him back. I'll make him listen.

Filled with determination, I rushed upstairs, and tripped in my haste. I wore his favorite button-down jean dress, fixed my hair and makeup, and applied red lip gloss. I hooked a red belt around my waist and slid my feet into my six-inch red wedges. Taking a moment, I checked myself out in the full-length mirror. I struck a few poses and considered my outfit. I paused a moment to think and decided to remove my panties.

Just in case.

The corner of my lips curled as I slid my panties off over my heels and took one more look at myself. *Josh Miller, I'm coming for you.*

Locking the door behind me, I jumped into Josh's golf cart and reversed out of the driveway. Then, putting the pedal to the metal, I drove toward his house. I made the left-hand turn onto Bay Street, and my phone pinged. My heart leaped out of my chest.

Is it Josh? Did he respond?

Stretching my arm across the golf cart, I fished in my purse, searching for my phone. Never taking my eyes off the road, I noticed a dark blue sedan up ahead on the other side of the street. My fingers felt my phone, and I clenched my hand around the case, and pulled it out of my purse.

I quickly glanced down and saw that I had received a text, another message from "unknown." I looked up to check the road and decided I had enough time to read the message. I clicked on the icon and saw the words, "I'm coming for you. Watch out."

Every hair on my body stood up. My eyes looked up as the dark blue sedan stepped on the gas, swerved into my lane, and smashed into the front of my golf cart.

With no time to react, the cart flipped over, and I was flung out. My head smacked the pavement, and then everything went black.

"Lizzie. Lizzie, can you hear me?" *Am I dreaming?* I heard the faint sound of Josh's voice. I tried opening my eyes, but my head was pounding.

Josh?

"Lizzie?" He had two fingers pressed against my throat, and leaned over me with his ear almost touching my mouth.

"Somebody call 9-1-1." Josh's voice was much louder now, making the pounding in my head feel like an orchestra was using my brain as a bass drum.

Josh, is that really you?

"Come on, Lizzie. Stay with me." His voice cracked.

What's happening, Josh?

"Oh, Lizzie. Come on, baby. Keep breathing. Stay with me. I love you. Do you hear me? I love you." His words sounded muffled. *Did he say that he loved me? Is this real?*

I tried to speak. *Josh. Are you here? I love you too. I love you so much. I'm sorry I hurt you. Josh? Are you there?*

"Please, step aside, sir. We need to put her on the stretcher," said a voice I did not recognize.

Josh? Where's Josh?

"You can ride with us in the ambulance or meet us at the hospital, but we need to go now."

"I'll ride with her, please," Josh said.

Oh, Josh. I'm so sorry. I was coming to tell you that I'm sorry. I love you. Please, Josh, don't leave me.

"Is she going to be okay?"

"It's hard to say. Her head is bleeding pretty badly. She's unconscious. She probably has swelling on her brain." The stranger's voice was intense. *Did he say I'm unconscious? Josh!*

"Lizzie. I don't know if you can hear me, but I love you. I'm sorry I gave you the cold shoulder. I shouldn't have done that. I got your text message, and I was on my way to see you when I found you on the side of the road.

"Please come back to me. You need to know how much I love you. I want to spend the rest of my life with you. I was scared, Lizzie. If you can hear me, I forgive you. I don't care that Gray kissed you. I believe you. I love you. Hold on, Lizzie. You have to hold on ..."

I squinted my eyes as the light poured into them. My throat felt dry, and I could feel a bandage tied around my head. Josh was sitting at my bedside, and Randy and Renee were at the foot of the bed.

"Lizzie!" Josh jumped up from his chair and rushed over. He laced his fingers between mine, raised my hand to his lips, and kissed my skin tenderly.

Randy stood and rushed to the door. "Let me get the doctor."

I put my hand around my throat and croaked, "Water."

The singular word was barely legible, but Josh understood. He reached over to the table next to him, grabbed a plastic cup, and filled it with water. Then, opening a straw, he dropped it inside the cup and brought it to my lips.

Sitting up, I slowly sipped the water. The orchestra was still banging the bass drum on my brain, but a little lighter now. My eyes squinted, not wanting to accept the light.

"Too bright," I managed to say.

Renee flicked the light switch off and joined Josh at my bedside.

"You gave us a good scare," Renee said as she touched my leg.

A tall man with salt-and-pepper hair, dressed in a white coat, entered the room. He held a chart in his hand as he flipped through the pages.

"Good news. You have a nasty concussion. We want to keep you here overnight as a precaution, but you should be able to go home tomorrow." He set the clipboard on the table and looked at Randy. "She'll need to be monitored around the clock for a few days." The doctor looked back at me and said, "You'll be good as new before you know it. You need to take it easy for a few weeks, and I'll want you to stop by my office once a week to check your progress. Someone will have to bring you. There's no driving until you're cleared."

Josh let out a sigh of relief, and Randy and Renee thanked the doctor.

"I need to ask, has she hit her head before? Any reason to believe she's had a previous concussion?"

Randy immediately said, "No. Not that we're aware of."

I opened my mouth to speak, but my words were barely legible. The doctor placed the cup of water in front of me and said, "We had to intubate you, so your throat will be sore for a few days." He set the water down and placed a notepad and pen in my hand. "Write it down."

I scribbled on the pad. About a year ago, I fell down a set of concrete stairs. I was in a coma for several weeks.

He read my words, looked back at Randy, and said, "Since this isn't her first accident, it may take her a little longer to recover. But I assure you she'll be fine." He looked back at me. "You're one lucky girl. No broken bones, just a few scrapes and ten stitches on your head."

Looking confused, Randy said, "What do you mean, this isn't her first accident?"

Handing Randy the notepad, the doctor stepped toward the door.

"Josh. Did you know about this?"

"I don't know anything," Josh replied as he rubbed my arm softly. I pointed to the notepad, and Josh handed it to me. Picking up the pen, I wrote, I have a lot to tell all of you, and I will. I promise.

Before walking out of the room, the doctor said, "The police will want to get a statement about the accident since it was a hit-and-run. I told them Lizzie needed to rest, but they insisted. They're on their way here now. Josh, they can start with you as an eyewitness."

A week had passed since I was released from the hospital. Josh had not left my side since I returned home. Sitting in my bedroom, I had written him all the love notes my fingers could manage.

"Lizzie. I told you a thousand times, I forgive you. I was on my way to see you. When I got your text about the stupid birds, I knew I needed to come. I love you."

I scribbled, *I'm sorry* on the dry-erase board Josh had brought over so I could communicate with him.

"I know you are. I'm sorry too," he said. "I've been wanting to ask you, though. Where were you going on my golf cart?"

I wrote on the board; I was going to see you.

"Is that why you weren't wearing any underwear?"

My eyes grew wide, and my smile stretched to a toothy grin. Uncapping the marker, I wrote again. When you didn't respond to my text, I decided I was coming to see you, and I wasn't taking no for an answer.

"When you're feeling better, maybe you can visit me again and leave your panties at home." His voice was smooth and sweet, like cutting butter at room temperature. I wiped the board dry and wrote in all caps. I LOVE YOU.

"I love you too." He walked toward the door. "Your phone's on the dresser. Do you want it?"

I nodded.

Taking the phone in my hand, I swiped up to bring the phone to life. I had a few missed calls and messages. Helen texted and left a voicemail checking on me. Detective Wilson also left a voicemail, and I had another text message from "unknown." For an instant, my heart stopped beating. *Delete it.* I swiped left to delete the message, then paused. *Maybe I should read it first.*

I opened the message and stared at the words on my screen, "I see you're feeling better. Maybe I'll have better luck next time." I yelped.

I can't take this shit anymore.

The next day my throat felt like I had swallowed glass, but I managed to get some words out. I needed to tell everyone the truth about my past. I had Josh plan a dinner with Renee and Randy. He insisted on staying with me while I got ready.

"I'm fine, really. I'm feeling much better. My headaches are gone, and my throat is only mildly sore," I said, and reassured Josh that I could handle going to dinner.

"I'll wait. It's okay. I'm not letting you out of my sight until I'm sure you're okay."

I put my hands on the back of his head, pulled him into me, and kissed him softly. My body felt his kiss from the top of my head to the tip of my toes. Bending my right leg at the knee, I pointed my toes and breathed deeply. He parted his lips, and I tasted his sweetness inside my mouth. It felt like an eternity since we had kissed.

Josh pulled away slowly. "Lizzie, we can't."

"We can't kiss? Wrong! I'm allowed to kiss you."

"Kisses lead to other things, and you need to rest. Doctor's orders."

"Are you saying you're incapable of kissing me?"

"I guess that's what I'm saying. It's been far too long. Every ounce of my body aches to be with you. But when you kiss me like that, I don't know if I can control myself." He took a few steps back to increase the space between us.

"We need to have breakup sex, makeup sex, you-almost-died sex, and slow, tender I-love-you sex. That's a lot of sex, and I'm doing my best to stay in control. So yes, if you could be a little more mindful of that when you kiss me, I'd appreciate it." His magnetic eyes winked at me playfully.

He's teasing me.

"You'll survive—it's only a few more weeks," I said, sliding my hands down to his ass, giving it a little squeeze. "I think I could manage some slow, tender I-love-you sex if you take your time."

"Don't tempt me," he said as he backed further away.

"Oh, I'm tempting you." I reached my hands under my skirt, pulled my lace panties slowly down my legs, and tossed them in his face.

"That's better," I said, and sauntered past him toward the steps.

Josh groaned. "Come on, we need to go. We're gonna be late."

I'm not sure we'll even make it to the front door. I climbed down the steps and paused to take in his reaction. When our eyes met, he looked flustered and a little tormented.

Following me down the stairs and into the living room, he said, "You drive me insane. Literally insane."

"We can do this now, or we can do this later, but either way. We're doing it. I can't wait another day," I said.

He sat on the couch with his hands on his head, pulling his hair as he thought about his next move. Unable to control myself any longer, I straddled him, looked him in the eye, and said, "Breakup sex, makeup sex, I-almost-died sex, or slow, tender make-love-to-me sex, the choice is yours, but I'm not getting off your lap."

He placed his hand on my head and laid me gently on the couch. Next, he slowly slid my skirt down and tossed it onto the floor. Reaching under my shirt, he slid his hands up my body as he kissed my stomach. His soft and gentle touch made all my pain disappear.

I craved his touch. I hadn't realized how much I missed him until this very moment.

"I love you," I whispered. "I've missed you so much."

Josh breathed in slowly and exhaled as he stood up. Standing in front of me, he removed his clothes, and my eyes scanned his beautiful naked body. I stood up and dropped my shirt; his lips met my breasts as soon as they became exposed.

I gasped. Josh's tender love and warmth rushed through me in an instant. This is where I belonged.

He slid his hands down my curves, and I wrapped my arms around his neck. Lifting me, my legs twisted around his waist, and he slipped inside me like pure perfection. He laid me gently on the couch, and I whimpered because he pulled away.

His eyes looked deeply into mine. "I love you, Lizzie. As long as I am able to draw breath, I will love you." I could tell by the longing in his eyes, that he missed me too. He slowly pushed himself back inside me. My eyes rolled into the back of my head. I not only wanted this moment, I needed it. I needed to share my deep intimate love with him, two souls fitting perfectly together as one.

He held me in his arms, and I closed my eyes as I thought about the rest of our lives together. This remarkable man, who loved me so fully, was almost gone, but I would never make that mistake again. I was done with Gray. He was gone and out of our lives for good.

"We should probably go. We're already late," he whispered but didn't move.

"We have thirty more minutes. I asked Randy this morning if we could push dinner back an hour. I didn't tell you in hopes that this might happen." Rubbing his chest gently with my fingertips, I kissed his shoulder.

"You sly little devil."

Dinner was delicious. Renee made her famous lasagna with meatballs and garlic bread. After we finished eating, I told them the entire story about New York City and Gray. I told them about the affair, the pregnancy, losing the baby, the coma, and my lengthy recovery in the hospital. I told them about the text messages I'd been getting, the word DIE on my mirror, and Gray showing up here out of the blue. I didn't leave out a single detail.

Randy was emotional. Renee consoled him, and Josh didn't know what to say. He stared at our joined hands while I talked.

"I can't believe you went through all of that alone," Randy said. "We would've been there for you. You didn't have to go through it alone."

"I thought you'd be disappointed in me. I was a jobless, single mother."

Renee looked directly into my eyes as she tried to reassure me and said, "None of this was your fault."

"I believe that now, but it took a while for me to get there." Fidgeting, I folded my napkin in half and then in half again.

"There's one more thing," I said. "The doctor isn't sure that I'll be able to have children. He said I could die if I tried." I looked directly at Josh to take in his reaction.

He opened his mouth for the first time all night. "I have no words for the trauma you endured. It's killing me knowing you suffered so much pain. I imagine you miss your little girl every day." He ran his hand through my hair. "I don't pretend to know what that must feel like. If we want to have children someday, we can adopt. So we're clear, this news changes nothing for me." He kissed my head and squeezed my hand.

Renee let out a small sob, pushed out her chair, and threw her arms around me. "I needed to hug you. I'm glad you told us. I wish you'd have told us sooner, but I'm glad we know now."

"I'm sorry. I didn't know how to tell you."

"I want to know who's been harassing you," Randy said sternly. "I think you need to go to the sheriff's department tomorrow in person and tell Deputy Wilson everything. If Gray Stone is harassing you, I'll kill him."

"Randolph Levine, you'll do no such thing," Renee said, and slapped him on the shoulder. "The police will handle it."

"I don't know that it's Gray," I said.

"Don't protect him, Lizzie," Randy snapped. "You've gotten cryptic text messages, someone was following you, your apartment was broken into, and they wrote the word die on your mirror, and most recently, you were run off the damn road. Someone tried to kill you, for Christ's sake."

"I just want to move on with my life. I came here for things to be simpler. But when you say it out loud, it does sound a bit ..."

"Stalker-ish?" Renee finished my sentence.

"I'll go to the police station first thing in the morning."

"I'll take her," Josh said as he looked at Randy and then turned his gaze back to me. "You aren't cleared to drive yet."

TWENTY-SIX

July

Red, white, and blue covered the town. The locals loved to celebrate Independence Day. Every occasion in Southport had its own parades, traditions, and celebrations, and the Fourth of July was the largest and most grandiose of them all.

Three months had passed without any "unknown" text messages, break-ins, and unexpected visits from Gray. After that, the police said the trail went cold, and they believed everything that happened to me was a series of unrelated events.

My love for Josh grew every day like a beautiful oak tree, strong and sturdy. I loved him with my entire being, and my life with him was magnificent. His love for me was even better. I had found my way here in this quaint, slow little town.

Over time, I gained a few marketing clients throughout North and South Carolina and converted my apartment living room into an office, because I spent most nights at Josh's house. I still managed to put in a few hours each week at the bookstore, so Helen was happy.

My past with Gray faded like a distant memory, and I finally forgave myself. I stopped sleeping with the pink baby blanket, but I still left it folded neatly on the nightstand next to my side of Josh's bed. Her blanket was the first thing I would see each morning after kissing Josh.

Sounds of waves, crashing gently against the sand, steadily rising and collapsing like the beat of a drum, swept through the bedroom.

"Good morning," I cooed to Josh as I opened my eyes to the sun shining through his bedroom window.

"Good morning, babe." He climbed on top of me and showered my face and body with kisses. "I love waking up with you in my bed every morning."

"Likewise," I said and slid out from under him. "I'm going to start the coffee."

"I'll get it. You lie in bed a few extra minutes."

How could I argue with him? I stared at his ass as he left the room. Reaching over to the nightstand, I ran my fingers along the satin elephant stitched in the corner of the pink blanket. *Mama loves you. My beautiful baby girl, I hope you're living an extraordinary life in the sky. You're so loved.*

Saying her name was still too painful. I hoped someday I would gain the strength to say it out loud. But that day hadn't come yet. I chose her name because it meant love. I knew then that she would be my special girl. I closed my eyes and imagined her dancing among the stars.

The vibration from my phone snapped me away from my thoughts. Reluctantly, I propped myself up on my elbow and grabbed the phone. The message was from Kit.

She wrote: I've got a surprise for you!!!

My lips curled into a smile, wondering what it could be.

I typed: YOU DO! Well, don't keep me waiting.

…

…

…

Finally, Kit replied: It won't be a surprise if I tell you now. You'll find out soon.

I sent back: You stink. Laughy face emoji.

I chuckled at my response, laid the phone on the bed, and rolled over to get a little more rest.

Josh returned several minutes later. He was carrying a tray that held two cups of piping hot coffee, caramel-flavored creamer, and sugar.

"Hot coffee, for my lady."

"Thank you," I said, kissing his lips.

Sitting on the porch outside his bedroom, I watched the sun sparkle on top of the clear blue water. My favorite part of each morning was sitting on the porch with Josh. It didn't matter what time we needed to start our day. We would wake up with enough time to drink a cup of coffee and talk. The daily dose of vitamin D was an essential part of our happiness. Of course, taking in the view wasn't too bad either. And by view, I mean Josh, but the water was nice too.

"I'm supposed to be at the bookstore in forty-five minutes," I said, sippin my coffee.

"I guess you don't have time to shower with me this morning." Josh stuck out his bottom lip and batted his eyelashes like a toddler.

A smile stretched across my face. "You're such a goober." I laughed. "We can shower tonight. How's that sound?"

"All right. I suppose I can wait if I have to." His voice sounded sad and disappointed. Stomping his feet up and down, he threw a silly mini-temper tantrum.

I put my empty coffee cup on the tray and walked back toward the bedroom. Josh grabbed my waist to block my pathway. He spun me to face him and pulled me in, causing me to fall into his lap. He glided his hand into my waistband and squeezed my naked butt. After all the time we'd spent together, his touch still sent butterflies to tickle every nerve in my body, which sent messages of warmth and love to each synapse.

Still massaging my bottom, he said, "Have a good day," between kisses.

"Come on," I said with a pretend growl. "Let's go take a shower." Rubbing the tip of my nose to his, I took Josh's hand into mine and escorted him into the bathroom.

Helen was helping a customer check out when I arrived at the bookstore with a soaking wet head. I set my things in the staff room and hurried back to the front of the store to see if she needed help.

"The bookcase in the back needs to be alphabetized. I rearranged some shelves a bit yesterday but didn't finish the mystery section. I put all the books on the shelf, so I could break down the boxes and clean them up, but I didn't have time to organize them. And the armoire glass needs cleaning. The hand marks and fingerprints drive me insane."

"No problem," I said. "I'm on it."

I walked toward the back of the store and started with the A's. Moving books one at a time, I alphabetized the top shelf, working my way across, then down. While I worked, I thought about Josh. I thought about how far I'd come and how lucky I was to have him by my side.

I heard the doorbell beep, but I ignored it.

"Well, aren't you a cutie?" I heard Helen say. She made raspberry sounds as she pursed her lips together and blew out noisy air. "We've got some great books for you. Let me show you." Her voice sounded like she was talking to a little puppy.

I heard another voice say, "She's precious. I'm the aunt that spoils her rotten."

Curious, I put down the book in my hand and walked toward the front of the store. When I turned the corner, I heard the voice call, "Surprise!"

Picking up my pace almost to a run, I screamed, "Oh my God, Kit." We embraced and then pulled apart to look at one another. "You look amazing. It's so good to see you."

"You look amazing, too," Kit said.

I turned to Helen and said, "Helen, this is Kit. My friend and nurse I was telling you about."

"Lovely to meet you, Kit. You look familiar. Have you been here before?"

Kit turned her attention to me. "This is my first time in town. I wanted to surprise Lizzie. My sister and I are here visiting a friend."

I bent down at eye level with the beautiful baby in the stroller. She closed her tiny fingers around my pinky and giggled. Her head was full of dark brown hair tied into two tiny pigtails, topped off with pink bows. Rosy red cheeks filled her face, and she looked at me with sweet, innocent chestnut-colored eyes. She was dressed in an adorable cotton jumpsuit with a pink T-shirt underneath.

"Hello, beautiful. You're getting so big."

Kit said, "She's growing like a weed."

"What's her name?" Helen asked.

"Sophie," Kit said proudly. "She's such a good girl. Walking all over the place, she keeps my sister on her toes." Sophie started to squirm in the stroller. She wriggled around like a worm trying to get out of her seat. I noticed a tiny red heart-shaped birthmark behind her ear.

"Wow, Sophie, did you know that you've been kissed by an angel?" I touched her head behind the ear, and then folded my ear over. Turning my head, I pointed to my red heart-shaped birthmark behind my ear. "My mommy told me when I was a little girl that spot was from an angel's kiss. Only special people have the mark of an angel's kiss."

I gently pinched the tip of Sophie's foot and wiggled her little toes. "Kit, she's adorable."

"She really is. I love her to pieces."

"Where'd you say you were staying?" Helen asked.

"We're staying at my sister's friend's house. 309 Bay Street, I believe," Kit said, and handed Sophie some goldfish.

"Mildred's place?"

"I'm not sure. My sister arranged everything. Little Sophie's getting restless. It must be naptime. I'll come back tomorrow for the books. Pick me some of your favorites, and I'll swing by and pay for them."

"Sounds good, Kit. Will do," I said.

Pushing the stroller toward the door, Kit said, "Are you free later? I'd love to get drinks and catch up."

"I've got to work most of the day, but we can go after. I'll text you."

"Sounds great. See ya then." She smiled and waved goodbye.

Staring at Kit as she left the store, Helen looked incredulous.

"What?"

"I know I've seen her before. Her hair was longer, but I swear it was her."

"No. She's never been here. You must be mistaken."

"Lizzie, I'm telling you. She's been here. It was a while ago, but she was rude. That's why I remember her."

Helen and I picked a few toddler books to put aside for Kit to pick up later.

"Helen, she's a dear friend. I've never seen her be rude to anyone. Truly, it had to be someone else. You can't possibly be sure."

"Yeah, you're probably right," Helen said as she packaged the books with Kit's name before going back to counting inventory. "But ..."

"Helen. Drop it." My tone was impatient. She was right most of the time, but I didn't want to talk about this anymore.

"I'm just saying, I think ..."

"Helen. Enough about it already. And even if she was in here before, so what? What's the big deal?"

"I don't know. My paralegal senses, I guess. I'm sorry. I know she's your friend. I'll leave it alone."

After organizing the mystery books and cleaning the pirate book armoire, I checked the daily to-do list for my next task. Tracy Stopler, an up-and-coming author, was hosting a book signing for the release of her new book, *We All Fall Down*, at the shop in a few days, and Helen wanted me to get things in order ahead of time.

Diligently with extra pep in my step, I worked to prepare the space. I assembled a pop-up display and decorated the table. I felt excited as I smoothed out the black tablecloth and placed a pink lace runner in the center. It had been so long since I'd seen Kit, and I looked forward to catching up with her tonight. Organizing the books, I placed a few on book stands for display and put the rest in stacks nestled in the corner of the table.

"I'm going to head out," Helen said. "It's bunco with the crew, and I'm hosting. So, I need to get things ready."

"Sounds good, Helen. I'll see you tomorrow."

"You can lock up in a few hours."

After finishing the display, I sat behind the counter and read. Positioning myself at the front of the store gave me a better view to greet any customers when they walked in.

Lost in a fantasy book about two star-crossed lovers separated by a galaxy, I didn't hear the doorbell beep, alerting me that someone had entered the store.

TWENTY-SEVEN

Leaving the store on her golf cart, Helen decided to take the long way home in the event she might catch Mildred outside. Mildred lived at 309 Bay Street, and she was an old friend of Helen's. They went to elementary, middle, and high school together.

Turning down Bay Street, Helen peered over the dashboard, and craned her neck to see. Mildred happened to be getting her mail. Helen pulled the golf cart to the side of the road and popped the pedal into park.

"Hey, Millie. How ya doing?"

"Hi, Helen. Doing great. It's good to see you."

Millie was a short, round woman. She was the same age as Helen, but looked about five years older. Bags had taken up residence under her eyes, and the blue shade in her iris had dulled to look slightly gray. Her hair had thinned and turned completely white over the years. She was full of energy, though, and gave the younger generations a run for their money.

"I met some friends of yours today. Said they're staying with you for a few days. A nice woman and her niece."

"Nobody's staying here. Maybe you have the wrong house." Mildred shrugged.

"That's odd. Have you seen any folks staying around nearby?"

Mildred tucked the mail under her arm. "No. Same old, same old."

"Interesting," Helen said. "Good to see you, take care."

Helen took her phone out of her purse and scrolled through her contacts. Finally, finding the one she wanted, Robert Stallard of Stallard Law, she pressed the call button. No answer.

Arriving home, she fired up her laptop and began searching online. She didn't know much about Kit, but she knew what she looked like and that she was a nurse in a New York City hospital. She spent over an hour searching for nurses named Kit at every hospital in New York City. Frustrated and about to give up, she did one last search.

"Jackpot!"

She grabbed her phone, purse, and keys, and ran out of the house. Hopping into the golf cart, she threw it in reverse and sped out of the driveway. She held up her phone and called Lizzie.

No answer.

"Siri, call Randolph Levine."

No answer.

"Shit! Shit, shit, shit!"

"Siri, call Josh Miller."

No answer.

Damn it, doesn't anyone answer their phone anymore?

Helen pulled the cart to the side of the road and created a group text with Randy and Josh. She typed, "Meet me at the bookstore when you get this message. It's important." Then, she pressed send.

She dialed Stallard again and left a message.

"Hey Bob, it's your old paralegal, Helen. I need some help. Will you dig up everything you can on a woman named Kit Maltisini? She was a nurse at New York Presbyterian Hospital in Queens. She no longer works there, and I need you to figure out why. Call me back."

Helen hung up the phone frantically and stomped on the pedal, and the golf cart lurched forward.

TWENTY-EIGHT

"Hey, Lizzie."

I jumped. "Oh my God." I put my hand over my heart, feeling like it was about to beat out of my chest. "You scared the shit out of me, Kit."

"Sorry, I thought you heard me come in. Do you still want to go?"

"Sure, I can lock up a few minutes early. Let me get my things. I'll be right back."

"Sounds great."

Kit had beautiful thick, light brown, almost sandy blond hair cut short slightly above her shoulders. Her face was a perfect oval, with a tiny, bulbous nose. Her skin was pale and smooth, like porcelain. She was breathtaking and had a body every woman dreamed of. She was thin but fit and muscular, with curves in all the right places. I was pretty sure her boobs were fake, and she had her fair share of Botox, but so did most women from New York City these days. If they could afford it, go for it. I was glad she surprised me, and I looked forward to having drinks with her tonight.

"Where ya want to go?" Kit said. Her voice sounded faint from the staff room.

Collecting my things, I shouted, "I'm good wherever. Just happy to catch up."

Exiting the staff room, I turned the corner toward the front counter. I saw Kit standing by the large wooden exit door. I looked down, rifling through my purse for the bookstore keys, when I heard the iron interior lock thunk into place.

"We need to lock the door after we leave, silly." I laughed.

"I want to lock the door now," Kit said with an eeriness in her tone. She was slowly walking toward me. Her eyes were filled with a darkened rage.

My mind ran through several scenarios as I processed my current situation.

Stop it, Lizzie. She's your friend. Don't be ridiculous.

Despite my best efforts to cast aside any doubts, my heartbeats hammered my rib cage, and my senses went on high alert.

"What's up, Kit? Would you rather stay here and chat?" I stopped dead in my tracks, my inner voice recommending that I not move any closer. "I think we've got some wine in the back. I'll get us a couple glasses."

"Yeah. I'd love to chat here. Let's start with you fucking my husband."

"What?" Confusion rippled across my face, and my pulse quickened. "Are you talking about Josh? I don't understand."

My breath was shallow, and I felt like the room was spinning.

Kit's Josh's wife? How could that possibly be?

I felt like the bookstore walls were closing in on me, and the room began to blur. Josh was my everything. I trusted him completely. *How can he have a wife?*

"No. You stupid bitch. Gray."

Kit's eyes were wild, like a rabid dog. Her porcelain white skin had turned a fiery red, and her teeth were clenched. My knees were shaking, and terror clawed at me from the inside out like a taloned creature lurking around a dark corner.

"I don't understand what you're saying. You're not making any sense." I wasn't sure how much longer my body would stay standing. My legs begged and pleaded for me to find a place to sit down.

"Let me spell it out for you. My name is Catalina 'Kit' Stone. Gray Stone's my husband." She reached behind the desk and grabbed the broom, smashing the chandeliers one by one as she moved closer to me. Glass rained down on top of the furniture and fell to the floor.

"He told me you were divorced," I said as tears fell down my face. "Truly. I didn't know you were still married."

Standing in the shadows, a sinister smile appeared across her face, and her down-turned brows made her look like pure evil. Her voice grew calm, almost tender, as she said, "He's been trying to divorce me for years. We've been separated on and off for most of our marriage. I'll never sign the papers."

"You must believe me, Kit. I didn't know. You're my friend. I never meant to hurt you. Let's talk about this."

"You think I came here to talk?" She bellowed an evil laugh that sent chills down my spine. "We aren't friends."

Thinking my best course of action was to talk her down, I pulled myself together and calmly tried again.

"But we are friends. I don't know if I'd have recovered without you."

I backed away slowly to keep as much distance between us as possible.

"You still don't get it. After all this time, you really don't remember." Catalina smashed another chandelier, causing more glass to shatter and fall to the floor. "You think I saved your life? The irony." She cackled again.

Working hard to keep my tone calm, I asked, "What don't I remember? What're you talking about?" The last thing I wanted to do was escalate the situation.

"Can you hear me, Lizzie? Can you hear my voice loud and clear?" She sneered.

"Yes, Kit. I hear you." *Catalina, not Kit.*

"I pushed you down those stairs."

Frozen in place, her words rushed through me like a kick to my gut. Distant memories flashed like paparazzi before my eyes, and I could see small snapshots of me standing in the stairwell that day.

"I pushed you, Lizzie. Did you hear me?"

Collecting the pictures, one by one, I strained to weave the memory together like a patchwork quilt in my mind. Then, like a movie on the big screen, everything came flooding back. A typhoon of realization crashed through my brain. My legs felt weak, and my hands shook.

I saw that moment in the stairwell, clear as crystal now. Her hair was longer and darker, but I remembered her face. When I had opened the stairwell door, Kit had been waiting for me. She had slammed my shoulders against the wall, and I'd struggled to get free. Her eyes had been full of revenge and hatred as she pointed a gun at my stomach. I had pushed her back into the railing and banged her arm against the wall until she dropped the gun. When I'd turned around, she'd punched me in the stomach and then pushed me down the stairs.

Snapping back to the present, I gritted my teeth and clenched my fists. Anger filled me with rage. I ran to the staff room and searched for a weapon to use. For over a year, this memory was locked away in a deep, dark corner of my mind. She pretended to be my friend. The feeling of betrayal swept over me, and my rage thickened.

Finally, I found a mop in the corner and unscrewed the handle. *Not many weapon choices at the bookstore. This'll have to do. Now I really wished Helen had bought a gun.*

I reached for the breaker box on the wall next to the fridge and flipped the switch for the overhead lights. The store went black.

"Are we playing hide and seek?" Catalina mocked.

Holding the mop handle, I stood inside the staff room door and waited for an opportunity to run. *If I could get to the front door, I could get help.*

"Come out, come out. Wherever you are." Her voice made my blood run cold.

She has no soul. She's completely crazy.

"When I discovered that you created a child with Gray, I wanted you dead. I tried to make it look like an accident." She snickered so churlishly that it made my blood run cold.

I breathed deeply through my nose and exhaled as quietly as possible.

Think, Lizzie. Think!

"But, nooo. You didn't die." She banged the broom handle along the edge of the bookcase, causing a repeated thumping sound as she moved. "What are the odds you'd show up at my hospital?" she roared, her laughter more menacing with each sentence she spoke.

The sound of her voice was getting closer. Remaining still, I took a huge breath and held it.

"Come out and face me, bitch," she shouted, then changed her voice to sound like a little girl. "Or hide like the husband-stealing fucking coward that you are."

Waiting quietly for her to reach the door, I stood frozen in the staff room entryway like a petrified statue. Anger and fear raged inside me, and I could feel the cortisol pumping through my veins.

Now's your chance.

I charged toward her and pressed the mop handle into her throat. "You killed my baby girl."

Knocking her backward onto the ground, I pressed down on her throat with every ounce of strength I had. "You're pure evil. You killed my child," I screamed.

She struggled and twisted her body from side to side as she clambered to break free. Finally, her hands gripped the mop handle, and she pushed against me. Her voice was raspy and strained as I squeezed her throat. Catalina scraped out two words.

"She's alive."

I loosened my grip on the mop handle, and my brow furrowed. Confused, I said, "What'd you say?"

"Your baby's alive," she said through gritted teeth.

I relaxed my grip and paused as I processed her words.

"You're lying. You killed her."

Determined that I would not die today, I pressed the handle down with every ounce of force I could muster. Of course, I didn't want to be a killer, but she wasn't giving me much choice.

Sobbing, I said, "You killed my baby girl." For months, I had blamed myself. I questioned everything. I thought God was punishing me, but the entire time Catalina Stone was the one to blame.

While I was lost in my grief, she threw me off her with one fast and hard push. Landing on my back, I succumbed to sadness and closed my eyes in surrender. Begging God to hear me, I prayed. Let me be with my little girl. End this, so I may see her and hold her for the first time.

Standing over me, she said, "Your baby's alive. You fucking met her today."

Like an electrical socket about to catch fire, every human emotion surged through my body simultaneously, and I felt vomit boiling in my stomach. Then, happiness pushed it back down. Love filled my heart, and then anger and hatred. My body convulsed for a few seconds as I expelled the emotional chaos inside.

I opened my eyes and paused to give my pupils time to adjust. I could barely see her expression.

"She's alive?" I said in a whisper. "But how?"

Her foot landed hard against my side, and my breath escaped out of me. Catalina screamed through her clenched teeth, "I."

Another kick to my stomach.

"Took."

Kick. Kick. Kick. I heard a crunching sound.

I think my ribs just cracked.

"Her." Her foot came down one last time. "That's right, bitch. I took her."

TWENTY-NINE

Knock, knock, knock.

"Don't make a sound," Catalina snapped.

Knock, knock, knock.

"Lizzie, are you in there?" Josh's voice bellowed through the metal slot in the thick wooden door.

I had managed to kick myself free and hide behind a bookcase. The pain in my side radiated into my chest, and my breathing was strained.

"I've got a gun pointed at the door. Tell him you're in here, and I'll shoot him in the face," she snarled.

She has a gun? Shit. Maybe she's bluffing?

Stretching my neck around the bookcase, I strained my eyes to find her in the dark. The store was completely black.

I can't see shit.

Knock, knock, knock!

The knocks grew harder and louder.

"Lizzie, it's Josh. Open the door."

Catalina whispered, "If you want to see him again, you'll keep your mouth shut."

Quietly, I waited. I could hear faint footsteps as Josh left the building.

"Why are you doing this?" I whispered into the darkness.

"Because I want you dead." She let out a deep, gritty howl. "I crashed your stupid Halloween party. I wanted to see the fear in your eyes. I tried to run you over, but somehow you survived. Again." She spat.

"Give me back my daughter, and no one will ever have to know," I said firmly.

Screaming, she said, "You gave birth to my husband's child." She slammed her fist onto a table. "Your baby's a part of him."

She banged the tip of the broom handle on the ground over and over. Then, speaking calmly again, she said, "After losing our twins, the doctors told me that I'd die if I got pregnant again and tried to deliver … So, I did the next best thing and took my husband's child."

Am I having a nightmare? That must be it. I'm going to wake up any minute in bed next to Josh, consoling me from a bad dream.

"You ended up in a coma, and I volunteered to be on your service. I figured I'd slip some air into your IV and kill you. But then, I held Gray's baby, and I had to have her." She sighed. "She has his mouth, you know."

I don't know. I don't know what my baby girl's mouth looks like because I've not spent any time with her. You stole her. Rage filled me to the brim. I wanted to kill her. Kit or Catalina, who gave a shit at this point, caused the crater of pain I'd carried with me all this time.

I could hear her getting closer.

"You were so out of it that you don't remember having the baby." She banged the broomstick frantically against the ground. "I slipped into the hospital late at night. I brought a duffle bag, unclipped the baby's ankle monitor, and nestled her inside the bag. Then I walked right out."

The throbbing pain in my side grew sharper, and filling my lungs with air became more difficult by the minute. *Think, Lizzie, think.*

"The attending doctor that night owed me big time because he had administered the wrong drug to a patient who then died, and only I knew about it. So, I got him to mark the chart that the baby was stillborn." She howled victoriously. "I can't make this shit up."

My skin felt clammy, and my pulse was racing. Nausea filled my stomach, and my side pounded like an ape beating on his chest. My eyes grew heavy and tired, and my body shook.

"You were in a coma, so there was nothing you could do. No next of kin. You were practically a Jane Doe."

The sound of her voice was like nails on a chalkboard. Her words were like little dagger epiphanies plunging through my heart.

"Shut up," I screamed. "Shut up. I don't want to hear anymore," I screamed again like a lion in the wild protecting his pride.

Choking back the vomit as it rose into my throat, I yelled, "You pretended to be my friend. I trusted you. You're fucking sick!" Spit and snot dripped down my face as I spat the words at her.

The door handle rattled, and I heard someone pulling on the door.

Thud, thud, thud. "Lizzie, are you in there?" I heard Josh's voice calling again from the other side of the door.

He came back.

Distracted by the knock on the door, I gave away my position tucked behind the self-help bookcase, and Catalina lunged at me from the darkness. She grabbed a fistful of my hair and yanked me off the ground toward her.

Sliding my legs on the ground, I scrambled to get my feet underneath me; I felt a chunk of hair ripped from my scalp. Kit reached her arm around my neck, squeezed tightly, and rammed me into the glass door of the pirate bookcase. Gasping for air, my lungs felt like they would cave in.

Thud. Josh slammed his body against the door again. "Lizzie, hold on!" Thud. Thud. Thud.

"I've been raising Gray's beautiful daughter for over a year," Catalina said, happiness spilling from her tone. "I'm her mother. I'm the one that rocks her to sleep at night."

My breath became shallow, and my head ached. My vision blurred between darkness and light, in and out. Then, staring at myself in the broken glass, I saw drool mixed with blood sliding down my chin.

Blankly staring into the shattered glass, I saw my parents. Katherine and Wayne Levine, and the brightest, most beautiful light, surrounded them. I reached out my hand to touch them.

Faintly I heard Catalina say, "I never imagined how good this would feel." She tightened her grip around my neck. "Don't worry, Lizzie, go to sleep. I'll take good care of my daughter."

My daughter. Janie.

My eyes widened at my reflection staring back at me. Janie!

Imagining my baby girl's face in the glass, I knew I had to find her. I had to dig deeper than I ever thought possible and fight back so I could hold my precious Janie.

Thud. "Lizzie, I'm coming." I could hear the faint sound of Josh's voice as I grew closer to unconsciousness. "This fucking door. I can't get in."

The light is so pretty. I felt its warmth surrounding me. It's so peaceful. My breathing was easier now, and my pain had disappeared. I was happy. Warm.

Josh. I'm here, Josh. Janie. Where's Janie?

Janie. Dig deep for Janie. Come on, girl; you can do this.

"Sophie thinks I'm her mother, Lizzie. She loves me. I'm the only mother she knows," Catalina sneered in an eerie, diabolical tone.

She's certifiable.

The sound of sweet baby giggles filled my head, and like a ball of fire shooting through a cannon, I opened my eyes wide and squirmed ferociously. I put my hands on Catalina's forearms and pushed with every bit of strength I had left. I swung my leg forward, reared back, and kicked her in the knee. I stomped on her foot and pushed hard on her arms, finally freeing myself from her grip as anger and adrenaline pushed me forward.

I turned to face her, and she landed a punch square on my jaw that knocked me off balance. I got my feet back underneath me. Running toward her, I wrapped my arms around her waist and sent her hurling to the ground with me on top of her.

I screamed as the pain radiated from my side.

"Something's happening to Lizzie. I can't get inside." I heard Josh talking to someone on the other side of the door.

"Move out of the way. I have the key," Helen said.

"Thank God. This damn door might as well be made of steel," Josh said.

Jamming her key into the lock, Helen said, "She's in trouble. I know it. No time to explain."

"Lizzie, we're coming."

Punching Catalina in the face with my right hand, then my left hand repeatedly, I screamed and cried, "You stole my baby." I kept punching. My arms were tired, the pain in my side was unbearable, and my breathing was difficult, but I didn't stop. "You stole my baby." Then I saw the gun on the floor, picked it up, and was about to pull the trigger.

I felt someone wrap their arms around my waist and pull me off. Screaming in pain, I kicked at the air. "She stole my baby. She stole my little girl." Sitting on the floor, Josh held my face. Blood and snot dripped from my nose and my eyes were swollen, almost closed.

"Look at me," he said frantically. "Lizzie. Look at me."

My eyes connected with his and suddenly became keenly aware of my situation. I fell into his arms, my head pounding, my heart racing, and I sobbed.

"She still has a pulse," I heard Helen say. "I'm calling the police."

Josh rocked me back and forth. "It's going to be okay, Lizzie. It's going to be okay."

"She has my daughter," I mumbled through my tears.

"You're in shock. It's going to be okay."

I cleared my throat, taking shallow breaths between each word. "No, Josh. Janie's alive. She stole my baby girl. Janie's alive."

"Helen, do you have a blanket? She's freezing," Josh said.

Returning with a blue fleece blanket, Helen wrapped it around me.

"I don't know exactly what's going on, Josh, but I felt like something was off this afternoon. So, I did some digging when I got home. This woman is Gray Stone's wife," Helen said.

I opened my mouth to speak, but no words came out. My throat was on fire, and my heart struggled to beat.

"She was also Lizzie's nurse last year in New York when she lost the baby. She showed up today with a baby of the right age and a birthmark matching Lizzie's. Now, I'm not saying that the baby is Janie, but I'm saying it's possible."

"This is insane," Josh said.

Unable to control my nausea, I leaned forward and vomited. Once I was finished, I flopped back into Josh's arms. My eyes rolled gently into the back of my head, and I danced between states of consciousness. I could hear sirens blaring in the distance.

"I'll contact the law firm I used to work for. They'll help Lizzie should we find out the baby's hers."

"What happened? What's going on?"

I thought I heard Randy's voice.

"Hey Randy, we'll fill you in on the way to the hospital," Helen said.

"She took my baby," I muttered breathlessly. "My baby, Janie. Janie. Janie. Janie." My words trailed off as I spoke, and my eyes slammed shut. Then, my body went limp, and the room went dark.

THIRTY

Stallard Law Firm was located in an old one-story home, remodeled inside with a lobby entrance, several offices, and two conference rooms. Sitting in the lobby chair, my knee bounced unconsciously as I waited for my appointment. Watercolor paintings hung from the walls, and the words Stallard Law sparkled in shiny silver metallic behind the front desk.

Josh put his hand on my knee and said, "Breathe, babe. It's going to be okay."

Chewing my bottom lip nervously, I looked at him. Compassion and confidence radiated from his eyes.

Looking around the room, Randy said, "We're all here to support you, Lizzie."

Their support meant the world to me. Josh, Randy, Renee, and even Helen came to the meeting with Robert Stallard. Today was the first step on a long road to getting custody of my daughter, Janie Katherine Levine.

Laws were made by men, most likely with the best intentions, but men are fallible, and so are the laws. I've learned this the hard way through personal experience.

"Bob will see you now," the sweet young lady behind the desk announced.

I stood up immediately, took a deep breath, and straightened my dress. My family and friends followed behind me as the young girl escorted us to the larger of the two conference rooms.

In the center of the room was a long polished wooden table with eight high-back leather chairs. We filed into our seats, and I crossed my hands on the table and sat up straight.

"Can I get anyone some water?" the girl said.

"Sure, that'd be great," Randy said. "Bring five."

Mr. Stallard entered the room. He was a tall man, standing at least six foot three inches. Wearing a navy blue suit, he removed his jacket and slung it over his chair.

"You're Lizzie, I presume," he said and extended his arm across the table to shake my hand.

Assuming the bruises that prominently decorated my face gave me away, I said, "Yes, sir. This is my boyfriend, Josh. My brother, Randy, and his wife, Renee. And you know Helen, of course," as I pointed to each person as I introduced them. I winced as I spoke, and my breathing was shallow because Catalina had left me with five cracked ribs.

"Thank you for coming today. We have a lot to discuss."

The girl from the front desk returned with water for each of us and closed the door behind her.

"Bob, I'm taking notes and can help Lizzie with any questions that come up after the meeting today," Helen said, and then pulled a small silver laptop from her bag and set it on the table. Opening the lid, she turned it on and said, "I'm ready."

"I want to recap a few things first, share some new information so that you're up to speed on the case, and then I'll explain all of your legal options," Mr. Stallard said after taking a sip of his coffee.

"I know this should be simple. Lizzie is the baby's mother, and she should walk out of here today with her, but unfortunately, the law doesn't work that way."

Randy cleared his throat and said, "I don't understand. Lizzie is Janie's mother. It really should be that simple."

"I wish it were," Mr. Stallard said, shaking his head. "Let me start by informing you that I obtained a copy of the police reports you filed. The reports detail everything you've been through and include eyewitness accounts when there were any. You've had quite a time with Catalina Stone."

I squirmed in my seat at the sound of her name. Reaching for a bottle of water, I removed the cap and took a sip to suppress the anger pumping into my veins. "Mrs. Stone has finally been arrested, and her arraignment is scheduled for tomorrow."

"What does that mean?" Renee said.

"It means the court will determine if Mrs. Stone will be granted bail. If she's granted bail and pays the bond, she will be released from jail until her trial. If she isn't granted bail or can't pay, she'll stay in jail until her trial. We also learned that Mrs. Stone has been renting a place in Wilmington for quite some time now."

My head was already spinning, and he had just gotten started. Standing up, I pushed out of my chair and stood against the wall.

Josh followed me and said, "Please continue. This has been an emotional time."

"Lizzie, please let me know if you need a break. We can take this as slow as you need to go," Mr. Stallard said.

"Thank you. I'm okay."

"Mrs. Stone is being charged with three counts of attempted murder, kidnapping, breaking and entering, endangering a minor, and assault and battery."

I shifted my weight, leaned on Josh, and slid my arm around his waist for support.

"I want to be brutally honest. I'm not sure that these charges will stick. In North Carolina, an appellate case says a confession, standing alone, is not sufficient to convict. You need additional corroborating evidence or eyewitness testimony." He took another sip of coffee, placed his hands on the table, and leaned forward.

His eyes softened as he continued. "I'm hopeful that something will stick, but I need you to understand that there's a possibility that Mrs. Stone could go free."

Renee sucked in a breath. Helen was clicking away on her laptop and froze. She lifted her head to look at Mr. Stallard.

"I need to use the restroom," I said, and ran from the room.

I collapsed onto my knees when I reached the bathroom. Heaving as tears splashed onto the floor, I felt excruciating pain shoot through my side, and my chest tightened, making it almost impossible to breathe.

How could this be? Catalina Stone has attempted to kill me multiple times. She stalked me, followed me, threatened me, and broke into my home. She stole my daughter. She's lived thirty minutes away for God knows how long. How's any of this possible? I just want to hold my little girl.

On all fours, I wailed.

Finally, I pried myself from the floor and washed my hands in the sink. Splashing water on my face, I breathed slowly and collected myself. Walking back into the room, I took my seat.

"Please continue."

"I'll inform you about the results of Mrs. Stone's arraignment and pending court date as soon as I have the information. I'm working closely with the DA on the case. We'll do everything we can to see Mrs. Stone behind bars, and your baby's home with you where she belongs."

Randy pulled off his windbreaker and folded it in his lap. Sighing, he looked at me, his expression full of empathy.

"You'll likely have to testify if her case actually does make it to trial. But we'll have plenty of time to prepare. The justice system doesn't move quickly," Mr. Stallard said. He took a deep breath before continuing again. "Now for the hard part."

"That wasn't the hard part?" Renee said, shocked.

"Sadly, no, ma'am. That's the information we have regarding the criminal case pertaining to Mrs. Stone's egregious actions against Lizzie. Now, I'd like to review Lizzie's different legal options to get her daughter back."

"This is ridiculous," Renee said. She leaned forward in her chair, and continued, "Janie's her daughter. Period. Done. End of story."

Helen stopped typing and placed her hand on Renee's shoulder. "I know this is difficult, but Bob's the best. Please hear him out. It sucks, but legally at the present moment, Lizzie has no right to the baby."

"It's bullshit," Renee shouted and slammed her hand onto the table. "DNA test, and bam, there's proof. Case closed."

Josh reached into his pocket and handed me a tissue. I dabbed my face to dry the tears streaming from the corners of my eyes.

"Please, Mr. Stallard. Is that an option?" I asked.

Loosening his tie, he said, "Yes, and no." He paused for a moment. "Mrs. Stone has a birth certificate listing her as the mother, and Gray Stone as the father of Sophie. A birth certificate is a legal document, and according to that document, they're Sophie's legal parents."

Listening to his words infuriated me to the point that my fingertips turned white as I gripped the table's edge.

Fucking stop calling her Sophie.

Narrowing my eyes, I took a slow, deep breath. "Call. Her. Janie. Her name is Janie." Mr. Stallard nodded.

Doing my best to suppress the desire to reach across the table and choke him, I continued. "Is Ki—Catalina legally able to maintain custody while her trial is pending?"

"Technically, no. So parental custody would fall to the father. Gray Stone is Sophie's biological father in this case, but that's technically irrelevant. He's Mrs. Stone's husband, according to the state of New York, and he's listed on the birth certificate as Sophie's father. So DSS will grant custody to him."

"For the last time, her name is Janie," I said with a forced smile.

"I'm sorry," Mr. Stallard said, his tone sounding genuine.

"If Gray acknowledges that he's the father, he will become Janie's custodial parent. You could ask him for permission to do a maternity test to prove that you're the biological mother. These tests take about three to five days to get the results and are ninety-nine point ninety-nine percent accurate. Once you have the results and prove you are Janie's biological mother, you can go to court and fight him for custody, like hundreds of married couples do every day."

"Okay, well, let's do that. I can call him right now. I'm sure he'd agree to a maternity test," I said hopefully.

"Right now, Janie's with Mrs. Stone's sister. Mr. Stone has been sent a letter and will have to accept custody. If he were to agree and you fight him for custody, and Mrs. Stone was to go free, the judge could decide that even though Janie is biologically yours, the mother she knows and has bonded with should raise her."

Shattering into a million pieces, my heart felt like it had stopped beating. I gasped for air as his words hit me like a ton of bricks.

Might the judge decide Janie should be raised by the mother she's already bonded with? I can't take this shit. It's all bullshit.

The room around me went blurry; I closed my eyes and rested my head on the table.

"Let me get this straight. So, the judge could agree that Janie is biologically Lizzie's daughter, but decide that Janie should be raised by the woman who stole her? Did I hear you correctly?" Josh said as he rubbed my back.

"I think we should take a break," Helen said. "Look, gang, I know this is difficult, and emotions are high. But, I promise, if I were Lizzie, Robert Stallard's the man I'd want on my side. He seems cold, but he does this every day. He simply wants to ensure you have all the facts and understand all your options so that you're fully informed before proceeding."

"I'll have Kelsey order us some lunch, and we can continue when we're finished. Unless you prefer to digest the information so far and come back tomorrow," Mr. Stallard said.

"Lunch sounds good," Josh said.

"I need some air," I said as I exited the room. "Josh, order me some soup, please."

After lunch, I sat staring blankly at the wall as my situation settled into the air around me. It was a stale, dank air with Gray, standing between Janie and me, and Kit clawing at us from the corner. I had been forever changed by my experiences this past year. Part of me wished I had never stepped foot into Gray Stone Marketing and never met Gray. But without him, I wouldn't have Janie, my special, beautiful baby girl. Now, I had learned Janie was alive, beautiful, and healthy, but I may be unable to raise her. How did I get here? In what world is a loving mother unable to raise her child? In what world would a thief be granted custody of my beautiful baby girl?

Mr. Stallard entered the room and took his seat. Then, looking at me, he asked, "Are you ready to begin again?"

"Yes." One word was all I could muster.

"We talked about if Mr. Stone accepts custody. Now we need to discuss if he doesn't. Do you think that's a possibility?"

Directing his question to me, I contemplated what he asked.

"Everything's a business transaction to Gray. So, it depends, I guess. He didn't want her when I told him I was pregnant."

"Well, let's say hypothetically he doesn't want custody. Then, a few different things can happen. One option would be for Mrs. Stone to choose a reliable friend or family member who would take care of Janie until Mrs. Stone could do so herself. Another option would be that DSS places her in a foster home." He said these words with the utmost delicacy and momentarily paused for my reaction.

I slumped into my chair like every ounce of life exited my body.

Foster care. This is too much.

I pressed my hands to my face and slid them to my temple. I sighed as I gently massaged my forehead and hoped to relieve the ache in my head. How could I allow my daughter to be put into foster care? The truth in his words cut deep.

"You have a few options in this scenario. First, assuming you take a maternity test, you could petition to care for Janie as her family member until Mrs. Stone could take care of Janie herself. At this point, we could fight her for legal custody. The other option would be to apply to be a foster parent. I think we could pull some strings between myself and your family to ensure that Janie is placed with you as her foster parent. Then we could apply for adoption of the child if her mother is incarcerated."

"I'm her mother," I snapped. I was losing the battle to keep myself in control.

"I'm sorry, poor choice of words," Mr. Stallard said. "There's another possibility to consider. If you could get Mr. Stone to cooperate and prove that you were biologically Janie's mother, then Mrs. Stone could be dismissed as a party to the custody action. As Janie's parents, you and Mr. Stone could enter into a custody order giving you physical and legal custody of your daughter. Having Mr. Stone on your side would help to eliminate the possibility of the judge deciding that Janie is better suited to stay with the woman who has raised her thus far."

Josh sucked in a breath and hesitated, then said, "Would Lizzie and Gray have to raise Janie together?"

"Well, that depends on Mr. Stone. Once they have legal custody, we could take steps for Lizzie to have full custody. But if Mr. Stone wants his daughter, he could fight for shared custody. He could demand that Janie live within a certain number of miles of his home. Given his business and financial status, you'll lose the location battle if it comes to that."

My head was reeling with information overload. I put my elbows on the table and dropped my head into my hands. Every option seemed long and painful.

"I don't know what to do. Mr. Stallard, what do you think our best option is?"

"First, you need to get that maternity test, also called a gene marker. Please don't be offended by my next statement, but everything needs to be considered. We need to be absolutely certain that Janie is, in fact, your baby. Just because Mrs. Stone said she was your daughter doesn't mean that she is."

In perfect unison, everyone gasped, almost depleting the oxygen in the room. I looked around the table, terror filled my eyes. Josh looked at me and waited for my reaction. Randy and Renee started to cry. Helen was totally at a loss for words, with both hands covering her mouth.

"After everything she put me through, I never considered she could be lying about my daughter. Why would she lie about that?" I said, almost in a whisper, as I stared at the wall across from me.

My body and mind were so exhausted that I felt like I could sleep for a week, and I'd cried enough tears to fill an ocean.

"Why has she done any of these things to you? She's clearly a mentally unstable person. You need to consider the possibility that your baby was, in fact, stillborn, and this little girl isn't yours," Mr. Stallard said matter-of-factly.

"Okay. I think that's enough. We're done for today," Randy said as he stood up from his chair and put his windbreaker back on. "Thank you for the information. We'll discuss this as a family and be in touch. You've been helpful."

"Bob, send me the information for Lizzie to get the maternity test. Then, if Gray accepts custody and agrees to that, we don't need the court involved in the test, right?" Helen said, putting her laptop back in her bag.

"Correct."

Still staring at the wall across from me, I was nearly catatonic. I was attuned to everything being said around me, but my body finally had enough. The constant ache in my side was getting stronger by the minute, and the sharp, stabbing pain caused me to wince with each breath I took. My eyes were open but not focused on anything in particular. I felt trapped inside my head with endless thoughts that pulled me into a deep, dark hole in the bottom of the ocean.

Josh grabbed my hand and said, "We can go now, babe. You did great. Do you need help getting out of your seat?"

Without looking at him, I nodded, and he assisted me as I stood. He draped my arm around his neck and put his arm around my waist. Escorting me out of the office, he said, "She's your daughter. I know it. It's going to be okay. We're going to figure this out."

Josh helped me into the passenger seat and closed the door. I heard him say goodbye to Helen and thank her for coming. Then he told Randy and Renee he'd take me to their house so we could all be together.

On the drive home, I stared out the window, the scenery passing by in a blur. I didn't speak. My eyes grew heavy, and I dozed off to sleep.

THIRTY-ONE

Sleeping through the rest of the day and straight into the morning was exactly what my body needed. I woke up for the occasional bathroom break and the meals that Josh made for me. The bruises on my face faded a little each day, and my ribs were still sore. The pain subsided to a dull ache, but that ache was a constant reminder of the trauma I had suffered and the unknown road ahead of me.

Getting out of bed with a clear head, I showered and dressed. I climbed down the stairs and discovered I was alone. Vaguely remembering that Josh mentioned he had a job site he needed to check on today, I picked up my phone from the counter and sent him a text, "Good morning, babe. I'm awake and feel good today. I'm heading to Stallard's to see if there's anything new. Kiss emoji. Love you."

I pressed send on the message and noticed a note taped to the coffeepot.

My love,

I made you a pot in case you felt up to moving around today.

Love you, Josh

I grabbed the *Fuck Off; I'm Writing* mug Randy had given me for Christmas. I wanted to be a writer when I started college, but I never completed the manuscript. Randy thought maybe now would be a good time to start writing again, so he bought me the mug as a bit of encouragement. Sipping my coffee, I scrolled through social media and checked the news. I thought maybe I would find some information about Catalina's arraignment. Having no luck, I threw my phone into my purse, grabbed my things, and opened the door. I locked the door behind me, hopped into Josh's golf cart, and drove to Stallard Law.

"Hello, Kelsey," I said, entering the lobby. "Is Mr. Stallard available?"

Kelsey stood up from behind the desk and said, "I'll go check. Give me a minute."

Mr. Stallard appeared a few minutes later, wearing black shorts and a light blue polo, and greeted me in the lobby. "Hello, Lizzie. You caught me at a good time. I'm playing in a charity golf tournament today, but I have a few minutes before I need to leave."

He led me into the smaller conference room this time. A square white table surrounded by four black chairs sat in the center of the room. The smell of freshly painted walls filled the little space.

"Please take a seat," Mr. Stallard said as he pulled out a chair for me to sit in.

"I wanted to see if you had any new information."

"I received quite a bit of news this morning," he said and poured me a glass of water. "Mrs. Stone was denied bail. The District Attorney argued that Mrs. Stone was a flight risk and that she'd most likely harm you again. Her court date's been set for about six weeks from now. This is good because custody of Janie will default to Mr. Stone while she's in jail waiting for trial. Her sentencing could take a year or more, so this buys you some time."

Relief washed over me, and I exhaled what felt like years of anguish. A small victory, but this news gave me a shred of peace, and my lips turned upward into a sincere smile for the first time in days.

"Thank you, Mr. Stallard."

"Don't thank me. I haven't done anything yet," he said. He pulled his phone out of his pocket, tapped the screen a few times, and then scanned the phone with his eyes.

"I'm expecting an update from a friend. Unfortunately, she hasn't sent it over yet." He put his phone back into his pocket and looked at me with compassion. "My friend's a social worker. She informed me this morning that DSS has been notified of the situation. They've contacted Mr. Stone and informed him that he needs to accept custody as Janie's current legal guardian, or DSS will file a petition and put Janie in foster care."

Taking a moment to digest everything Mr. Stallard just said, I took a sip of my water.

"Do you know if he accepted custody?"

"He's on his way here now from New York. He's rented a place nearby for a week. She's supposed to text me the address."

I allowed endless possibilities to roll through my mind as I sat quietly in my chair. It must have been obvious that I was silently weighing my options because Mr. Stallard looked at me and said, "I'll give you the address, but I need you to understand that every action you take from this point forward will be scrutinized if you end up fighting for custody in court."

He looked at his watch and then back at me.

"Every person you interact with, every social media post, every text message or email can be brought into discovery, so you must be smart."

Slumping into my chair, I took a deep, painful breath.

Every inch of my life will be scrutinized.

"How's it that I'm the innocent party, but I feel like the criminal?"

"The law is messy, but you'll get through this," Mr. Stallard said reassuringly. "I can draft a document to send Gray asking his permission as Janie's legal guardian for you to take a maternity test. We have no reason to believe he wouldn't agree. Assuming the test proves you're the biological mother, I can draft a complaint stating the facts and petition for you to have custody of Janie."

"And if I don't want to do that?"

"What do you mean? I thought you wanted custody of your daughter."

"I mean, I might have a better chance if I talk to Gray myself. Maybe I can avoid a legal battle."

"I advise against that, but you're the client. I can't stop you."

"Please send me the address. I'll keep you posted on how it goes."

As I was leaving the law firm, I called Randy to tell him everything I had learned. Then, I texted Josh to see if he wanted to meet for lunch. I wanted to tell him in person that I planned to meet Gray at his rental house. I didn't want a repeat of last time. Josh responded right away. He texted, "Meet me at your apartment. I'll pick up lunch on the way."

Pulling up to the apartment, I felt my phone vibrate on the front seat. I parked the golf cart and reached over to get my phone.

My screen displayed 212 West Street. I had worked through a plan in my head as Josh and I ate lunch. It was a good plan. I updated Josh on my visit with Mr. Stallard and told him I was going to meet Gray to discuss Janie.

"I want to go with you." Josh insisted.

"Thank you. But I need to do this on my own." I kissed his cheek and then his lips and hugged him tightly.

"I don't like it, but okay, Lizzie. I understand."

One block from the Intercoastal Waterway, Gray had rented a condo on the first floor equipped with all the amenities, including a pool, tennis court, and boat dock access. I rolled my eyes as I rang the doorbell.

My breath accelerated with the anticipation of seeing Janie, and I popped a Life Saver into my mouth to calm my nerves. No one answered. I rang the bell again. Still no answer. I knocked three times and waited.

Finally, Gray opened the door wide, and allowed space for me to enter. As he closed the door behind me, I noticed that he was in nothing but a towel, beads of water sliding down his perfectly tanned chest like a fitness model.

"I was in the shower. Give me a second to change," he said, noticing my rolled eyes. Moving toward me, he placed his hand on the small of my back and said, "Unless you prefer me to stay in this."

"No, please put on some clothes."

I glanced around the condo and didn't notice any signs of a one-year-old. No clothes, no toys, and no child. Gray reemerged, pulling his T-shirt over his head, and said, "Crazy week, huh."

"You could say that."

"You okay?" He sat on the couch and motioned for me to sit beside him.

"I've been better."

He touched my face and gently ran his fingers over my bruises. "Yeah, looks like she did a number on your face."

"You should see the other guy," I said and removed his hand.

"You didn't deserve this, Lizzie."

Dropping my head, I said, "Thanks."

His words seemed genuine, tender even.

"I'm sure you're here about Sophie. I'm going to take custody of her. I'm supposed to sign the paperwork tomorrow."

A mixture of emotions surged through me. On the one hand, I was relieved because Gray getting custody should make things easier, but on the other hand, I know he doesn't want Janie. Carefully considering what he had to gain, I chose the following words purposefully.

Assuming what he had to gain was me, I scooted a little closer to him. "With your permission, I'd like to get a maternity test."

"It's ironic, isn't it?" he said as he put his hand on my knee.

"You insisted you were pregnant with my child, a child I didn't want. Here we are over a year later, and I have custody of that child, and you're desperate to prove that she's biologically yours."

Stay calm. Don't let him get under your skin.

Shifting nervously in my seat, I said, "She's our child, and her name is Janie." I paused, deciding exactly what words to use next. "I'd be grateful if you'd give me permission for the maternity test."

"You'd be grateful," he said, raising an eyebrow. "Exactly how grateful would you be?" He slid his hand up my thigh, looked directly into my eyes, and watched for my reaction.

Repulsed by his touch and doing my best not to show it, I picked up his hand and placed it in mine. I said, "I'm in love with Josh. You didn't want to be with me, so I moved on." I kept my voice steady.

"Here's the deal," Gray said as he stood and walked toward the kitchen. "I don't want the kid. Hell, I'm not convinced she's mine, but the law says I'm her father, and I've been awarded custody. So, I'm accepting custody because I want you. Your job offer still stands, and the board has allowed me to double your pay. Move back to New York with me, and you can spend every day raising your daughter."

I tossed his offer around in my mind, and I felt sick at the thought of living a life with Gray Stone again. On the other hand, the idea of Janie going into foster care made me want to die. What kind of mother would I be if I didn't do everything I could to keep that from happening? Finally, I swallowed the bile rising in my throat and said, "My life's here now. I'll return to the firm, but I want to work remotely from here."

"And what about Janie?" he said, looking perplexed. "I don't want to raise her."

"As her father, you could sign a power of attorney authorizing me to raise Janie here in Southport," I said, hopeful my plan would work.

I held my breath, waiting for his answer.

"I don't like that option. I need to think about it. In the meantime, have lunch with me," Gray said. He was already wielding his leverage over my head.

After returning to my apartment, I explained everything to Josh.

"I want to know what you really think. How you feel." I said with my head in his lap as I lay on the couch.

He rubbed my head and said, "I want to be honest, but I feel like it's not my place to have an opinion. I'll support you no matter what."

Groaning, I rolled onto my side and sighed. "Your opinion matters to me. I want to know what you think."

Josh leaned his head back on the couch, stared up at the ceiling, and said, "I think you're in a pretty shitty situation, and you've been so strong. I hate the idea of you working for Gray Stone, and I hate even more that he'll use your daughter to his advantage. However, I understand that the power of attorney may be the quickest and least painful way to get Janie back. It's easy to say that I prefer you work with Mr. Stallard and pursue legal options, but that won't be an easy road. No matter what, I love you. I'm here for you and excited to meet your little girl and be a part of her life."

Gray texted the following morning and asked me to meet him at his rental house at 1:00 p.m. When I arrived at the bookstore, I filled Helen in on everything and asked her if I could leave a few hours early.

"I'm hopeful that Gray will do the right thing, but I'm afraid to let my hopes get too high. I need to get off this rollercoaster," I said as I straightened the chess pieces sitting on the table in the center of the store.

"My heart breaks every time I think about what you've been through, but I know it's all going to work out," Helen said as she fluffed the pillows on the couch. "You understand that if you get a power of attorney, your legal ability to raise her lasts only while Catalina is in jail. As soon as she gets out, she can walk right into your house and take her from you."

"I'm aware, but this is my best option to have Janie with me now. Hopefully, I'll have custody before that happens."

I finished checking out the customers in line, packed my things, and said goodbye to Helen. The sun shone brightly in the sky and beamed down on my skin as I walked to Gray's condo. Anticipation was building in my chest, and my nerves caused my hands to shake.

When I arrived, I pressed the doorbell anxiously. The door opened almost immediately, and Gray welcomed me inside. He was wearing shorts today but no shirt. His laptop was open on the kitchen table, and papers were sprawled on either side. A dirty plate and fork sat on the counter next to a half-full glass of water.

Sitting in front of his laptop, Gray said, "I've accepted custody and will meet the social worker in about an hour to pick up Janie."

My stomach did a flip-flop. Instantly, joy filled my heart and pumped through my body. Soon, I could meet my beautiful baby girl. My precious Janie. I wanted to drop to my knees and beg Gray to take me with him.

"That's great news." I suppressed my elation, not wanting to give him more leverage than he already had.

"Also, I decided I will not accept your proposal."

Despair instantly replaced my joy; this time, I couldn't control my reaction. "You hateful piece of shit," I snapped.

"Whoa now, Lizzie. Is that any way to talk to the father of your child?" he said smugly. "You didn't let me finish."

He looked at his laptop and started typing again. My frustration was boiling over. I sighed, shifted my weight, and did everything I could to remain calm.

He lifted his eyes above his computer, examined me, and said, "This is my final offer. I'll sign a power of attorney allowing you to raise Janie here in Southport. In return, you'll work remotely for the firm and agree to come to New York and work from the office once a month for a minimum of three days. The offer expires in twenty-four hours."

This wasn't the perfect situation, but I could make this work. I wanted to scream yes, but I remained cool and collected. I knew the smart thing was to take some time to process his proposal before answering.

"Thank you, Gray. I want to discuss this with my family before I agree, but hypothetically, if I say yes, could we agree to my old salary for three days a week?"

"Easy-peasy. I honestly don't give a shit how much you work. The three days in the New York office each month are non-negotiable."

"Understood." I couldn't believe he would use a child, our child, to manipulate me into working in the city once a month so that he could try to win me back. On second thought, I could believe it. It's exactly something Gray would do. Internally, I rolled my eyes, but kept a straight face.

"I can have my attorney send you the paperwork tomorrow. If you want your attorney to look at it, that's fine. Once you sign, Janie's all yours."

Janie's all yours. Hearing those words took every bit of control I had not to break out into a full-blown happy dance right in the kitchen of his rental condo.

I'm going to meet my baby girl.

"Do you want to come with me to meet the social worker?" The question was music to my ears, like a symphony playing at

Carnegie Hall. Finally losing control, I let tears of joy spill onto my cheeks. My smile grew wide, exposing my teeth, and I said, "Yes."

"I want to remind you that what I really want is for us to be together, and I always get what I want." He closed his laptop, grabbed his keys off the counter, and said, "By the way, I bought this place, and I plan to visit often. Now, let's go get your daughter."

THIRTY-TWO

Seeing Janie for the first time was indescribable. My heart filled with more love than I knew a single person could hold inside. Janie sat quietly beside the social worker, swinging her legs as they dangled in the chair. I stared at her. Scanning every inch of her face with my eyes, I committed it to memory. For as much joy and elation as I felt at the moment, bitter sadness swept over me. Thoughts of the days, weeks, and months I had lost with her took over my mind. *Lost?* I didn't lose her. My sadness turned to seething anger. She was stolen from me, taken from my womb. I was robbed of the opportunity to grow and bond with my newborn baby girl, and now she was a toddler. Time that I would never get back. *Pull yourself together. You can't change the past. You can only move forward.*

Gray signed more paperwork and shook the social worker's hand. He kneeled down and said something quietly to Janie. He helped her out of the chair and held her little hand. I wanted to run to her and smother her with kisses, but I knew that would scare her. My heart yearned to hold my baby girl, my child. The child that I had made with Gray. The man who now held the fate of my daughter in his hands. As I watched Gray and our daughter walk toward me, I saw a glimmer of what might have been. How things could have been different.

As fast as the glimmer appeared, it disappeared, and Josh flooded my mind. I couldn't wait for him to meet Janie. I couldn't wait for him to be the father to her that Gray could never be. Finally, holding her father's hand, my daughter stood before me. I kneeled.

"Hi," I said as my voice quivered.

Choking back the tears, I held my breath. She doesn't even know me. I am both her mother and a stranger. Her mother, the woman who gave birth to her. The one who dreamed of her and loved her every single day since she was born. I am also a stranger, a person whom Janie does not know.

Janie smiled at me and shook her body from side to side. Revealing two perfect little baby teeth, she said, "Hi-eeeee." A tear trickled down my cheek and I knew in that moment my life was complete. Everything I'd do from this day forward would be for her. They say that children are resilient, and my Janie girl was the most resilient of them all.

I had to pinch myself to ensure my new reality wasn't a dream. This morning, I was granted power of attorney, and Gray returned to New York. Tangled in his web, I knew he would control my life for the foreseeable future, but I had my sweet baby girl.

Janie was dressed in a purple sundress with white daisies, her hair was like a sprout tied into a ponytail on the top of her head, and her new white sandals lit up when she walked.

I unbuckled her from the car seat and carried her to the front door. Renee must have been standing at the window waiting for us because I didn't even have time to knock before she flung open the door. Tears instantly filled her eyes as she bent down to meet Janie.

"Hello, Janie, I'm your favorite Aunt Renee," she said, and handed Janie a stuffed white unicorn.

One by one, Randy, Josh, and Helen met my little girl. The house had no shortage of love and tears of joy. A gigantic banner covered the living room wall with pink letters saying Happy Homecoming. White, purple, and pink balloon arches decorated every doorway. A giant white unicorn cake surrounded by matching cupcakes and paper plates covered the kitchen counter.

Sitting on the couch, I looked around the room, and my heart was full. Life was complete. Encircled by family and friends, I reveled in the moment. I watched as Janie giggled and played with Randy. I had expected her to be more cautious, even afraid of us, but somehow, I think she knew she belonged.

I watched as Janie and Renee played peekaboo. I watched as Janie sat on Helen's lap, and listened to a book. I watched as Janie fell asleep on Josh's shoulder. I watched as my family welcomed my little girl into their hearts. I watched with a joy I had never felt before.

Josh and I laid Janie down in a pack-and-play Renee borrowed from her neighbor. Focused on my time with her now, I did my best not to think about the time we had lost. The months of maternal bonding. The months that Catalina took from me. I wanted to stay in the guest room and watch her sleep all day. They say babies can have separation anxiety, but I had mom separation anxiety. I wanted to be with her every second of the day. Wrapping his arms around my waist, Josh stood behind me and held his hands in mine. He kissed my cheek tenderly and said, "She's beautiful, like her mother. I'm excited to be part of her life."

His words meant the world to me. I turned to face him. I gazed into his eyes and said, "I love you," and then pressed my lips to his.

Holding hands, we walked downstairs into the living room.

"I can't believe my little sister has a baby," Randy said as he shoveled a bite of cake into his mouth.

"It's so surreal," I said. "Thank you all for your support. I couldn't have done this without you guys."

"What happens now?" Renee asked.

"Right now, I'm enjoying this moment. Tomorrow, Josh and I are going to put the nursery together and get all the necessary baby supplies."

"That's so exciting, but I was referring to your next steps for custody," Renee said.

"I want to get everything we need to take care of her first. Then, I'll do the maternity test and talk with Mr. Stallard about petitioning for custody."

"What about Gray?" Randy said.

I groaned. "Gray's going to be a pain in the ass, but I have to play his game. I've got a better chance of getting custody of Janie with his help."

Hearing my words, Josh looked down at the ground as his shoulders slumped. He didn't sign up for this battle, and he certainly didn't ask for Gray Stone to be smack in the middle of our lives.

Not wanting to continue the conversation, I cleaned up the dishes. Helen must have sensed that I wanted to move on because she said, "So, what color are you going to paint the baby's room?"

"I haven't decided, but I'm thinking of maybe doing a beach theme with lighthouses, so Janie can always find her way home."

"That's a wonderful idea," Renee said. "And, of course, she'll have a room here too."

"Of course, she will. She has to spend time with her favorite Aunt Renee," Helen said, and everyone laughed.

THIRTY-THREE

New York City

Gray reluctantly agreed to give me time to acclimate to life with Janie before making my first trip to New York. I put off the work visit for as long as possible, but he grew impatient. Standing on the sidewalk in front of Gray Stone Marketing, I sighed and took in my surroundings. Once upon a time, the hustle and bustle of the city thrilled me. Today, as I watched the mobs of people walking here and there, hurrying to their destination, I felt a pang of disgust. I had become accustomed to my small southern town's slow, quiet life. *How did I do this for so many years?* Taxi cabs honked, and lines of people stood at the stands on the street—overcrowded coffee shops with people everywhere.

Uneasy about what this trip would bring, I pulled open the front door and walked toward the elevator. *Let's get it over with. You won't have to do this forever.* A man scrolling on his phone stood waiting for the elevator. He looked up. We made eye contact, and I smiled. The elevator dinged, and we both stepped in.

"Twenty, please," I said politely. The ride felt too quick. I wasn't ready to waltz back into my old life. My throat went dry, and my hands began to sweat. As the elevator stopped on the twentieth floor, I swiped my hands down my body as if straightening my skirt would provide me some courage, took a deep cleansing breath, and slowly exhaled. *Confidence. You are Lizzie fucking Levine. Show them confidence.*

I walked toward the front desk, my shoulders back and my chin up. My feet were already hurting; it had been a minute since I had worn six-inch heels. "I'm here to see Gray Stone," I said to Claudia, his assistant. I had not noticed before, but Claudia was young. Her beauty radiated from her perfect skin as if she were the poster girl for a dermatologist's office. *You're in the wrong business, honey.* Her thick, naturally blond hair was down to the middle of her back, and her shirt was cut low enough to accentuate the perkiness in her breasts.

"He's expecting you," Claudia said.

When I entered Gray's office, the past came rushing back like a mallet hitting me in the gut. Flashes of our first night together panned through my mind like an old movie. My bad choices, like shiny trophies on display, sat on his bookcase. *Confidence. You've got this. Exude confidence.*

Gray stood from his desk, walked toward me, and said, "I'm glad you're here. You look beautiful."

Always about the looks. I fought hard not to roll my eyes. "You can work from the large conference room. It's available all day except for our meeting later today." He stepped closer. I could practically feel his breath on my skin. He started to wrap his arms around me.

Backing away from him, I said, "Great. I'll get to work."

I made a beeline for the conference room. Sitting down at the table, I opened up my laptop. I called Claudia for reports on the last six months of marketing subscriptions, and I was shocked at how easily I fell into my old routine.

Several hours passed as I sorted through the data and mapped out a plan for the next steps. Lost in concentration, I didn't notice Gray enter the room. "How's it going, gorgeous?" he said.

"Fine," I said flatly.

"I have no doubt." He smiled. "I'd like to take you to dinner tonight. Like old times."

"Thank you, but I'm not interested. Our last dinner didn't go too well." Wanting to appear busy, I shuffled the papers and hoped he'd go away.

"Why do you think I wanted you here?"

I continued looking at my computer and organizing the papers on the conference room table. Gray drummed his fingers as he waited for my answer.

"So I could work," I said and let him know I was inconvenienced by his question.

"Work's a bonus." He moved to the seat beside me. Grabbing the handle of my chair, he spun me to face him. "I want to spend time with you. Have dinner with me tonight."

My eyes looked up from my computer and peered at him. "I'd rather have my toenails pulled."

He laughed. "Ouch. I'll let it slide this time, but these visits are required, and you'll do what I ask." The magnitude of the agreement I made became clear for the first time. I had made a deal with the devil. *What was I thinking?*

He grabbed my hand and cupped it inside of his. "Next visit, I want you to bring Janie."

"What?" I said in disbelief. I scrunched my eyebrows and looked at him. "I thought these trips were for work?"

"I want to spend time with my girls. We've got daycare here at the office for Janie when you're working. And I'd like to take you both to the zoo."

"We're not your girls." My face turned three shades of red as anger welled inside me like hot lava bubbling to the top of Mauna Loa.

"You will be." He smirked and rested his hand on my knee. Slowly, he slid his hand upward, and his fingertips rested under the hem of my skirt. *Note to self. Wear pants.*

We received results from the gene marker test a few weeks ago confirming that I was Janie's mother and Gray was her father. I still had power of attorney to raise Janie, and she lived with me, but he had threatened to take that away if I didn't allow him to spend some time with Janie. So, I agreed to supervised visits.

His hand proceeded further under my skirt, in between my thighs. Slamming my laptop shut, I yelled, "I can't do this!" Incensed, I stood and packed my things to leave.

As I approached the door, Gray said, "Walk out that door, and it's over, Lizzie. Remember, you've got Janie because I've allowed it, and I can take her from you anytime."

I stopped; tears stung my eyes. I felt defenseless. I turned to face him as a tear trickled down my cheek. He walked over to me, touched my face, and gently wiped away my tear.

I clenched my teeth and inhaled. "Gray, I won't let you control me. You say you want to spend time with me, then you'll have to earn it." I lifted my hand to rest upon his and gently removed it from my face. "Keep threatening me, and Janie and I will be gone forever."

He looked down, his eyes meeting mine. "I'll never give up on you."

"I'm leaving, Gray. First flight tomorrow, I'm going home."

His body softened. He hugged me tight. I let him. I don't know why I let him, but I did. He hugged me tighter and whispered in my ear, "I messed up." He kissed my cheek. The once uncontrollable desire for his kiss was replaced with repulsive disdain. "I love you." He smiled.

I forced a smile back.

"I'm going to get a coffee. I'll see you later, Gray." He let me go.

THIRTY-FOUR

October

A dazzling display of crimson, gold, and amber leaves spread across the oak trees on the drive back into town. I had just returned from another trip to New York City and could not wait to see Janie and Josh. Gray insisted my office visits continue, but I refused to bring Janie. The Uber driver dropped me off in front of Josh's house. I wheeled my bag up the driveway as the front door flew open, and Janie came bobbling out, with Josh following behind her. Her arms were outstretched, and she uttered the most fantastic word I had ever heard. "Mommy!"

I scooped her into my arms as tears of joy danced down my cheeks.

"Did you hear that?" I said to Josh.

He smiled and folded his arms around both of us. Then, breathing deeply, he kissed me and said, "We missed you."

Feeling his body against mine made my skin tingle. Two days away from him felt like an eternity.

"Don't make any plans for tomorrow night or Saturday. Janie's spending the night with Randy and Renee, and my dad will watch her on Saturday." He said and rubbed his nose against mine. "I've got a surprise planned."

Setting Janie down, I said, "I'm supposed to work with Helen at the bookstore on Saturday and then go to Randy's Grand Opening."

"I've already talked to Helen, and she agreed to give you the day off. Randy's Grand Opening's part of the plan."

Josh left for work, and I took Janie for a stroll along the water. I spent every minute with her that day. We even snuggled during nap time, and she fell asleep swaddled in my arms.

Later in the day, we visited Helen at the bookstore. Janie loved books like her mama. Sitting on the beanbag chair with Janie in my lap, I read several books to her. I thought back to my happiest memories of my own childhood and was grateful for every minute I could spend with my daughter.

Balancing motherhood, Gray's bullshit, and work at the bookstore hadn't left much alone time for Josh and me. I was looking forward to the surprise he had planned. I showered, gave Janie a bath, and packed her bag. Renee was on her way to pick her up.

Hearing the doorbell ring, I threw on my bathrobe and headed down the stairs with Janie to answer the door. As I opened the door, Janie shouted, "Ren Ren." She clapped her hands and smiled at the sight of her aunt. Renee picked her up and kissed her cheek.

"Have fun tonight," Renee said. "We'll see you tomorrow."

"Thank you for keeping her for the night."

"Are you kidding me? We're excited about her first overnight with us."

Renee carried Janie outside and buckled her into the stroller. She waved goodbye, and I watched them walk down the street until they disappeared over the hill. A little ache formed in my heart as they left. I knew that Janie was in good hands and would have a blast, but I wasn't totally comfortable letting her out of my sight yet.

Turning on my heel toward the house, I heard a voice say, "Nice outfit." I looked behind me, and my heart sank. Gray was walking toward me. "I just passed our daughter," he said as he approached.

He's such an ass. I'm certain he's hanging around to annoy Josh and drive a wedge between us.

"Yes. Janie's spending the night with her aunt and uncle," I said flatly. "What're you doing here?"

"I've fallen in love with this quaint little town. I'm working from my condo for a few weeks. Right now, I'm out for a stroll."

His constant holding Janie over my head infuriated me. I had to break this cycle, but life wasn't that simple. Instead, I was a prisoner of my choices and shackled to Gray Stone for at least the foreseeable future.

"Well, have a great day. I've gotta run." Walking inside, I leaned against the door and closed my eyes. I exhaled the stress and frustration he brought to my day. I had plans with Josh, and I wouldn't let Gray ruin this night for me.

Josh said to be ready by 6:00 p.m., and the clock said 5:30 p.m. I only had thirty minutes to finish getting ready. I dashed up the stairs, rummaged through my closet, and looked for the perfect dress.

Settling on a purple cotton maxi dress, I slipped it over my head. I tightened the straps, ensuring my breasts nestled perfectly inside the V-neck top which rested on the smocked waistline. The bottom flowed to the ground with a large slit up the right side.

I fixed my hair and makeup, applied Josh's favorite red lip gloss, and studied myself in the mirror.

I'm ready. I wonder what we're doing.

"I'm home," I heard Josh shout from downstairs. "Pack an overnight bag really quick. You don't need anything fancy, but we won't be home until morning."

Josh greeted me with a quick kiss and jumped into the shower. I grabbed my toiletries and put some clothes in a bag. Then, sitting at the kitchen table, I waited for him to finish getting ready.

He appeared in the kitchen with a rhinestone blindfold and said, "Turn around. You need to wear this."

He tied the blindfold around my eyes, picked up my bag, escorted me to the golf cart, and assisted me into my seat.

"You look beautiful," he said.

"Thank you."

I heard the clutch pop and felt the cart roll forward. The wind blew through my hair as we drove. Parking the golf cart, Josh said, "Stay here. I'll be back to help you in a moment."

In the darkness, I sat alone with my thoughts and waited for him to return.

I wonder where we are?

I hope Janie is okay and having a good time.

Maybe I should text Renee.

Janie's fine. Stop it.

Should I peek?

Ugh, the waiting is killing me.

Hearing the sound of feet crunching on the pavement, I called out, "Josh?"

"Yes, babe, I'm here."

He took my hand and escorted me several steps to our destination. "Just a few more feet," he said. "Okay, big step."

"Big step," he said again. Then he lifted me and carried me a little further. Putting me down to stand on my feet, he removed the blindfold and said, "Keep your eyes closed."

With my eyes squished shut, I waited in anticipation. A few seconds passed before Josh finally said, "Okay, open your eyes."

Gasping, I threw my hands up to cover my mouth, and my eyes grew wide. I was standing on Josh's boat. Every inch seemed to be covered in twinkling lights. At least one hundred electric candles decorated the cabin, and an archway of lilies adorned the glass doorway. Randy, Renee, Helen, Janie, and Len were all there, smiling happily.

Josh pulled a black velvet box from his pocket and bent down on one knee. Tears formed in my eyes as I stood there, taking in the moment.

"Lizzie, I fell in love with you the moment I knocked you over in the Southport Market." Everyone laughed. "I can't imagine not spending the rest of my life with you and Janie."

Renee, holding Janie's hand, walked toward me. She wore a beautiful white dress with a puffy skirt decorated with tiny pink flowers. Josh opened the velvet box, pulled out a little pearl bracelet, placed it on Janie's wrist, and said, "Janie, I'd like to be your daddy if you'll allow me. I'll guide you, protect you, and love you with all my heart."

Janie giggled and said, "J J." Opening her arms, she stepped forward and put her hands around Josh's neck. Tears spilled down my cheeks, and I looked back at Josh.

Holding the most gorgeous pear-cut diamond, he said, "Lizzie, I'd like to be your husband in good times and bad. I want to love you more tomorrow and every day after that for the rest of our lives. Here with our closest friends and family, I profess to be by your side, to love and support you always. Will you make me the happiest man alive and agree to be my wife?"

Without hesitation, I said, "Yes!"

I threw my arms around his neck. He scooped me up and cradled me into his arms. Dipping me back, he kissed me. Everyone clapped, cheered, and wiped away tears. When the kiss ended, he put me down, and we stared into each other's eyes. Surrounded by complete and total silence, our eyes spoke a thousand words, and I knew God sent me this man to be by my side and love me in a way that I probably didn't deserve. I was the luckiest girl in the world.

Red snapper and filet were served, and we toasted our engagement with champagne. After the evening ended, everyone said their goodbyes. We walked off the boat and down the dock toward the parking lot. Josh thanked everyone for coming, and Randy hugged me and said, "He's a good man. I'm so happy for you, sis."

I gave Janie a big hug and kiss and buckled her into the stroller. We waved one more goodbye and walked toward the boat. Climbing aboard, I said, "I can't believe you did all this."

"I love you, Lizzie. I can't wait to spend the rest of my life with you and Janie."

"I love you too. Sometimes, it doesn't seem real, but I'm happy raising my daughter with you. The past few months have been a little slice of heaven."

Running his hand along my hair, he said, "I can't imagine our days without her."

Stars twinkled in the sky, and the air was crisp. Feeling a chill, Josh wrapped his arms around me, and I said, "I can't imagine life without her, either. I'll feel better when I have full custody, but I'm grateful to raise her with you."

"Lizzie, when you have custody, I'd like to adopt her legally if you'll allow me the honor."

His words were so genuine and tender. I loved him more at that moment than I did five minutes before. "I would love it if you adopted her."

I smiled as he reached his hand inside the slit of my dress and caressed my thigh. His touch was full of love and adoration. He tenderly kissed my face, and I tilted my head back. He moved his lips down my cheek and onto my neck. I let out a breath as he kissed my collarbone. Massaging my thigh, he worked his way up to my hips, lifting the bottom of my dress slightly. He gently moaned and whispered, "You aren't wearing any underwear."

My lips curled at the corner of my mouth, and I giggled coyly. "Nope. I didn't have any on all night. I didn't realize you planned to have our entire family here."

Unable to control himself, he picked me up into his arms. I squealed as he carried me inside the cabin. Setting me on the couch, he pulled the straps of my dress down and ran his fingers slowly along my shoulders. Our eyes met, and he stared into my soul, causing my pulse to race. I untucked his shirt from his pants, and pressed my palms into his back as I slid my hands under his shirt.

Finally, he kissed me, and I could taste the smooth Maker's Mark whiskey he had been drinking.

Desire burned inside me as I pulled him to me from the couch. He put his hand in mine and led me downstairs toward the bedroom. Reaching his hands under my dress, he slipped it off and pulled it over my head. Unable to wait any longer, I frantically undressed him. Our lips met again, and my insides exploded like a chorus of angels begging him to be inside me.

He laid me down and slowly eased himself inside. I could feel his love as he rocked in and out, and kissed every part of my body he could reach. He whispered over and over in my ear, "I love you," as he made sweet love to me again and again.

Several hours later, we climbed the stairs to the upper deck. Naked and covered with blankets, we lay on the lounge chair and gazed at the stars. My heart was full, my world was complete with Janie in our lives, and I knew that no matter what may come, I'd survive with Josh by my side. I felt safe in his arms.

I rolled to face him, kissed his lips, and tangled my legs between his.

"I love you," I said, resting my head on his chest as I saw my phone light up on the table beside me.

"Unknown."

Acknowledgments

Writing any book can be challenging. It is difficult to put yourself out there and hope you can find the right audience who'll appreciate your story. There were times I wanted to give up, times I didn't think I would finish, and times I wanted to cry from exhaustion.

I couldn't have done it without the help of my team, who encouraged me every step of the way. I am so grateful for the amazing editors I've found and how wonderful and diligent they are. Thank you, James, Jenn, Kim, and Adele, for your hard work helping to make this story come to life.

Thank you, Mo, for putting up with my numerous cover design revisions, essentially scrapping three covers before we found the perfect one. Your patience and willingness to get it right are astounding.

My husband, Chris, sat up with me and discussed each character like they were real people, living real lives, that we might go out and have dinner with. I appreciate your participation in the process and reminding me it is okay when I don't have all the answers. You're always my biggest cheerleader and fan. I thank God for you every day.

My children think it's cool that their mom writes books, and my daughter is my best salesman. Thank you for putting up with mom's late-night and weekend writing sessions. I love you both to the moon and back.

I must acknowledge my college roommate Steph, who is by my side cheering me on every step of the way. Reading draft after draft, discussing plot holes, and character development, and even giving me awesome ideas that help create shocking plot twists. You are my book muse.

I would also like to thank Robin Strickland, who took time out of her busy schedule to help me make sure that the legal aspect of Call Her Janie was as accurate as possible. I am forever grateful.

My launch team—there are hundreds of you and you know who you are. Marketing Call Her Janie would be a daunting task without you. Thank you for your time and effort in spreading the word. I will always be grateful to each of you for your support.

Writing can be lonely, since falling into the land of your story means no one quite understands it but you. I am lucky to be surrounded by amazing people who will jump into the book with me and buckle in for the crazy ride.

Last but definitely not least, to my family and friends who support and root for me. I am grateful to you. I could not do this without your love and encouragement. I love you all.

From The Author

Several years ago, I decided I wanted to be a writer. I started with my debut novel, The Secrets We Conceal, a coming-of-age fiction based on a true story. After releasing the book and deciding, I wanted to write another. I needed some time to figure out what my next story would be.

I was going through some personal difficulties, struggling to find gratitude each day. My siblings are a huge part of my life, but I rarely see them because we live in different states. I decided I needed to take a trip to visit, and I did. Spending time surrounded by the comfort and love of my brother and sister was exactly what I needed to get back on track. Enjoying the beautiful weather and the small town of Southport, NC catapulted me into a story. I couldn't move my fingers fast enough to write. I was sitting at a picnic table on the water and whipped out an outline and feverishly developed characters and plot lines. It was exhilarating.

What I didn't know when I started was how special and unique Southport NC is. Going down the rabbit hole to learn everything

I could about the town opened my eyes to the wonder and beauty of the quaint beach town. I wanted my story to capture the essence of Southport and the healing it provided me during my trip.

Everyone should have someone they can lean on to lift their spirits and show them they have the strength to get through anything. In Call Her Janie, Lizzie leans on her brother and Helen to lift her up and find her way again. I hope you enjoyed reading Call Her Janie as much as I enjoyed writing it. Stay tuned for book two and many more books to come.

Do you have a story to tell? Would you like me to join your book club and discuss Call Her Janie? I'm happy to help, reach out any time to srfabricoauthor@gmail.com. If you feel so compelled, please leave an honest review on Goodreads, Amazon, or anywhere books are sold.

Book Club Questions

1. Who was your favorite character and why?

2. Who was your least favorite character and why?

3. Who would you choose to play the characters in a movie rendition of the book?

4. How did the book impact you? Do you think you'll remember it in a few months or years?

5. Are there lingering questions from the book that you are still thinking about?

6. Are you team Gray or team Josh? What do you think will happen in the sequel?

7. What was your favorite and least favorite part of the book?

8. Which scene stuck with you the most?

9. What did you think of the author's writing style?

10. How did you connect with small-town Southport, NC?

11. Do you believe the legal system would function the way it is described in the book?

12. Did you race to the end, or was it more of a slow burn?

13. Was the book realistic and original?

14. Would you want to read another book by this author?

15. If you could ask the author anything, what would it be?

About the Author

S.R. Fabrico is an award-winning author whose literary talents have captivated readers worldwide. With her debut novel, The Secrets We Conceal, she has emerged as a rising star in the literary realm.

With a remarkable 25-plus-year career in business, marketing, and sports, S.R. Fabrico brings a unique perspective to her writing. As a World Champion Dance Coach and esteemed speaker, she infuses her stories with passion and insight.

Residing in Tennessee with her husband and children, S.R. Fabrico continues to create captivating narratives that will transport you to new and extraordinary worlds. Prepare to be enchanted by her exceptional storytelling prowess.

In addition to her passion for writing novels, she has published a series of sports journals and a journal for women.

Turn the page for a sneak peek of book two in the Southport Series.

Available in 2024.

Keeping Janie

ONE

Hues of orange and yellow swirled through the sky as the sunshine engulfed the eloquent beach town. Today was May 18th, Janie's second birthday. Sitting at a table on the Johnson Lawn, I felt like an onlooker, watching my daughter's two-year-old birthday party. *I knew I shouldn't have trusted him. This party is out of control.*

Fort Johnson Museum is a large two-story brick mansion with four tall white pillars adorning the entryway. Sitting on several acres of land, the fort was the first constructed in the state of North Carolina back in 1749. Gray rented the Johnson Lawn to throw Janie her birthday party. When he asked if he could have a birthday celebration with her, I thought he meant a cupcake at his condo. Little did I know that the entire Princess brigade, complete with pumpkin-shaped carriage rides, would attend today's event. White tables and chairs decorated the lawn with Cinderella castle centerpieces. Front and center stood an archway decorated with twinkling lights and white flowers. Through the archway was Janie's very own pink throne. *Thank God she won't remember this.* I rolled my eyes. *How long am I going to have to play this game with him?* Face painting, clowns crafting balloon animals, and magicians were scattered around the area for kids and parents to enjoy.

"This is quite the party," Josh said, interrupting my thoughts.

I looked at him with sullen eyes. "Sure is."

He leaned over and kissed my head. "We'll get through this. Have faith." Josh was as handsome and kind as ever, wearing his usual perfectly fitted jeans with a short sleeve blue button down. His shirt accentuated his exquisite blue eyes, and the five o'clock shadow he was currently sporting highlighted his square jaw.

"I know we will. I'm just frustrated." Frustrated is an understatement. Gray had been using my daughter to manipulate me daily, and I felt like a prisoner, caged inside my own life.

Josh reached out and took my hand, pulling me to my feet. He said, "You're raising Janie every day. That's a wonderful thing. Let's try to enjoy the party."

I shot him a sideways glance and followed him toward the birthday crowd. "*We've* been raising Janie," I said, wrapping my arm around his side. I leaned into his chest and said, "I love you. Thanks for always finding the silver lining."

He squeezed me and said, "I love you, too."

Janie sat on her throne, clapping her hands, and watched the princesses dance in unison before her, their dresses belling out as they twirled in circles.

"Look, Mommy," Janie squealed as I approached. "Daddy JJ, watch," she exclaimed. Her eyes glimmered in the sunshine as happiness oozed from her every pore. I scooped her up, rested her on my hip, and we danced to the music before sitting back on the throne with Janie on my lap. Josh stood beside us, and we did our best to enjoy the moment. I looked out at the crowd and noticed I barely knew anyone in attendance. Eventually, I spotted Randy, Renee, and Helen, which made me smile.

Gray sauntered throughout the grounds, shook hands, and spoke to his guests. As he approached, Janie giggled; holding out her arms to him, she blurted, "Daddy." My heart sunk low into my gut. I could practically taste each heartbeat as my blood pumped through it. *Daddy.* The words might as well be nails on a chalkboard. *I want to vomit.* I kissed Janie on the cheek and handed her to Gray.

Gray proceeded to parade her around the party, showing her off to his friends. The child he never wanted—the child he uses to control my life. *I've got to get out of this tangled web of bullshit.* I watched as Gray waltzed toward the carriage rides, and my eyes darted toward Josh. "I'm not letting him take her without me."

"Go," he said, urgency pouring from his words. I took off, briskly walking toward the carriage.

"Do you have room for one more?" I said to Gray as he and Janie climbed into the carriage.

"I always have room for you," he said with his menacing green eyes piercing right through me. I climbed into the carriage, looked back at Josh, and smiled reluctantly. Josh supported me every step of the way. *He has the patience of a saint. I love him so much.* I could feel my cheeks getting hot and turning red at the thought.

The carriage lurched forward, and we were off, heading down Bay Street along the water. Janie was propped onto her knees, gripping the open carriage window as she looked out at the seagulls diving into the water. She pointed her little finger. "Gulley's, mama, gulley's."

"That's right, Janie. Seagulls," I said, leaning forward to get a better view. Gray sat on the opposite bench and snapped pictures of Janie and me.

"She's beautiful, you know. Gets it from you," he said as he looked at the photo he just took.

I sighed. "She's beautiful and smart."

"I've fallen in love with her. I know you don't want to hear it and don't believe me, but I have. I'd love nothing more than to be a family."

"You don't know what love is," I snapped. "We've already discussed this. I'm engaged and madly in love with Josh. You agreed to let Josh and I raise her."

"Well, I changed my mind. I'm crazy in love with you both, and the thought of not having you in my life sickens me. The thought of not spending time with Janie makes me feel like I'm suffocating."

"You can't do this. Gray, we've been over this a million times. I'm marrying Josh. Janie will live with us. There's no family here," I said, pointing my finger at him, then toward myself, and back to him again. "It's never going to be us."

The carriage came to a stop by the picnic tables along the water. "Come on, Janie. Let's blow some bubbles," Gray said, stepping out of Cinderella's pumpkin. I followed behind and rolled my eyes.

"Why are we stopping? We should get back to the party," I said in a huff.

"I want to talk for a minute."

I crossed my arms and said flatly, "Talk."

"I understand I hurt you." Gray unscrewed a cap of bubbles and handed it to Janie. Then, placing his hand gently on my shoulder, he continued, "I know I don't deserve a second chance, but I'll do whatever it takes to win your trust." He looked at Janie, who was distracted, playing with her bubble wand. "Our daughter has changed me; I want to be a better man. I love you both and will fight for you, Lizzie."

"There's nothing to fight for. You say you love us. Love isn't pony shows and diamonds, Gray." I shifted my weight and flailed my arms. "It's unconditional. It's being there for the hard parts. Not long ago, you didn't want to have anything to do with us, especially Janie. I moved on, and now you want us in your life." I rolled my eyes and let out a sigh. "I gave you a second chance once; you called security."

"You need time. I get it, but I will prove that I've changed."

Janie was giggling as she smashed bubbles with her hands.

"Sure, Gray. Yep. Time. Time's what I need." I turned away from him. "We should get back."

"I'll be part of my daughter's life, whether you like it or not. She's my daughter. And need I remind you that I can take her from you at any time." His words filled me with rage, and I balled my fists and gritted my teeth. *Calm down, Lizzie. Don't make a scene.* "You're spending time with her now because I've allowed it." *Not for long, hopefully.*

"And there it is. That's the Gray I know." I put the cap on the bubble jar and lifted Janie into my arms. "Come on, sweetie. We need to return to the party."

"Par – teeeee," Janie said as she wrapped her arms around my neck.

"If you're genuine and want to be a better person, you can start by not threatening me whenever I don't do exactly what you want. Janie needs stability. She needs her mother. If you love us, you'd understand that and never threaten to take her away." I placed Janie into the carriage and climbed in behind her, closing the door. "You can walk. It'll give you time to think about what I just said." I waved and said, "Wave bye to Gray, Janie."

Later that night, Janie was exhausted. She passed out in the stroller on the way home. I felt terrible admitting I hated the party. Janie loved the party and had a blast, and I hated that even more. Josh and I tucked her into her crib and sat on the balcony attached to our bedroom, looking over the water.

"I'm exhausted," I said.

"I know, babe. At least Kit's still in jail. That's a plus."

"For now, but..."

"Just focus on today. For today, she's in jail. She's been found guilty. We wait for her sentencing now."

Part of me feels a little sorry for Kit and Gray. Gray has been trying to divorce her for over a decade, and she won't sign the papers. On the other hand, I often wonder if Kit became the psycho she is because she was married to Gray. Maybe she was always crazy. Who knows? Either way, she stole my child and needed to pay, but the legal system has been slow and daunting.

"Gray threatened to take away the power of attorney today," I said, looking at Josh.

"He did what?" Josh gasped.

"He wants to be a family. He didn't outright say it, but he might as well have. 'Lizzie, if you don't allow the three of us to be a family, I'll take Janie from you.' He gently reminded me that he controls my life right now." I rocked slowly in the chair and rubbed my temples. "Please don't say I told you so. I know. I know. Everyone thought a power of attorney was a bad idea. What was I supposed to do, let them put my child in foster care? Let Gray have her? I made the best choice out of the shitty choices I had."

"I know. The entire situation sucks." He took my hand in his and squeezed. His touch sent warmth pulsating through my body, melting my worries away. He stood, pulling me out of my chair toward him. He wrapped his arms around my waist and pressed his lips to mine. He lifted me, cradled me like a baby, and carried me into the bedroom. He undressed me slowly, occasionally pausing to kiss my body. He laid me down and massaged my back, slathering sunflower lotion on my skin. He pressed gently, working his way up to my shoulders and neck.

Releasing the stress I had pent up, I groaned. "Ugg, you're so good to me," I whispered. "I'm tense all over."

"Tense all over, you say?" he teased. "I can certainly help with that.

He placed gentle kisses on my neck and down my back. He massaged my hips and buttocks, down my hamstrings, then my calves, and onto my feet. Barely able to speak, I muttered, "That feels amazing."

"I'm glad. You've had a tough day," Josh said between kissing his way up my leg. He gently rolled me over and kissed my stomach. He placed his hands on my thighs and spread my legs. I felt a rush from his touch that stretched down to my toes. His lips were like an artist painting a masterpiece as he worked his way downward.

Working his tongue back and forth, I gasped. Tingles shot through my body, and I wanted to cry out for more, but guilt took over. I ran my fingers through his hair and pulled him toward me.

"What, babe? Are you upset? I only want to help you feel better."

"I'm not upset. I'm sorry. You're incredible, and I practically have zero self-control with you."

"Your self-control seems pretty on point to me lately," Josh snickered. The words cut deep into my soul. I didn't want to hurt him. But he's right. Lately, I've been unable to allow myself to be with him. I was sure my denials were hurting him, but that was not my intention.

"I'm starting to think you don't want to be with me anymore."

"That's not it all," I said, kissing his lips. "I love you. I love you so much. It's just..."

"It's just what, Lizzie? I don't think we've been intimate for months." He stood from the bed and began to dress. "I'm trying to do my best here. I'm trying to be patient and understanding. I know this must be hard for you. But being with me should be easy."

"You're right. I'm sorry." I rolled onto my side to face him. "You're amazing, and your touch sends a rush through my body, but then I feel guilty. I'm trying, but I can't help it. The guilt kicks in, and I feel I need to stop."

His shoulders slumped, and he said, "I don't understand, but I want to help. What can I do?"

"I don't understand either. I guess I feel like I don't deserve you. I don't deserve to feel good with you. I'm a mother doing my best to hold on to my child, and I feel every ounce of me should always focus on that." I scooted toward the middle of the bed to make room and patted the sheets. "Come, lay with me. Hold me. That's what you can do."

I've got to get through this before it takes over my life. But how can I let myself be with Josh when all I can think about is keeping Janie?

Josh climbed into bed, wrapped his arms around me, and pulled me into him. His desire was still at attention, poking me. Tears burned my eyes as I lay quietly in his arms. *I genuinely don't deserve this man.*

Also by S.R. Fabrico

Connect with S.R. Fabrico

Subscribe and follow S.R. Fabrico to receive additional Chapters of Keeping Janie and stay up to date on the release of the second book in the series.

Email srfabricoauthor@gmail.com to set up a virtual book club meet and greet with the author.

Ingram Content Group UK Ltd.
Milton Keynes UK
UKHW040632140723
425136UK00004B/211